# The God of the Cucumber Vine

# THE GOD OF THE CUCUMBER VINE

Daniel G Opperwall

Later on Sunday Press
Hamilton, Ontario

*In memory of Dom James Deschenes,*

*who always encouraged me.*

# AUTHOR'S PREFACE

Here I share a novel that I wrote nearly ten years ago, and which has been sitting in my (digital) trunk ever since. The novel is titled *The God of the Cucumber Vine* and takes place on a fictional Pacific island called Milau. It is not really a finished book, not in the fullest sense anyway. It is a complete story from beginning to end, but it never went through the process that any truly completed book must, which is to say it has not been fully rewritten and no editor has touched it. All real books are created several times by at least two people—usually more—who take an author's draft and craft it into something complete. Not so with this one. *Cucumber Vine* is also a very green book written by a man not yet thirty who even ten years on knows very little about writing.

*Cucumber Vine* is, fundamentally, about God the Father and His presence in the economy of salvation, which is something deeply mysterious indeed. Especially when one considers death. That, by the way, is the other thing this book is about: death. And the symbols of water, the night, the little girl, and many others mingle around the question of death and the Father's place in it (to put it thus) throughout the story. It is a work of theology in fiction, then, but as you will see it is not explicitly religious, barring at most a short flourish near the end. And the book is meant to be funny, which makes for a little bit of an odd combination.

I have left many stories, poems, and novels behind over the years as any writer does. There is no need to finish or publish everything. But there is something at the heart of *Cucumber Vine* that haunts me even ten years later in spite of it being green, and flawed, and incomplete. There is an idea at the centre of it—that idea about God the Father—that I still think matters. It feels like the time has come to take the Doc's advice from the very end of the novel and just let things be what they are, let them float out into the darkness of the ocean night with no expectation of building (or writing) something important, but rather as a sign of just being here, reflecting and wondering.

I hope, then, that you'll enjoy this novel simply for what it is, and pass it along to anyone else who might appreciate it the same way. May it be a solace, somehow, to know that however terrifying it may be to recognize God's literally infinite depths, by faith in His love (faith which is never quite certainty) we are steadfast in our hope that we will reach Him and the life for which we have been created.

Daniel G Opperwall, Hamilton, 2022

# 1

Somebody once told me to memorize a passage from Seneca—in Latin, no less. Referring to death, Seneca says *"Scopulum esse illum putamus dementissimi; portus est..."* and that, very loosely translated, means, "we, like lunatics, imagine death to be a barren atoll; but it is a harbor..." It's from *Epistle* 70, and I want to say right off that I'm pretty sure it's complete bullshit. But, after everything, I find myself dutifully repeating it in the mirror now and then. So, it seems like a good beginning. Maybe a decent end, too.

What I know is that every single soul on the island but three went out into the water, and that I am the last living person to have set eyes on them save possibly one. What I do not know is what they found out there–harbor, atoll, or something else.

I have my guesses. But so did Seneca. And I expect you don't need my thoughts on that, even if you believe me in the first place.

---

I found out about Milau at a brief meeting three years ago in January. It was a moment vivid, awkward and confusing. As you know, I was working in supply-chain for Saf-T-Set Foods, keeping tabs on facilities producing things like "Catsup" (as we continued to call it in the South-East), hamburger buns, pasta in a can, and that sort of thing. I had a little windowless office at headquarters on the second floor, which was a bit of a big deal when I first got it. I'd been working there for about five years—it was my first real job out of college. Which, again, you already know.

The meeting itself happened on one of those mid-winter days in Grand Rapids when the snow has gone crystalline and vacant, and everything is empty gray light; people lower their eyes and try not to exist until they're inside, only to find out they don't feel like existing there either. As I was heading to my office, Doug Bacon poked his head around a corner like he had been waiting there listening for my footsteps. Doug was just about the only person on our floor who was near my age (I'm 33 now), and therefore the only thing close to a friend I had in the company, though I didn't know him all that well. He had a good enough sense of humor, though, so we had lunch together once a week or so. He liked to wear flannel shirts to work, which was both anachronistic and against the dress code. But he had been doing it with so much exuberant frequency, and for so long, that no one actually seemed to care. Doug was a properly trained architect, and worked on any projects where we constructed a new plant or tore something down. We had actually been doing a fair bit of building around that time since we were the type of company that does well when the economy's bad.

"Hey," he said when he saw me, "you heard about the thing, right? The meeting? We should get up there now."

"No…" I said slowly, heading towards my office door where I could put my bag down, "I just got in. What's up?"

"Oh!" said Doug with a little too much surprise in his voice, "you didn't see the e-mail, then? They want you and me up in the big conference room…to talk to John Feilsma." Feilsma was the company's CEO and grandson of the founder.

"What?" I said, opening my door and starting to take off my coat, "about what?"

"No idea," said Doug, "Must be something big. I've never even met the guy before, have you? And I heard around the office that there were some feds around today looking like they didn't know where to stand."

"What do you mean 'feds?' Like…government agents?"

"Yeah…something—I don't know. We're supposed to be there in five minutes."

"Shit…" I said, opening up my bag quickly and grabbing a notebook. "Do I look okay for that?"

"No," said Doug with a smirk, "you look like you need a cup of coffee." I told him that that was true and we headed for the elevator.

"Did you have a good vacation?" Doug asked as we stood there. I said yes in that automatic way you do when you don't mean it. "You were out of town, right?" he asked.

"Yeah, I was down in Phoenix visiting my parents. They just moved there for good."

"Did you take Melissa with you?" he asked. Melissa was my girlfriend of about a year and a half—my wife now.

"No," I said, "she wanted to stay up here with her family. I don't blame her. Phoenix basically makes me want to kill myself." Doug laughed and I looked down somberly at the bagel crumbs on the carpet. The elevator showed up. We got on and hit "36"—all the way to the top. A loose door panel rattled at every floor as we went.

When we emerged, a secretary with one of those headsets was standing right there waiting for us. She was holding a clip-board with that bitter shifty arrogance that only a sycophantic underling is capable of cultivating. "Are you Doug and Edward?" she asked, using my full name awkwardly. We nodded. "Come this way."

She walked ahead of us down a hall to a big wooden door and opened it. Out from the conference room poured the scent of cherry-wood and velvet drapery—the odor of a bygone concept of high style and power decorating. The room was huge. The light of the sun, breaking through a weak spot in the overcast sky, streamed helpfully through the window so that the big corporate logo (it's a picture of a safety pin twisted into the letter "S") cast its shadow down over everything. The secretary left us as we stepped in, and the door closed with that loud-soft thud that only lots of money can buy.

There were four people in the room, sitting as far away from the door as possible. Three men in suits, and one woman smartly dressed. I didn't recognize any of them. "Welcome, gentleman," said the heavy man in the most central chair. He was red-faced and looked like he had had a few Bloody Maries to start the day. Still, he spoke fairly clearly. His voice was low and booming. "Have a seat, please." Doug and I looked at each other a little awkwardly. "Please," he said again, signaling once more. We sat.

"My name is John Feilsma—I don't believe we've met." We both shook our heads. "That is my grandfather there." He motioned to a massive painting on the wall across from the window. It was a portrait of a slightly cross-eyed old man in a Louis-the-Fifteenth pose. We looked up in feigned admiration. Feilsma looked up, too, with a little twinkle in his eye. Then he took a deep breath as if to start in on a significant speech. "Gentlemen," he began, "my grandfather founded this company one hot summer eighty years ago when he first began selling deli salads in a tent on the banks of the Grand River. He was just a simple Dutch immigrant with a wealthy family and a dream. From that first day in the heat, he knew what he desired: to grow that dream. And he did—summer after summer, year after year—into an international conglomerate. He grew it not just from dressing and diced ham, and not just from stock and capital, but from determination and opportunism. Today my grandfather would be proud that we carry on his legacy. I lay awake at night just imagining the look on his face if he were to see our annual revenue. Revenue, gentlemen, the blood that circulates in the very veins of an American company, sustaining it—making it live and breathe!" he looked up dreamily for a long moment at the portrait. "But it's not about the money, gentlemen. No, it's about the mission. We feed a nation for less—it's a great responsibility." We both nodded our heads like we meant it.

"Why, when this company was founded," he went on, "Grand Rapids was just a backwater town. Now look at us! Here we sit on the top floor of the tallest building in all West Michigan, looking down on everyone like…like soaring buzzards…our wings nobly akimbo. And the people below are looking up—dreaming of one day sitting where we sit—of being what we are: a symbol of everything that hard work and plenty of seed money can achieve! You should be proud to work here, gentlemen. Proud indeed." He seemed completely serious, so we nodded again. Feilsma opened his mouth and took a deep breath like he was actually planning to continue, but just then the man sitting next to him, like an angel called suddenly to the panicked work of our salvation, interrupted him.

"Good morning," he said, "my name is Josh Plank, and I am director of overseas operations." His voice was thin and nasally so that we could barely hear it from all the way across the room. "We've asked to meet with you about an issue with one of our plants. Are you gentlemen familiar with our popular brand of pickles…North Pacific pickles? We sell them in US regions one and two" (that means the Midwest) "and across Canada. A navy blue label with an island on it—block writing in a sans font, if I recall. Yes? Number five brand of pickles in the United States, and number one right here in Michigan!" Doug and I confirmed that we knew what he was talking about.

"Good," said Plank, straightening himself up. Then he haltingly pronounced the sentence that molded our meeting into that uncomfortably memorable creature that occupies my mind to this day. "Well," said Plank, "North Pacific pickles are made exclusively on an island…in the…in the North Pacific…I mean, the North Pacific ocean…it's very remote…very exotic…and we're proud to call it home for the brand." Here he paused, cleared his throat, and looked up at us as if we should speak. Instead, there was silence. I remember the moment as one of slow confusion—the kind you experience when someone has told you something that doesn't even make enough sense to be absurd. Doug gave me a look of questioning confusion, which I only met with a vacant stare as we both waited for Plank to continue.

"Uh…yes, that's right," he finally went on. "It's quite a small island, and it is known as Milau—a territory of the United States and also a completely independent republic. It's located exactly on the tropic of Cancer—I mean, like, exactly on it…which is odd. Anyway, it's a bit hard to get to, even with the Air Force base, but it's absolutely beautiful. And the plant is a cornerstone of our long-term North American plan—we really cannot maximize our presence in the pickle market without it. That is why we are very concerned that, as of about eight months ago, it has stopped delivering shipments." He stopped again, this time his eyes practically begging us to respond. It took us a good long moment, though.

"So…" said Doug, finally breaking the ice, "you want us to…help fix the problem?"

"Yes!" exclaimed Plank. He stuck his finger awkwardly in the air for emphasis.

"Okay…" Doug said, looking like he was still shaking off confusion, "can I ask a couple of questions then?" Plank nodded. "First, why do we have a pickle factory in…in the middle of the Pacific? I mean…do they grow cucumbers or something? It seems like a logistical nightmare."

"Right!" said Plank smiling gently, "no, we opened the plant in exchange for some tax breaks and a big grant. The governments of the US and Milau wanted to create some industry there…to help build a future for the people beyond just getting enough to eat and enjoying life in the sun. So, they contacted us. It didn't really make sense from a shipping point of view, but we worked with the two administrations to make it worth everyone's while." He stopped and chuckled to himself, but wisely did not elaborate.

"I see…" said Doug, fixing his posture. "Alright…so, what have our people on the island said about the shipments, then?'"

"Oh!" said Plank, "I forgot to mention all that! No, we haven't had any contact with the island for about the same amount of time as the shipments have been stopped. We've tried to call, and apparently the phones are down. In fact, I was just meeting with some people from the State Department this morning to discuss what could be going on. I guess there was a pretty big storm out there about ten months ago, and we're worried—well, mainly the folks from the government are worried—that that has damaged their infrastructure. Milau is very vulnerable to storms, apparently, because it's particularly low down. I think it might even be below sea level…can an island be below sea level? Anyway, there have also been some complications with local politics that I guess we need to keep an eye on. But, at the moment, the shipments are the big concern."

"Okay," I said after a pause, Doug having proved stubbornly mute this time, "so, how were we getting product off the island before, then. I mean, before the stoppage?"

"Well," said Plank, "everything would basically just show up at port in Toledo. Our people on the island had just been taking care of things for us, and that was working fine. The Milauans are very diligent—very trustworthy. We used to have a rep go out there every year or two, just to touch base. I even went out myself once to finalize a new hire. But it's been three years now without anyone visiting, and, like I said, the phones are down." Plank stopped and started laughing to himself, "I was just thinking this morning that maybe the plant has up and vanished or something like that. Wouldn't that be something? But, no…can't be…right?" Plank went a little bit flush, like the evaporation of our major facilities was a secret worry of his. We all sat quietly for another long time.

"So, basically…" the heretofore silent woman next to Plank finally said, "we need some people to get out to the island and get some information on the stopped shipments. We also need you to return with some schematics of the plant as well as the necessary information on what would be required for a tear-down and operations transfer from the island, should that become necessary. We're hoping the solution is simple out there, but everything is on the table. I'm Lisa Dykstra, by the way. Director of operations for Saf-T-Set Pacific."

"Yes," said Plank happily. "You'll fly to Honolulu first, and then you'll get on a little plane that can take you to Milau. Three weeks there, and then you fly home. It's practically a vacation for you guys—all expenses paid, too."

We both paused again. "Oh," said Doug, "So…you were assuming it would be us…specifically, then? Going out there? Not just coordinating…?"

"You're absolutely right!" Feilsma suddenly butted in, speaking as if we had accused him of a hidden emotional weakness, "you're not sending out lackey interns on this one! Don't even think about it!" His head wobbled slightly and he went a little green as he tried to glare at us. He must have been drunker than I had thought.

"Yes," came the woman's voice again, "we figured we should have you both there in person, especially since it's going to be so hard to communicate. And you'll really like it on the island. I've been, and it's lovely."

Plank nodded with a weak smile, glancing over at Feilsma with a touch of worry. "So, that's the situation. Do you have any more questions?"

Doug and I looked at each other for a moment. "Well, when do we depart?" Doug asked finally with an awkward smile.

"On Wednesday. You're flying out of Detroit, then via San Fran," Plank responded. "Oh, you'll need your passports. Also, we've got briefing folders for both of you. We'll have them sent down. If there's any confusion after you look through them, you can just get in touch with my secretary, whom I believe you met."

After a brief moment, Feilsma (who seemed to have gotten control of himself again) said, "It was a pleasure to meet you, gentlemen," in a meeting-is-over sort of way. The two of us got up and went out the door. The air in the little coat room now tasted like chocolate and acid. In a moment we were back in the hallway. The secretary was gone.

We headed to the elevator. "What the hell was that?" Doug asked as soon as we were out of all possible ear-shot, laughing under his breath. "I mean, Feilsma, and three top-level people at a meeting just to tell us about a plant visit? They could have written that up in an e-mail like the usually do—even if it is in the middle of nowhere."

"I know…" I said, in a perplexed murmur. My brain still felt like it was full of foam pellets, and I shook my head like I was honestly trying to get them out. "Something's really off. I mean, do we seriously have a plant on a Pacific island in the first place? I'm not sure I actually even believe that…no government grant could possibly be big enough. Any idea what the profit margin is on a jar of pickles?"

"Yeah, bizarre," said Doug, taking my questions as rhetorical, "but what can we do? Hey," he continued after a moment, "hadn't you heard of this place? You sounded like you didn't know about it."

"No," I said as the elevator arrived and we stepped in, "I've run into that brand, but as far as I knew, all those pickles were coming from some-where around here. But…yeah…I guess we could be putting them on a boat and sending through the Panama Canal or something. That's not the kind of thing I'd really know…or want to know…"

"Well, why not all the way around Cape Horn while they're at it, right? And they could put them in canoes just to make it exciting." Neither of us actually laughed. "Well, look," he went on after a moment, "this place sounds beautiful, and there's definitely a whole lot of something they're not telling us. Maybe this'll be fun, for once." He was starting to really rope me in. One thing about Doug was his sweeping enthusiasm. I stood there nodding gently as the elevator descended.

"Yeah," I said when we hit the second floor, "I guess we might as well look at it that way."

Doug laughed and nodded as he walked away toward his office. "I'm playing hookey tomorrow, no doubt about that," he said. "You know what? I'm leaving right now! Can't fire me two days ahead of something like this. I'll come in and grab those forms tonight, maybe. See you Wednesday!" And he was out of sight down the hall already. I headed back to my office and shut the door. I was still shaking my head to myself as I sat down at my desk. I don't remember getting much done for the rest of the day.

# 2

I was sitting at home with my girlfriend.

"This place is in the middle of absolutely nowhere," she said, staring at the computer screen in my living room that night. "I mean—just totally out in the middle of the Pacific. Closest place is Midway, but it's not that close. What if you get stuck out there or something?"

"I don't know," I said, "I guess they would have to come rescue us."

"There's barely even anything online about it. I guess the whole island has a population of fifty thousand. Can that even be right? It's a coral atoll…with a lagoon. It says here there's a little resort up on the northern tip of the island. That's it—that's the whole place."

"Wow," I said as she glanced up at me pleadingly for a moment. "Anything else there?"

She looked back at the computer. "Oh Lord," she said, "They have a parliament that meets in a tent by the beach three times a year." She shook her head and muttered over a few more lines of the article. "Elected president.…they somehow had a university there twenty years ago, but now it's closed. It says that they have a language called Milauan, but basically the whole population speaks English. But…this is odd…it's…not

a Polynesian language? It says that the Milauans aren't ethnic Polyne-
sians."

"What do you mean?" I asked.

"I don't know…" she said, "there's just a note here that says that the
Milauan language and culture aren't related to anything else."

"Does it say anything about an Air Force base?" I asked, recalling
Plank's brief mention of one.

"No, nothing about that. This article is like two paragraphs long. Where
the hell are you going, Ed?"

"You just told me everything I know about it," I was trying to tease her,
but she wasn't having any of it. "I guess I'll have to find the rest out once
I'm there."

She frowned. "I don't see why you don't just quit or get somebody else
to do it."

"They were pretty emphatic," I said, "but it's not even that. It's just that
I think this might actually be kinda…fun. And it's only three weeks,
Melissa."

She nodded. "I know. It just sounds so stupid."

"Of course it's stupid," I said, "it's mind-boggling, in fact. Having a
plant on a Pacific island in the first place…. But, that's why it'll be interesting."

Melissa sighed, and stood up from the computer. "Alright," she said,
"Don't get into any trouble over there."

---

Two days later I was yanking my bag from the back of a black airport
limo at about 6:00 in the morning with the crepuscular light just begin-

ning to stir my blood. I had slept most of the drive. The driver was a Mexican guy and wore one of those little limo hats that everyone likes. I tipped him handsomely, and then proceeded to worry whether that seemed patronizing. He was happy enough, though. Security was pretty quick heading in, even with a pat-down. I always get a pat-down, by the way—I hate those naked picture machines. I mean, if you need to get up-close and personal with my every nook and cranny then you're going to have to do it for real; none of this cowering in a dark room. After security I spotted Doug staring at a monitor, looking for our gate.

"Hey, Doug!" I said, heading towards him.

"Hey, Hill," he said, waving me over, "we each got our own limo, huh? Didn't expect that."

"No, me neither," I said, "still cheaper than the extra flight from Grand Rapids, I'll bet. How was your ride over?"

"Fine, just fine. Too early, but whatever. Hey, looks like we get to take the little red monorail thing to gate A77!" Doug was honestly excited about the little red monorail thing. Well, there are worse ways to start a trip to a pickle factory on a Pacific island. After our ride, we had a cup of coffee and each read a newspaper waiting to board. I called my parents to give them a last update on my itinerary. It was a short conversation.

The flight to Honolulu (there was a transfer in San Fran like Plank had said) was long and boring. On both legs we were in the very last row of the plane, back where you can't recline your seat at all on those older jets. Our flight attendants were, as usual, overly friendly and underly attractive. As one of them on the second leg swiped my card to the tune of eight dollars for a Gin and Tonic, I wondered where the old stereotype about foxy stewardesses comes from. Must have been a pre-union thing, back before giving people peanuts on a plane turned into a real job. Not that it shouldn't be. I mean, I think it should.

"So what are we supposed to do when we get to Honolulu?" I asked Doug at some point over the Pacific, just as he was tossing back a whole bag of peanuts at once.

"Um," he said, trying to chew them down quickly, "there's going to be someone there holding up one of those little signs for us." He finished chewing and swallowed…stopped, held up his hand, took a swig of his drink (Jack and Coke), shook his head in a shivering sort of way, swallowed again, and took a deep breath. "Sorry about that," he said in a now clear voice. "Yeah, someone is going to meet us, and then I guess we leave the main terminal and head over to the little private plane section, and there will be a prop or something there to take us out to Milau. Then we're supposed to just find the one hotel on the island and get ourselves a room. We might be booked, but they couldn't confirm that because, you know, no phones or anything right now. They gave me a bunch of Yen—said it would be hard to get cash there."

"Like—Japanese Yen?" I said. Doug said yes. "Odd…" I shook my head.

"I guess they just never stopped using the stuff after the Japanese occupation in the 30s. And they're way too small a country to print a currency of their own or anything."

"Yeah," I said, mulling it over. "Makes as much sense as anything, I guess. So, what are we actually supposed to do when we get there?"

"Oh, yeah," said Doug, "they gave me a big packet of stuff here." I hadn't actually received anything myself, and had made the strategic decision not to go inquiring after further information. Come to think of it, that was a pretty big risk since Doug could very well have done exactly the same thing. Anyway, it worked out. Doug leaned over and rummaged around in his bag, eventually taking out a thick manila folder. "There's a bunch of paper work, maps of the island, spreadsheets—all sorts of stuff. I've got it all in .pdf on my computer, too…hopefully they've got electricity there at least. Anyway, we're supposed to meet a contact person when we arrive on the island. She should be waiting for us when we get there. Her name is Martha Tok. Says she's some kind of manager for us. Makes it sound like she'll just be standing there when we land, basically—so, I'm not really sure how to find her if we have to go looking. Cross our fingers, I guess."

"How does she know we're coming?" I asked.

"It sorta sounds like they do have mail service still," said Doug, "though it takes a really long time. So, maybe they just sent her the information through the mail a while back? That would mean they've been planning this for a good month at least and decided to just lay it on us a couple of days ago."

"Sounds like Saf-T-Set," I said.

"Definitely. Anyway, if she's not there to meet us we're going to be wandering around like idiots for a little while. It's a small island, though. Regardless, after we make contact with her, we're supposed to tour the plant and get settled in, meet some of the management, figure out why the shipments have stopped, and then basically just get to work setting up all the paperwork for a plant shutdown. That's regardless of what the actual problem is, by the way—the stuff they gave me says they want a shut-down report either way, even if we can fix the problem there."

"Well, pretty run of the mill, then," I said, "albeit in the Pacific ocean."

"Yeah, basically," Doug said. "Three weeks is probably way too much time—but that's good. We'll have some days to just relax and enjoy the beach or whatever."

"So, why are they even sending you—all that stuff is usually on me."

"Oh, yeah," said Doug, "I forgot to mention that. There's some kind of glitch with the plant architecture. See, they say that if they have to move operations over, they would want to rebuild the new place on the exact same layout as the one on the island. They're being really hyperactive about not wanting any changes to the way the product is made—like, which hallways it goes down and when. They kept talking about the 'salty sea air' and how it affects the pickles and stuff like that. Gotta protect that brand! Anyway, that's not so strange except that the architectural side turns out to be a complete nightmare. Evidently we have absolutely no record of the plant design that I could access. So, I've got to dig up a schematic on the island, and failing that I have to actually go out there and *draft* this damn thing again *from scratch*—unbelievable! But it'll give me something to do." He smirked and sat back in his seat.

"Great…" I said with a sigh. I paused for a while. "Hey, so how long will the ride from Hawaii out to Milau be?"

"Depends on how fast the plane is, but I would think a couple of hours. Pee before we go!" he grinned at me to emphasize this piece of advice, then he wiped the peanut residue from his hands, filed the documents back away and pulled his book out from the seat-back in front of him. He was reading *Jane Eyre*, which I thought was extremely bold. But, then again, if he was going to read a romance novel, at least a Victorian one showed class. Anyway, I don't like to read on planes, and I declined to purchase a headset for three dollars, and no, I hadn't brought my own, so I was forced to watch *Bananas*, the old Woody Allen movie, without any sound. Where they got a copy of *Bananas* I don't know. Anyway, it's always interesting to see how much of a movie plot you can gather without the dialogue.

When we got to Honolulu, at about 2:00, I think, we located our sign-bearer and began following her. She walked briskly, apparently annoyed with our existence. We snaked our way through the main terminal, through some strange back entry-way that circumvented security somehow, out of the terminal, back into the terminal (skipping security again), and finally over to a little corner office in a distant back hallway of the airport with a little blue banner that said "Lightface Charters and Aerial Rescue." She unlocked the frosted glass door and let us in. Then she turned around and left, still without saying a word, and we stood in silence alone.

Inside the office there was a single small desk with no one attending it, a rack filled with a collection of National Geographic magazines so old they had probably become valuable again, a coffee vending machine, and a unisex bathroom. Doug repeated his advice from the plane and headed straight for this most important amenity.

An hour and a half, four cups of coffee and several more visits to the can later, someone finally came in. We had been talking for a while about what we ought to do if nobody showed up, and had determined that calling Saf-T-Set would only be a waste of time. Anyone we might easily reach was certain not to have the slightest idea who we were, or what our project was, and probably wouldn't even have much sense of the basic business model or geographical catchment of Saf-T-Set itself. In short, we were at the mercy of whatever distant god or secretary had built the machine of our current arrangements. We had gotten to the point of doing some of the cross-word puzzles in the NatGeos, and Doug was just starting to read a few of the racier articles, when, like I said, somebody finally came in.

Tom (the pilot) was more or less a walking stereotype. He had on a leather jacket and, I kid you not, aviator sunglasses with a little Top Gun hairdo along with a mustache that covered about half his mouth. Really! He removed the jacket and sunglasses (these he basically ripped off his face like he was proving a point about his masculinity), hung the jacket up on a rack just behind the desk, and offered his hand to both of us.

"You must be the fellas from Saf-T-Set, right…what'd they say, Doug and Edward?" He had a drawl which seemed oddly placed in Hawaii.

We smiled and shook his hand. "Everyone calls me 'Hill,' or maybe

'Ed,'" I said, "only my great-grandmother and my first girlfriend ever called me Edward."

"Well, I'm Tom, and I'm going to be getting the two of y'all out to Milau t'day. Now we're gonna have a real safe flight, but I want y'all to know that we're headin' out over a whole mess 'a water—I mean, it's a lotta water, the Pacific ocean is—biggest ocean in the world, did y'all know that? I just found that out this week. Anyway, if we go down into that much water, we're gonna be in for a real 'good mornin' and how'd ya do' sorta situation, if you know what I mean. Now don't panic 'cause the water ain't too cold and the sharks ain't too hungry around these parts, not like where y'all are comin' down from, so don't worry." Doug and I gave each other worried looks—not necessarily about the sharks.

Tom explained that we would be flying on what turned out to be a four-seater single-engine float plane—the kind that can land on the water, I mean. The flight was going to take four and a half hours, though Tom noted that we would get two more hours back from the time change so as to be there in time for dinner. Dinner would be happening the next day, though, because we were crossing the international date-line. Just look at a map if that doesn't make sense. Actually, Tom mentioned something about a kerfuffle during the cold-war regarding which side of the line Milau should be on; evidently some Americans thought it was unacceptably communist for the islanders to want to be in their natural time-zone. Anyway, Tom had done the flight two times before, both eight years previous, "back when the airport was still open over there," he noted. "You used to be able catch a commercial flight on Milauan Airways, but when your company called me I went an' checked on the internet an' there ain't no more flight! How 'bout that?" He then gave us a specific rundown of the various safety procedures on the plane, and I'll spare you that. The basic gist was that if we went in the water, we should wear our life-jackets, and that way we would die of exposure floating on the surface rather than drown.

Tom whisked us through a back door into a corridor that led to the runway. The plane was parked a few steps away. It was a little red number painted with a pin-up style figure of a woman reclining across one of the pontoons, a carnation firmly in her mouth and a look of "here we go again" sublimely illuminating her face. The expression looked like it had been meant to connote sexuality, but the artist hadn't been quite skilled enough for something so subtle. Just above the woman, in a white script tailing off into a little cloud design, were the words "Jet Red Sadie," which, presumably, was the name of the plane.

"This here's the Sadie," said Tom, who had somehow gotten a lit cigarette into his mouth in the time it took me to glance at the plane. "She's a good plane—engine runs nearly always, and I ain't never crashed her beyond repair. She's fast, too—souped her up a bit so she'll clear four hundred the whole damn way in a head-wind if we need 'er to. She blows a little smoke when she does, 'course. I mean she gets awful hot runnin' like that, but it don't seem to hurt nothin'. Yep—she'll do us just fine. She's my favorite plane, I think."

Tom showed us where to put our bags and shuffled them around a bit to get the weight just right. Then he sat us down in the cockpit with me in the front seat first, whereupon he switched us so that Doug was riding shotgun. I'm not sure which one of us was fatter than he looked. Tom put on his headset, lit his fifth cigarette without asking if it was alright, and started pushing buttons and talking in jargon to someone in a tower somewhere. This was followed by about ten minutes of sitting in silence before some more jargon was spewed, some more buttons were pushed, and the plane's engine flipped on, lurching us forward to a distant tarmac at the other end of the airport. It took us about ten minutes to get there.

"Alright boys," Tom shouted over the engine roar when we were settled in to place, "this here's the fun part—up an' away! Milau here we come!" He let out a sudden, gleeful cowboy shout and tilted his head back, unsettling his headset slightly. Cigarette still firmly in mouth, he pushed up the throttle shouting "balls to the wall, boys, balls to the wall!" and in a few moments we were off the ground watching the runway shrink behind us. I took a last deep breath of low altitude oxygen as the world gave in to its more gentle nature and the engine hum filled the air with a cacophonous silence. It's always free in those spaces between—it gives you the sense that you haven't really opened your eyes before, or at least not in a long time. Palm trees and resort hotels and ocean, ocean, ocean, and we were gone.

We didn't talk very much on the flight over, mostly because it was so loud in the plane. Absolutely everything rattled in some way, giving us a lot of uncomfortable insight into the science of mechanical gerontology. Tom was right about the smoke, which you could see streaming by us most of the time, though we were going so fast that it didn't seem to really get into the cabin at all. He tried to chat a little bit about the Tigers (the baseball team), figuring correctly that that was our "club," as he called it. When Doug turned out to know anything at all about baseball, Tom got rambling about more shortstops and middle relievers than I knew existed anywhere in God's creation. Doug kept nodding like he neither understood, nor wished to become better informed, though that was no deterrence to Tom. Then we asked him a few questions about Milau.

"What's it like there?" Doug said.

"Oh, it's beautiful," said Tom, looking away from the wind-shield for much too long, "yep—just gorgeous. They've got this pritty lagoon—you should see it! I mean…you're gonna see it, so I guess I don't need to say that. Uh, anyway, the women are beautiful too, and so are the beaches, and the trees're also beautiful. There's some places t' skin-dive 'round there, and those're beautiful. There used t' be a resort up on the top 'a the island, and that was just beautiful. And they've got all these birds that land there—some special type that only ever come

there, y'know, called Striped-Footed Boobies, I think, and they're beautiful, let me tell ya. And the women are beautiful…I guess I already said
that. They wear these flowin' dresses a lot—look a little like kimonos or
something—all white, sometimes with flower patterns, and those are just
beautiful. Between you fellas an' me, the men are beautiful too—I'm just
saying, y'know, just an observation—I can appreciate when a man's got
good looks. Yeah, I guess I'd just say it's beautiful, pritty much." Doug
and I nodded, which Tom was able to notice because he still wasn't looking in front of him.

"So, you'll be coming back for us after the three weeks are up?" Doug
asked.

"Yessir—I'll be there right on the dot. That won't be any problem. Me
getting' home is a bit more complicated, though. I've only got enough
in the tank to get out there, so I'll need to scrounge up some gas on the
island which—gets a little tricky 'cause they don't have a regular station
or nothin'. Gotta go door-t'-door, and haggle for a good price. I've got
plenty 'a Yen, but whatever I don't spend on gas I git to spend on drinks,
so I like to negotiate. Sometimes gotta wait some people out for a day or
two, so I might be around for a while—maybe a week even. Yeah, and
that reminds me, there's only one bar, and all they got's a liquor they
make over there from bread-fruit and pineapple. Tastes like rubbin' alcohol, they call it Aijee, that's short for Island Gin. They mix the stuff with
pickle juice and a little sea water, and, you know somethin', it doesn't
taste half bad—at least not after the first couple. Gets you movin' fast,
if you know what I mean. Anyway, when I've sobered up I'll be back to
Hawaii and then back out to get you boys."

"Oh—will you have to do that again when you come back—I mean, the
asking around for gas?" Doug asked with a worried look.

"Nope—I'll bring my own fuel on the way to git ya. Won't have you
boys to carry, so I can fill up the plane with jerry cans. I love the smell
when the plane's all full like that—makes the trip go awfully fast, if

you know what I mean. I just shut my eyes for a minute or two and I'm there—like a baby nappin' in the car, ain't that right?" He laughed from his gut and turned around to look at me while I tried to take a deep breath and smile. We hit a patch of turbulence and the plane shuddered hard while the stall horn screamed. "Giddyup, boys!" shouted Tom, "it's gonna be a bull ride the whole way, I'll betcha!" Doug smiled like that was good news, and I lay my head back. Maybe it was the thin air, or maybe the slowly growing sense that this really might be my last flight ever, but before too long I actually fell asleep. I don't know how long I was out, just that I was awoken again by the sunlight suddenly hitting me square in the eyes through the still rattling window.

# 3

The plane was descending in long wide loops over a crescent-shaped atoll curving around a blue lagoon. I rubbed my eyes a bit and peered out the rattling window. The island was outlined by a strip of white beach surrounding several elongated patches of green brush, one of which, to the south, was quite substantial. There were maybe a dozen boats of various shapes and sizes out on the lagoon. You could see a little town near the center and just to the north a cleared out grassy area jutting out on the ocean side of the island that looked like some kind of landing strip. On the other side of the town sat a big gray box—our factory—with a couple of exhaust chimneys flipping us the bird as we circled past. This was surrounded by an astounding number of brining vats (it's eight hundred, to be precise, not that I was counting on the flight) that seemed to stretch along about half the outside coast. Not far from the plant on the lagoon was a pretty hefty mass of concrete that looked like an old shipping port of some kind, in serious disrepair. On the far north end of the island we could see a sprawling complex which, even from the air, was quite obviously a resort hotel—or had been, at some point.

Tom was beaming all over the place, but flew in silence, ever lower, in broad circles. He apparently wanted to flirt with the tops of some of the palm trees as we got ready to land. His grin gave the impression that there was some kind of game he was playing inside his mind with its own set of rules about how to best tempt death. With one last loop over the trees, he let out a barely audible prayer—yes, a prayer—and with a sudden look of deep seriousness he closed his eyes completely. Bracing the controls with his knee, he put his hands carefully on his lap. With a deep breath and a look of placid sublimity, he nodded as though listening to some silent voice, and we hit the water with a silken touch, easily the smoothest plane landing I've ever witnessed. Doug turned back to me and we widened our eyes at each other. He mouthed the words "who is this guy?" and I shook my head in erstwhile terrified disbelief. Tom suddenly sprang up from his transcendent silence.

"Here we are, boys!" he said with a smile, looking over at us like nothing was the slightest bit out of place. "Welcome to Milau—hope you brought your passports. Ha…I'm only kidding, they don't check for passports here. You can just stroll right in." He winked at us.

We were now afloat on the lagoon in the middle of the island, and Tom piloted us toward a small wooden dock jutting out from the beach close to what appeared to be the town. "The hotel's just up on the main road there," he pointed behind a row of palm trees at the only two story building that we could see, "right there—can't miss it. The bar's next door, and you can get some food there or at the hotel most every day. Other than fish and everything, they eat a lot 'a goat—consider it a big treat, in fact. I like it barbequed myself." We nodded in a "sounds delicious" sort of way.

I looked around from island level at our surroundings. The lagoon was that bright kind of pale blue, almost sky-like and streaked with moments of emerald and white. The palm trees swayed a little in the breeze while soft waves lapped up on the white sand shore. Some boats and people were visible along the beach, fishing or swimming, mostly smiling all over. It was, in sum, a big tropical idyll—as much as you could ask for. As we floated into the dock, a deep sense of peace settled over me—one of the only times I was ever glad that I had come. If the trip was going to be a headache, then at least it was a headache in paradise.

We bumped up against the dock, and two young men in bathing trunks without shirts suddenly appeared, climbing up a little ladder from the water. They started tossing lines about to tie us off. Tom gave them a wave, then killed the engine, unbuckled himself and hopped out onto one of the pontoons, nimbly working his way around to the dock itself. Doug and I waited until the plane seemed settled before we opened our doors and stepped out. A couple of old fishermen were smoking cigarettes and sitting on a beaten-up motor boat tied off near the plane. They each gave us a casual little wave like seeing people arrive on the island this way was pretty routine, or had been at one time in the past.

"Well, there you are, boys," said Tom with an already half-smoked cigarette dangling off his lips. "It's been a real pleasure flying with you. Like I said, I'll be around for a bit, so if you need me before I leave, just ask over at the Conch and Dodo. That's the name of the bar, did I mention that? Anyway, if I'm not there, they'll know where I am. Otherwise, I'll see you boys in about three weeks." He had unloaded our bags from the back hold while he was talking, and we picked them up. "Thanks fellas," he said to the two young men, handing them a few coins each. They stuffed these into their pockets and immediately dove back into the water, laughing and splashing at one another as they had evidently been doing before we arrived.

By the time I turned around from straightening out the handle on my duffel, Tom was half-way down the dock already, and a figure in a flowing white dress was approaching us from the shore. The tropical air circled around the light fabric she was wearing—apparently one of the flowing dresses Tom had mentioned—sending it up in billows. She walked with a slowness and confidence, carrying a small stack of papers in her left hand. She was on the short side, about thirty, with big round eyes, quite an inviting face, really, though she held on it a serious and professional look that seemed more genuine than affected. Her beauty struck me as a simple fact of no particular consequence. Not so for Doug. He was staring at her with his mouth literally ajar, like a retriever on the wrong side of the IQ curve.

When she had made it to us, she extended her hand to me. "Martha Tok," she said in perfect English, with a very slight and difficult to place accent. "Corporate Liaison for Saf-T-Set Milau. Welcome to our island." I shook her hand and introduced myself. Doug just stood there like an idiot. She didn't seem to notice, though she also didn't try to shake his hand. "I am quite happy that your plane arrived as planned," she said, "I had been worried there might be a delay. Let me take you over to your accommodations," said Martha, turning around. "You can get settled in there, and then I will return and take you both for dinner where we can discuss business."

We followed her up the dock to the beach, through a row of palm trees, and onto a dirt road with occasional patches of pavement so broken and isolated that they probably would have destroyed an average car suspension. Turning down the road, we passed through a neat row of clean white buildings. They all looked like they had been built on the cheap in one go—just flat boxes each of the same shape and size. They were all painted white, and as such they made the place feel somehow both Spanish colonial and post-apocalyptic. The only exception was a large building near the middle of town bearing a sign which proudly declared "City View Hotel" in green letters. This building, like I've already mentioned, had two stories, with two little balconies visible up on the second floor. Next to it there was a simple looking convenience and grocery market, evidently closed, and finally there was the bar, the Conch and Dodo, which had an elaborate neon sign, switched off in the waning daylight. The other buildings in the town appeared to be houses. On the door of one such house, just across from the hotel, there was taped a piece of yellowing newspaper with the word "Bank" written on it in thick black marker. And that was that: the commercial district of downtown Milau.

Just next to town, such as it was, a long and really beautiful stretch of beach ran as far as the eye could see down the lagoon. Behind the hotel you could see a church steeple with a little bell in it, and the roofs of a good number of houses spilled out on a disorganized series of side streets. Near the beach there was a single lonely flagpole flying a flag with a purple field and a very small dot of slightly darker purple in the center. That's the flag of Milau, which I'm told represents the island itself and its surroundings (the ocean) and makes a veiled reference to the eventuality of the island's destruction by the sea.

Martha led us into the hotel. There was a young woman sitting behind a tall old-fashioned desk, the kind with the little key boxes behind it. Martha said something to her in Milauan, and she smiled and handed over two sets of keys without putting down her book. Evidently we were checked in. We walked up the stairs to the second floor where Martha politely opened up the doors to our two rooms and gestured to show us in. Our eyes popped, or at least mine did (Doug might still have been staring at Martha). The rooms were spacious, with big king beds, decorated in lavish blues, reds and golds, tapestries and ebony carvings on the walls, fine wicker furniture, small comfortable ensuite bathrooms and each with a balcony and a spectacular view of the beach and lagoon. Everything was clean but with a warm and inviting aroma. I blinked my eyes before I set my bags down. I had been expecting a dingy hole in the ground.

"They will have breakfast in the restaurant downstairs every morning at eight, except Sunday," said Martha, "the islanders tend to eat caviar—well, it is a local fish roe more technically, from flying fish—very simple, but if you would prefer grilled goat and eggs, that can also be arranged."

"Uh," I said, looking back at her from where my eyes were fixed on the brilliant water, "uh, caviar is fine…" I trailed off. Doug had disappeared into his room, and Martha stepped over to give him the same information.

"Please take your time to settle in," she said when she returned. "I will be back in half an hour and escort you to dinner." With that, she was gone. I took a deep breath and slid open the door to the little terrace. The gentle salt air curled up through my nostrils.

"Holy crap!" Doug exclaimed, charging into my room, "Look at this place! I can't believe it! I mean, this has got to be one of the nicest rooms I've ever stayed in. And in this little nothing city—what the hell?" he stopped and pushed his hand through his hair, "and if the rest of the women are anything like Martha…"

I nodded, "Very pretty," I said.

"You ain't kiddin'!" Doug practically shouted. "Man…well, I'm gonna take a shower then, and freshen up a bit. This is gonna be great!" and he was gone.

I sat down on the bed and slowly started to unpack my things, my eyes trying to stay glued to the view of the lagoon while I worked. The sun was setting right over it, like somebody had done up the scene for one of those tourist brochure photos, lacking only the requisite sexy thirty-something leaning against a palm-tree with her back to the camera. Even without her it was pretty magnificent. After unpacking, I decided I had time for a quick shower, so I took one. I was sitting out on the terrace watching the last purple shades from the sun dissipate into black when a knock came on the door. Martha opened without waiting for me, and signaled that I should follow her. She disappeared and I heard her knock on Doug's door. After a couple of minutes waiting silently for him to emerge, we were off.

Martha walked quickly ahead of us down the stairs and through a small door beside the front desk. The girl behind the counter was still there, and smiled at us over her book as we passed. Beyond the door was a lovely little restaurant, with dark wood tables and furniture in good repair. Martha sat us down at a round table in the corner. The room was lit up in a welcoming orange emanating both from the tasteful sconces on the walls and the last bits of sunset tumbling through the windows. The only other thing really notable about the place was a tall wood statue standing in the corner. It was a male figure with long legs, reaching up into the sky and making a face like he had just bitten into something both bitter and sour.

"It is from the old religion of our people," said Martha when she saw me looking at it, "a god which our ancestors worshiped. This was the god of the shore of the lagoon. Now it is only a statue…decoration." She didn't seem interested in talking about it, so I didn't press her for more information. A waiter with a white apron approached us, with a pad in hand, but no menus.

"Three tall glasses of Aijee," Martha said without asking, "and three glasses of water." She turned to us, "since you have just arrived, it is the custom for us to eat an elegant meal. You may order your goat how you prefer. I will have it traditional, please," she said, turning to the waiter again.

"Me too!" Doug nodded eagerly, then asked Martha, "what's traditional mean?"

"Oh," said Martha, not expecting the question, "yes. It is first boiled in vinegar, then encrusted in salt, and it is served with oyster sauce. Very chewy and delicious."

"Uh," I said slowly, remembering Tom's recommendation, "barbequed please." The waiter nodded again and was gone. In a few moments he returned with six glasses, three a pale green color, the other three filled with clear water. He also had a tray full of pickles in about eight different cuts. Gerkins, sandwich slices, ridged, sweet, some kind of waffle-cut pickles I had never seen before, and I think a few others. He set every-thing down and disappeared again. Doug fell to on the waffle-cut pickles and I sipped my Aijee. My lips puckered up, but there was a sweet floral aroma to it that made it pretty drinkable despite the barbaric level of salt.

Martha placed her stack of papers on the table and opened up a folder. Doug paused for a long moment before straightening up and clearing his throat, at which point he took out his own papers and tried to look like he was interested in the business of why we had come.

"I have received a package of materials pertaining to your visit by post, gentlemen," she began, "and I understand the situation as well as pos-sible given the information that I have. I will let the plant and opera-tions manager discuss most of the specifics with you tomorrow. Forgive me, I should have mentioned it…I will bring you for a tour of the pickle facility after breakfast. After that, you will have complete access to it, and any information there that you might need to fulfill your duties. All records for Saf-T-Set pertaining to operations on the island are housed there." We smiled and nodded.

She went on. "I am also sorry that we have not been able to communicate with you more easily on these matters. As you know, the phones have been down for quite some time. That is because of a cyclonic storm—a hurricane—which passed over Milau some months ago. The necessary repairs have not yet been made. You, however, should be made aware of the reason for that." She paused ominously and gave me a very serious stare-down kind of look. "There has been a great deal of confusion on Milau of late—a lot of distraction which has kept us from attending to simple pieces of business like the phone lines. Our political situation…is bad, gentlemen…it is, at present, extremely volatile. There are serious concerns—I will spare you any details now—about the ecological and economic condition of our country. At the present time, we are exactly ten days from a major election. It appears that the opposition party is likely to capture the presidency and may well capture most of the seats in parliament as well. And, gentlemen, I am afraid to report that that may have consequences even for your work here." She trailed off quietly.

"Oh?" I asked, prompting her.

"Yes," she continued, looking back up at us. "The opposition…is quite unfriendly to the American government, and strongly opposes the presence of Saf-T-Set here on the island. They have opposed the company from the very beginning, in fact, though they were a small minority at that time. Now, however, they seem to have gained the support of most Milauans. What is more, they are becoming increasingly open about their ties to a small group of…" she stopped for a moment and looked around at the empty restaurant to see that no one could hear her, "a small group of activists on the island who have been accused of…terrorism…by the current party in power." Doug's eyes got pretty big as he looked over at me. "I don't know what else to tell you about the situation, gentlemen," she said sadly, "but your visit comes at a difficult time." We were silent.

"Still," she said eventually, "you should be able to compile the necessary reports in regards to the plant, and I am very happy to carry out my duties assisting you in that capacity. With some good fortune, you will not encounter any problems. However, it seems to me that you might do well to meet with the American ambassador on the island at some point—at least to make him aware that you are here. I believe he is expecting you, in fact. The ambassador is a pleasant man, I am sure he will be happy to help in any way he can."

"Great," said Doug, as though everything were straightforward, "Sounds like we've got a plan. Talk to the plant manager, talk to the ambassador. Easy!"

Martha smiled brightly at Doug's reaction to what she had said. "Good, then," she replied, "then we will simply proceed tomorrow."

About then our food arrived, along with a new tray of pickles (Doug had polished off all the waffle-cut ones and requested some more of those) and another round of Aijee, which was starting to taste pretty good. I cut into my barbequed goat and ate it. It tasted about like you'd imagine—the sauce was basically Kansas City style, but zipped up with some pineapple. Doug and Martha began chewing on their goat-meat, Doug doing so quite loudly while Martha managed to make it look elegant, even while opening her mouth really wide as if she were trying to reveal its contents. Martha started looking up at Doug periodically with an elusive smile. I got the impression that she liked something about both his optimism and his chewing skills, but I don't know for sure which was more important.

I ate pretty quickly, but it took the two of them about forty-five minutes to finish their dinner. I ended up having five glasses of Aijee, and was feeling pretty comfortable with the ambient sounds of teeth-gnashing and lack of conversation by the time they were done. For dessert the waiter brought out a tray of sweet gerkins rolled in powdered sugar. With all the booze in my stomach, I recall them tasting pretty good. Doug ate them with the élan of a person chowing down on a piece of his mom's famous apple pie for the first time in years. Martha politely took one and left the rest to us. After dinner, Martha paid the bill, explaining that everything was being covered by the company. She wished us a pleasant evening and confirmed that we knew our way back upstairs. Then she departed with a bow followed by handshakes for each of us. Doug sat back in his chair in satisfaction.

"Sounds like things are a bit crazy here, huh?" he said. "At least the food and weather are good. And, it probably won't matter for us. We're doing our own thing, right? We've got lots of time to take it nice and slow. No stress."

"Yeah," I said, "sounds about right, I hope. Seems a little funny to be meeting with an ambassador—but, I guess it's a pretty small place. Still…disconcerting."

"It'll be fine," said Doug with a wave of his hand, "she's just being thorough, I'm sure. It'll be fun, too. I've never met an ambassador before."

We both took the last swig of our drinks. With nothing else to do, we looked at the wall for a few minutes before picking ourselves up to go get some sleep. I gave a hazy wave to the girl behind the counter, still reading, and in a moment I was lying in bed. I didn't even manage to turn off the light before I slipped from consciousness.

# 4

In the morning I got up, took a shower, and headed down for breakfast. I had expected to be feeling pretty hung over after going through so much alcohol and salt water on top of a few hours' jet-lag, but whether it was the island air or something else, not only did I not feel awful, but on the whole everything seemed better than average. I grabbed a table in the restaurant near the window and ate the roe and toast that they brought me. They made a good cup of coffee there, too—really good, in fact. The waiter mentioned that they grew the stuff on the island, but islanders basically never drank it. It had a nice rich flavor, no bitterness. Doug came in just before nine looking like complete crap. He sat down across from me, eyes boggling around the room.

"Ugh," he said, "what the hell, man? Aren't you feeling…I mean…you're, like, fine…"

"Yeah, I feel great," I said, "Slept better than I have in years. Hey, flag the waiter over—this breakfast is top notch." The waiter brought out Doug's food. "Eat up," I said, "fish eggs are good for a hang-over." He screwed up his courage (I guess he had never had the stuff before), downed some on a piece of toast, and seemed to perk up a bit.

A few minutes later, Martha came in wearing a pant suit with the same stack of papers in her hand. She pulled up a chair and sat down next to us. "How is your breakfast?" I complimented the meal profusely. Doug just rubbed his head a little and had some more coffee. "As soon as you are finished, we can go up for the tour of the plant."

"Are you feeling up to it?" I asked Doug.

"Yeah," he said, not really sounding like he meant it, "I'll be fine…eventually."

I finished my last swig of coffee, and we all got up to go. Martha led us back out of the hotel, past the girl at the desk, who was midway through a new volume, and out into town. The whole place was filled with the sound of birds—the Striped-Footed Boobies, I guess. Martha mentioned that it was their breeding season, and apologized that they were so loud. I told her I rather liked the sound of birds in the morning, and she gave a crooked smile.

"I took care of one of them as a little girl," she said, gazing off, "from a nest the mother had abandoned. It would eat from my hand. They are silly creatures, and not very pretty. But they are good…they leap about in a dance when they start to learn to fly—they do the same dance when they are looking for a mate. Funny things. It liked watching it fly away." She turned to me and smiled.

She led us up the main road toward the dock and then veered off on a little path through a patch of trees. It ran through a few palms back into the clear where the ugly gray box of the plant greeted us. We entered through a small door. Inside, the place was loud and hallow. A handful of workers swished back and forth like the last swig of beer in a bottle. Well, what can I say?—it smelled like pickles and metal. We were in a big open room that they apparently used for cleaning and cutting cucumbers. In the middle of the room, looking right at us and sitting on a small cheap-looking desk chair (without a desk, mind you), was a short man with a long nose and tiny circle-rimmed glasses. He stood up when he saw us.

"Good morning, sirs," he said in a heavier accent than Martha, "it is a pleasure to meet you here today."

Martha motioned to him as he extended his hand. "This is Baya Vin, the plant and operations manager. He has been working for the company since its very first day on the island."

"Very pleased to meet you, sirs," he said as we greeted him, "and very glad that you have come here to examine the facility. It has been quite some time since we have had any communication or written contact with headquarters. We are very pleased to welcome you for the inspection and report. I am sure you will find everything up to speed and in working order as it should be. And entirely according to protocol! I am a believer in protocol, sirs. I very much stand by it. I am known throughout the island as the grand Babu of company policy, if you know what I mean." We, of course, had no idea what he meant, "Please, please, come this way and let me show you around."

He started in on a short tour. The plant was basically one spacious room with a bunch of cutting and cleaning machines for prepping the cucumbers, a room with all the jarring machines, and a storage space. It was all a pretty standard design, acceptably efficient, nothing miraculous, nothing odd. "These are the vats," Baya indicated, drawing us over to a window to take a look. The vats were set up in rows outside, as usual for this kind of place, and, as I think I've said, there were an exceptionally large number of them. That made sense, though, since we were evidently sourcing all of our North Pacific pickles from the facility. Baya continued, "they are all state of the art technology, the most up-to-date vats available, which we have kept in excellent repair and in fine condition since the founding of the plant those many years ago. Yes, very clean, but not soapy—it would be very much against the protocol to have soap in the pickling vats, as I am sure you are well aware. But clean, of course, unless there are pickles in them in which case they are quite pickley. And through here is the jarring line where we fill the jars and put the pickles into the jars. It is also quite clean and sanitary, everything up to protocol. There you can see the jars moving around on their little line. Ah—they are not running at this very moment, but you can see where they would be running. I like to think of them as ants all marching—marching to pick up the pickles and then marching away from the colony. I always feel like a queen ant, sirs, as I am sure you can understand, for I have no children of my own. It would be nice to be a queen ant, would it not, sirs?" We nodded, and Doug seemed like he actually meant it. "And here is where the pickles are stored once they have been placed in their jars and where the jars are kept once they have pickles in them. They just stay there in storage, not moving, until they are sent out."

"About that," I interjected, "how do they actually get from here to the United States anyway?"

"Oh, I am not at all certain, sir, precisely how they get all the way to the United States. I have never been to the United States, and I do not know correctly how far away it is. It is a sizable distance I believe, is it not? I suspect that the jars cannot just be floated there, is that correct sir?"

"Uh…" I said, "you mean, just floated out across the ocean…likes logs down a river or something?"

"Yes, that is what I meant, but as I said, I should suspect that they cannot be floated in such a way at any point in the journey, though the jars do float, sir, it would not be a problem with their being floatable, but most probably it would be impossible due to distance, yes? So I suppose that that is not how they arrive in the United States. Is there perhaps a large port somewhere in the United States at which they could arrive on boat? I am uncertain, sir, I am afraid I am not an expert in these matters."

"Okay…" I said very slowly, "where do the pickle jars go from here."

"Oh!" he said with sudden understanding. "From here we would…I mean, we have in the past…and are…still taking them now, are we?" He seemed really confused here about what was going on, "to the large concrete dock…to be loaded onto…freight ships. From there, I believe, they are taken to another island or perhaps all the way to the United States, as I was saying? Of this I am not certain, for once the pickles have left this factory they are no longer under my control and are no longer any of my concern. I do not know who is responsible for all these various and diverse activities after they are loaded onto the freighters, but it has been working this way since the plant was built."

"Alright, then." I paused and mulled over how to ask the next question. "So," I decided to go for the sidle-up approach, "have the pickles been getting shipped out…as usual lately? I mean, have there been any disruptions at all?"

Baya's eyes got large and he sighed like he was letting out a breath he had been holding for the past hour. "Uh…" he said slowly, scratching his neck, "uh, yes…yes, there have been some disruptions…with the main shipping company…yes. That is why you are here, of course and indeed. Yes, there is one primary company…a fairly small company that we rely on for most of the island's supplies…and…one of their boats…is in need of repair…it has shut them down temporarily, and so we have been simply storing…the product…for now. Nothing at the fault of the plant—everything is running exactly to protocol, yes! The shipping…company…it is their responsibility from that point, and they have been dragging their heels. I have been putting pressure on them for some time, but to no avail."

"Okay…how long has that been going on—the problem with the shipping company?"

"Well…" he said, "let me see…I suppose perhaps nine months now—perhaps a little less."

"I see," I said, "well that explains where the shipments have disappeared. We haven't gotten one in the United States for eight months now."

"Yes, I am very glad we have solved the mystery!" He was suspiciously excited here. "This is most certainly the problem you have been having…with the boat! Now that we are aware of the problem, I will speak with the shipping company further. Yes, it has become unacceptable, the situation! Do not trouble over this, I will be certain to deal with it tomorrow, and have it fixed right away. And we would indeed have contacted you about it, but as you know it is very difficult—the phone disruptions, as you know…from the storm."

"Yes, Martha mentioned that to us," I looked over at her. She looked at me nervously. "So, how have you been receiving supplies here, then?"

"Right this way!" said Baya, still nervously. He led me over to a loading bay door and barked an order at a passing employee who opened it up. "Right through here, sir, everything comes in here and is placed in this holding area until we are ready to use it."

"Yes…" I said, trying to remain patient, "but I mean, how do you get your supplies here on the island? The same company, or someone else?"

"Oh!" he said, "yes…we do receive supplies…from the same company, I believe. That would explain why we have been short on supplies of late. We will soon have to slow production, I believe, and stop storing our products, perhaps."

"Alright," I said turning to Doug, "So, I guess it's the shipping company that is creating the problem here. Probably why most companies don't build these things in the middle of the ocean—but what do I know?" Doug smirked.

"As I said," Baya interjected, "I will speak with the shipping company tomorrow."

"Okay," I said. "And what's the name of the company? Do they have an office on the island or anything—is there a way to get a hold of them?"

"Uh…" said Baya, his eyes getting wide with apparent anxiety, "I do not even recall the name, I am sorry sir. I am sure our records at the plant will show. I do believe that they have a representative on the island…or an office, yes—for me to speak with. I do believe so. Please, check the records, sir, and you will perhaps be able to make some progress that way."

"Alright," I said slowly, beginning to wonder about Baya's continually strange responses to everything I said, "that was my next question. Can you show us where you keep records and all that?"

"Yes!" exclaimed Baya happily, apparently eager to change the subject, "Yes, let me show you into the plant office where you may examine the various records and documents pertaining to all of our operations. I am sure you will need this in order to compile your report and find the information you need." He walked us quickly through a set of two small doors and into a little office with a desk, several filing cabinets, and an old computer terminal with a green and black screen and the words "Nort Pacific PIc" burned into the face of the monitor like you used to see sometimes. On a shelf in the corner there was an intricate little wood carving of what looked like a chubby baby somehow trapped inside an egg, confusion and perplexity on her face. Baya noticed me looking at it. "Yes, that is an old carving from our ancestors," he said, "it is a god they once worshiped. This was the goddess of the seeds of the grass. It is a very beautiful carving."

"Definitely," I said, "I take it these things are common around here? We saw one in the hotel."

"Oh?" he asked somewhat proudly, "yes, we have kept many of them—tokens of our past—decorative, now. We are proud of the artists who made them. Anyway, sirs, this is the office, and all our records and documents are here—you may examine whatever you like. This cabinet contains the data since the last inspection, so you will most probably wish to focus on this cabinet—oh, but I am not trying to give you any undue instructions, oh, no, no! That is not my place, sirs!"

"Thanks, Baya…" said Doug, "this is great."

"Very good, sirs," he went on, "and please do not hesitate to approach me should you require any assistance with the documents or any other matter regarding the plant. You may inspect any of the facilities at your leisure, at any time. Please take this ring of keys," he handed Doug a thick rattling hoop of about fifty keys, "which will allow you into any door in the facility, and will open any of the locks as well, though I might request that you not unlock the drainage tubes on the pickle vats without letting me know—though you are well within your rights to do so! You may drain all the pickles completely if you choose! You will hear no complaints from me or any of the workers here if you do!"

"We won't do that," said Doug, "thanks for the heads-up."

"Very good, sirs, whatever you like," said Baya, "if you will excuse me, I do need to return to my work—always very busy as I am sure you would assume. Always making sure everything is up to protocol. And everything is, sirs, I can assure you—please believe me. As I said, I will speak with the shipping company right away. Consider the problem solved!"

"Thanks, Baya," I said, "you've been very helpful. We'll come find you if we need anything else." He bowed deeply and left the room.

"May I be of any further service at the moment, gentlemen?" asked Martha deferentially.

"Uh," I said slowly, "no…I don't think so." Doug seemed like he was trying to think up a reason for her to stay, but came up short, and just shrugged his shoulders in agreement.

"Very good, then," she said, "I will leave you to your work."

"Oh!" said Doug, "where would we…find you, if we need you?"

"Yes," said Martha, "my office is located in my home, which is very easy to find from the hotel. It is simply up the road which runs along the north wall, leading past the church." She explained in detail where it was. We proved ourselves by repeating her directions back like a couple of teenagers studying for a driver's test with their dad. Then she headed out the door and was gone.

"What in the hell is going on here?" Doug asked after the door shut, "that song and dance from Baya was just…what was that?"

"Yeah," I said, sitting down. "I don't know. How could he think we wouldn't know about the stoppage in deliveries?"

"Exactly. Could he possibly not have known why we're here?"

"No," I said, "he must have known. He was sitting here waiting for us. Something is going on."

"Well," said Doug, "not that I'm eager to get to work or anything, but maybe we should look through some of these files. I'm hoping there might be a blue-print in here somewhere anyway."

"Yeah," I said, "and I think I'd like to see if I can figure out who the shipping company is that he was talking about and maybe track them down. I mean, first he insists that he'll take care of that right away and everything is as good as fixed, and then says he doesn't even remember their name? Fishy as hell." Doug agreed.

So, we started looking through some of the filing cabinets to see what we could find. I think you've already seen most of the important documents. If you haven't, you should take a look on your own time. I couldn't tell you very much about them from memory. But, I guess there are a couple of general things that I should say here. To begin with, there were four filing cabinets in the office that were completely empty, which seemed odd. However, the documents that we did find in the other cabinets were in decent shape. We had numbers dating back for ten years on everything going in and going out, budgets and ledgers, legal documents (which didn't have much bearing on me), employee and payroll logs and records—the works, as far as we could tell. But, and this is important, we *only* had numbers going back ten years. There was nothing—not a scrap of paper that I could find that first day—referencing anything to do with the previous decade of the plant's existence (I think I've mentioned, and you already know, that the plant was twenty years old). So, there was a big gap. And despite that very important anomaly, there was one more thing that was even more strange about what I found. The basic figures in terms of the plant's operations, I mean the ones I was interested in regarding the actual production of the pickles, while diligently recorded, didn't make the slightest bit of sense.

So, most people know that most commercially marketed pickles are basically made out of cucumbers and vinegar with some salt and a handful of run-of-the-mill food-safe chemicals, plus, for the sweet ones, some kind of sugar or corn syrup or whatever. Now, given our location in the Pacific ocean, all of those ingredients had to get shipped in from somewhere. And the ledgers, indeed, showed they were. But there were a whole lot of red flags.

So, salt and vinegar for instance. According to the logs, the plant was really only taking in enough of those ingredients for maybe a few thousand jars of pickles a year, absolute tops, and that meant that the theoretical maximum output of the plant (which should have been about fifty million pounds a year) was several thousand times what the salt and vinegar could have supported. After noticing that, I started looking at the rest of our ingredients. Cucumbers and corn-syrup matched again for a total maximum output of almost nothing. That, in itself, struck me as good news because it seemed to indicate that I was simply misreading something or missing some other stack of records. But it became clear that something else was afoot when I noticed what was going on with the supply of polysorbate 80 and yellow 5. According to a couple of rough sums I did, the plant was signing for as much yellow five by weight as it was for cucumbers, and it was doing so at astronomical prices—hundreds of thousands of dollars of food coloring every month. You could have turned the whole lagoon bright piss yellow ten times over if you wanted, and you still would have had plenty left over for the plant while running at its *actual* full capacity, which, again, it could not have been doing given the supply of other ingredients. Same story with the polysorbate 80, though I haven't a clue what it would do to the lagoon if you dumped that in there.

So, basically what we appeared to have on our hands was a pickle factory that provided all of North America with its entire stockpile of a top-five brand of pickles, and which did so while only making enough pickles to supply no more than three or four grocery stores for about three weeks. Either the company had Jesus on a receiving dock in Toledo working a loaves-and-fishes miracle to the benefit of Saf-T-Set's bottom line, or something was terribly wrong. Mind you, North Pacific pickles really do get produced. They exist—they're on supermarket shelves. And while I recall briefly considering the possibility that no one *ever* bought our brand, and so all those shelves were just stocked with the one original shipment that ever made it to the US, I quickly concluded that that was probably even more absurd than the Jesus hypothesis. So…there you go.

Okay, like I said, you ought to just take a look at the numbers yourself if you want more detail.

That first day at the plant, I basically just did a quick mental audit of those numbers. Doug rifled around trying to find a schematic. He even tapped on the little computer for a while, though it quickly became obvious that that was pointless. In fact, the thing was so loud when he turned it on that we were honestly concerned it might blow, and after all the noise starting up, it didn't actually do anything except proudly display the same misspelled message already burned into the monitor. Anyway, despite going through files for several hours that day while I was doing the same, Doug never did find any kind of plan for the plant. After I had gotten a decent grip on the "situation," if you could even call it that, I set my papers down and explained to a still vaguely hopeful Doug what was going on with my end of things.

"So there's no way this plant is producing what the company says it's producing?" he asked after I gave him the numbers.

"No, no way. The plant isn't claiming that it *is*, in fact, which is the strangest thing about it." That reminds me, I ended up noticing that the output numbers matched the low input numbers. "So, our pickles have to be getting made somewhere else, I guess."

"Well, maybe they do make a lot of them back home, then," said Doug, "maybe Plank just didn't know that. I mean, he believed you when you made up a distribution center after all."

"Could be," I said, hoping to death that that was it. "And if that's the case, then this whole situation is pretty straightforward. We just shut down operations. A capacity loss of a few thousand jars would never even be noticed—it's probably less than what we lose to theft."

"Well, great!" said Doug, "let's assume that's the deal, then."

"It would be nice to be able to communicate with the company somehow to confirm that, though. But, nothing can be easy, can it?" Doug laughed at me.

"Look," he said after a few more minutes, "I've done about all I care to do here today. I'm not going to find any damn plans, and this place is stuffy as hell." I'm not sure if I mentioned that, but it was indeed stuffy as hell in there. "Why don't we knock off for the afternoon and head over to the Conch and Dodo for a drink or two, and then maybe check out the beach up the way or something."

I agreed to the plan and we picked up three or four folders that I really did want to look at in some detail, and headed out the office door. And that was when one last unusual and suspicious thing happened. When we got out from the office into the main cleaning and cutting room, everything was completely dark and utterly silent. Not a soul was there, including the supposedly busy and hard-working Baya—at least not as far as we could tell.

"Looks like we're not the only ones quitting for the day," Doug said, looking around in the little bit of light soaking its way around the exterior door and through the small windows.

"What the hell?" I murmured, looking around. "What time is it?"

"Looks like it's about three," said Doug, looking at his watch. "I switched this to island time while we were riding through that turbulence with Tom. Maybe they just quit early here—I mean, how much work can there be to do anyway? Don't the pickles just need to sit there for a while?"

"I don't know," I said, shaking my head, "let's just go. I don't want to think about it right now." We stepped towards the door on echoes, the kind that ring with particular cold clarity in the dark. The sunlight outside was a bit dazzling for a moment until our eyes adjusted to the blue-white glitter of the sky, a sight which, once we could really bear to take it in, made us feel like we were main-lining the essence of a more peaceful reality. I took a deep breath and tried to let everything just go. Maybe I really did.

"To the Shell and Bird!" said Doug, merrily christening the bar to which we had so far never been with its natural cockney nickname. We headed over there, back through the patch of trees and along the beach.

When we arrived the place was empty. A little bell rang as we came though the door. The joint was pretty brightly lit, and had formica table tops and red vinyl seats. It basically looked like a fifties style diner or some place like that. Behind the bar stood a slightly bored looking bartender staring out the window (which had no ocean view, just the little main street and the row of houses across the way). When he saw us he smiled in a genuinely friendly way, and without saying anything headed for a rack of glasses behind him and started in to mixing two drinks.

"You're the Americans," he said without looking back as we sat down on a couple of stools right in front of him. We said we were. "I don't take an order—you understand?" he turned with an inquiring expression. "No orders—all the same." We told him Aijee would be fine.

I was watching him mix our drinks when I noticed another one of the statues that now seemed to be everywhere on Milau, a small one standing on the shelf near the glasses. It was a male figure, extremely fat to the point that he was almost completely spherical. He had a look of maniacal laughter on his face.

"Which god is that?" I asked the bartender, pointing.

"Oh!" he said, looking up with a smile, "the god of alcohol, what else?" He turned to me and winked. I smiled back as he kept working on the drinks.

"Quiet afternoon in town, huh?" Doug asked when the two pale green glasses were slid our way.

"Yes," said the bartender, "yes, very quiet today." He enunciated pretty hard, but, like basically everybody we met, his English was close to perfect. "You two…are the first visitors in a long long time. You two are very welcome here, to our island." He smiled broadly and warmly. He was one of those guys who seems to have a genuine calling to tending bar.

"So, everybody knocked off early up at the plant today," Doug said, in a making-conversation kind of tone. "Is it a holiday or something?"

"Oh no," said the bar tender, "The holiday is coming up, but not today."

"So," I said, "does everybody just quit at three around here?"

"Not sure," the bar tender shook his head, starting to wipe the bar. "Barely anybody working at the plant at all anyway. Just a few, nothing like years go. Ten people, maybe. Baya Vin goes up—a couple others. Only busy day there is Monday when everyone from the island…they go up to buy pickles there."

"You mean to say just ten people are working there?" I asked.

"About," he said with a shrug.

"Do they actually make pickles at all, then?"

"Not sure," he said again, "they sell 'em, for sure. That's all I know." We fell silent. After a moment he smiled and stepped back through a little door into the kitchen.

"Well, shit," said Doug to me, "it's even worse than you thought, isn't it?"

"Yeah," I said shaking my head and taking a big sip of my drink.

"Sorry, man," Doug said, in a genuinely sympathetic tone. "Look, don't worry about it anymore for right now. We'll just have to track down Martha tomorrow, and probably Baya, too…and…see what they have to say. Nothing to do about it here." I agreed.

About that time, Tom the pilot showed up and sat down next to us, giving me a slap on the back as he did. The bar tender, who had reemerged from the kitchen, greeted him by name and started mixing up a drink for him, too.

"How you boys doin'?" Tom asked us jovially. We lied and said that we were fine and enjoying our time so far hanging around on the island.

"Yeah, looks like you two got a good sense of how t' organize your day 'round here. Three PM's about right for getting over to the Conch, ain't that right?"

"Have you rounded up any fuel yet?" asked Doug.

"Yeah!" Tom nearly shouted, "got it all in one shot, can you believe it? Ran right into a fella I met over here last time I was on the island. He actually remembered me, aint' that somethin'? Anyway, he's got some connections or somethin' like that, because, I'll tell ya, he had a stock-pile 'a gasoline likes a' which I ain't never seen. Couple 'a barrels of the stuff tucked away in a little hut on the north side 'a town up there. Other types 'a fuel, too, he said—anything that burns, practically, ha! Anyway, sold it to me for next to nothin', so I'm all set up here to just hang around for a few days an' live the good life a bit—maybe a week. Fella's name is Dominic Vin, if you boys happen to need 'im for somethin'.'"

"That was Baya's last name, wasn't it, Hill?" Doug asked.

"Yeah," Tom jumped in, "that's his brother, I think. Mentioned that he works for your plant or somethin' a' that sort, is that right?" We explained that we had met Baya earlier in the day. "Well, it really is a small world out here, that's for sure," Tom noted happily, "everybody is everybody's brother or cousin or somethin'. You boys met any nice island girls yet?"

"No," I said, while Doug was in the middle of nodding his head, "haven't really been looking."

"Oh, you should!" said Tom, "they're just the sweetest things. They'll fall in love with ya as soon as look at ya, most of 'em! You wouldn't regret it—but suit yourselves." Doug seemed really pleased.

After an hour or two the place had a decent pack of customers in it. We chatted it up with Tom pretty well, especially after several more rounds (he really must have gotten his fuel for cheap because he insisted on buying all our drinks) and had a generally good time. Once we got sick of hanging around there with him, we headed out in the darkening evening to explore a little bit of the island. That was the first night that the island darkness started to sink in a little. It's not just that there's no light, you know—it's a darkness that's real, I guess—a black liquidy thing that has a kind of presence that it brings like it's just sitting there next to you, not talking but aware of you. Anyway, it's probably only the coolness of the air there right on the ocean, but maybe you know what I mean. Doug and I roamed about in the moonlight, looked up at the stars, and just sat in the sand for a while. Aimless stuff, basically, but it was nice.

"Hey Hill," he said at one point late in the evening. He was pretty well drunk, but not obnoxiously so. "I'm glad you came out here…with me, I mean."

"Yeah," I said, "no problem."

"No really," he said. "I'm glad it's you. I mean—look at all this—this white moonlight everywhere. Look at it! Just stars and air and water. Most people wouldn't be sitting here. I don't know. I've been thinking for a while—I've been feeling holed up back at home. But it's not stuffy out here, do you know what I mean? I think maybe I'm growing crooked where I am."

"Yeah," I said, "I know how that can feel."

"But you don't mind it, do you?" he asked.

"Grand Rapids?" I said, "no. I like it fine. But I can understand."

"It's not that I don't like it," he responded, "I do. I just want to feel like I am where I am—not like I just woke up there confused. I forget what cold water tastes like, sometimes. Sitting out like this you remember." He paused a good while, then continued. "Maybe *that's* my problem—I should be *more* dead to it. I don't know…I just come out here and see everything all over like crazy, and then I just want more of that, I guess."

"Like some kind of beauty addict?" I chuckled almost under my breath.

"Yeah, man," he said, "exactly like that. It's not like I'd want it another way, but still—it can make you crazy, that's all. Then I worry, though—that everywhere becomes dead if you stay long enough. You can't run forever. But maybe it's all just me, huh? Maybe I've just got to look around better. But I just want to see it all, you know—get it digested. Then you can look back on it and remember. You filter things out that way. They're locked in. But, they're not alive either, are they?"

"I suppose not," I said, not sure if I was really following him.

"I'm sorry," Doug said, turning away, "it's all just the booze. Anyway, I just wanted to say I'm glad you came. That was all." I nodded with a smile and we fell silent, just looking up at the moon for a long time.

# 5

The next morning I got up for breakfast once again feeling fantastic. Evidently Aijee was some kind of tonic for my system. Doug, on the other hand, must have disimproved from his previous experience, because he didn't even come down to the restaurant during the time I ate my breakfast. He said later that he had been up half the night puking his guts out, and had only managed to get a few hours of headache riddled sleep in the late morning. Anyway, in his absence I had nothing much to do, and so was encouraged by the waiter to take a look at the island's newspaper. I was surprised to hear that there was such a thing, but there sat two copies of it, one for me, and one for Doug, now sentenced to loneliness by his hangover.

The paper was printed out on old scrap so that the back of each page (it had about five pages) had a bunch of inscrutable type-written words on it, presumably in Milauan. The fronts of each page were laid out pretty nicely in fairly classic style, though the headlines seemed exaggerated in size, perhaps in order to get the edition to look bigger than a leaflet. The paper was called The Milau City Plain Dealer, Sun-Times and Post-Gazette. I don't even know what to say about that.

Anyway, the paper that morning had something like seven stories in it along with one cartoon strip, a Blondie which looked to be about twenty years old (though it's always tough to tell with Blondie). The punchline, because I'm sure you care, was Dagwood eating an enormous sandwich. That's always the way with Dagwood. Three of the other stories in the paper were part of an ongoing exposé series about a local fisherman who called his wife a particularly nasty name in public. I confess, I got a bit sucked in to those, but I won't bother about them here since I'm getting way off the point. The reason I bring up the paper at all is that two of the stories were pretty important to what happened.

The first was on the front page. The headline loudly screamed that the National Front for Milauan Liberation and Ascendancy (the current opposition party in the Milauan parliament, I gathered) was now leading in the polls for the upcoming election with seventy percent of the projected vote. The story noted with great excitement that it was the only time in history that a party's lead before the election was actually big enough to surpass the outrageous margins of error common to Milauan polls due to tiny sample sizes, and so for the first time ever the Plain Dealer, Sun-Times and Post-Gazette was ready to make a real projection about what would happen if the election were that day—a true journalistic tour-de-force, apparently. The second important story was the last in the paper. It was really just a blurb—a six or seven line bit explaining that some scientists somewhere had altered their projections about rising sea-levels around the world. According to these new numbers, Milau had no more than five years before it would sink completely into the ocean. The story made note that previous figures had given a prognosis of more like twelve.

Now, this was all complete news to me at the time—the fact that the island was going under, I mean. Plank had mentioned something about Milau being particularly susceptible to storms, but I hadn't really thought further about it. Anyway, it seemed from the story that the situation was pretty serious—downright alarming, in fact, and it was hard for me to figure why such a piece would be relegated to the very end of the paper, even if it was just a few pages in total. I was just looking up and getting ready to drain my coffee in a worried sort of way when Martha Tok appeared next to my table with a smile on her face.

"Are you enjoying the paper?" she asked, looking rather proud.

"Yes…" I said, slowly, "yes, it's a good paper. But I was just reading…"

"About the rising sea levels," she stated flatly, cutting me off. "Yes, I decided not to bring that up with you yesterday. It seemed unimportant for what you are doing here."

"So, you all have known about this for a while, then?" I asked.

"We have been concerned about it for a few years now, but have only had concrete proof of the situation for just under one year. That is one of the key problems driving the political situation which I mentioned yesterday. It is in large part because of these reports about the risk to the island that the Black Salmon and the opposition have gained so much traction with the people."

"I'm sorry," I said, "The Black Salmon?"

"Oh, yes," she answered apologetically. "That is the name of the activist organization I mentioned earlier…the one which, forgive me…which some call a terrorist organization." She fell silent as if ashamed to bring it up again.

"I see," I said, "so…is there a plan or something for what to do? About the sea-levels and all that, I mean."

"Well," said Martha hesitantly, "there are many ideas circulating…but, I am perhaps not the ideal person with whom to be speaking on this matter. In fact, I came to find you because I have been contacted by your American ambassador about meeting you, and I was hoping to take you and Mr. Bacon to him this morning, if possible. He will know much more about what is going on if you are interested." I explained that Doug had not showed up, was probably pretty hung over, and so was unlikely to appear any time soon. "That is no great problem," Martha answered, "I am certain you can pass on any vital information to him after the meeting if you go alone. Please do come, however. The ambassador was clear that he wanted to meet with you right away."

Having not much else to do anyway, I agreed to go. After giving a smile apiece to the waiter and the girl reading at the front desk, we were out the door. Martha led me up a small road next to the hotel toward perhaps the most neatly kept of the depressing white houses that defined the town. It had a little English garden in front surrounded by a wrought-iron fence on which was attached a brass placard reading "Embassy and Consulate General of the United States of America." We strode through the gate up to the door, and Martha lifted and dropped the heavy brass knocker with a thud. Almost immediately, the door creaked open and a fifty-something blond woman, still attractive in a way which you'd call "pretty," peered out at us with a smile. "Oh, good!" she said, opening the door for us, "so glad you came. The ambassador is just in his office meeting with the president at the moment."

"Ah, very good," said Martha as we walked into the house. We found ourselves in a little sitting room, with a fairly large desk and a big fireplace. The rug was a lovely burgundy Persian number, and there were some decent quality oil paintings on the walls. In one corner stood another wooden statue, a bit like the one in the restaurant, though this one was short and fat and depicted a female figure. She had a look of anxiety on her face. I complimented it aloud.

"Oh, yes, thank you. It was donated by the Milauan government—it's from the old island. I guess it represents the goddess of the roots of the palm trees. They have a god for that—or they did—isn't that interesting? Anyway, we just love it. An Embassy has to look good, that's what Reg always says. I'm Linda, by the way, Linda Stryker—the ambassador's wife. I'm also serving here as his secretary, assistant, and so forth. We're a tiny operation, as you might expect—it's just me and Reg." We shook hands, and I began to sit down on one of the beautiful leather waiting chairs they had set out in the place. "Oh, no," she said, holding out a hand to stop me, "no, the ambassador would like you to head straight into his office."

"But, the president?" I asked.

"She would like to meet you as well," said Linda. "And you may join Mr. Hill if you like," she said to Martha, who bowed politely and gave me a look to ask permission, which I gladly granted. Linda stepped over and opened up a heavy looking wooden door next to her desk, sticking her face inside. "Reg," we could hear her saying, "Mr. Hill is here with Ms. Tok. No. No. I don't know." She turned to me, "Mr. Bacon is not with you?" I explained again. "He's got a hang-over," she said into the door. We heard a sudden delighted peel of laughter before the door swung open all the way and a tall gentlemanly fellow in his mid-fifties appeared, hand already extended, with a broad smile on his face. He was wearing a button-down without jacket or tie and a pair of high-end blue jeans. His hair was cut slightly long and slicked into a really suave little do, with a few stylish streaks of gray running right through the middle. A darn fine looking fellow, I must say.

"Reginald Stryker, US Ambassador," he said, greeting me. "So glad you're here. You and your buddy out late with the island girls, were ya?"

"Well, no girls sir, but out late, yes."

"No girls?!" Stryker beamed, "Well, aren't you boys just the picture of good character, eh? Ah, but I shouldn't expect anything less out of a town like Grand Rapids, should I? I'm a Buckeye myself, hate to tell ya, Columbus born, raised, and hope to die, once I'm done with my work out here, of course. You a Michigan man, Edward?"

"Oh, everyone calls me 'Hill,'" I explained, "If you mean the University of Michigan, no, I went to Michigan State."

"A Spartan, is it? Well, not quite as good as a Buckeye, then, but you'll do in my book as long as you're not a Wolverine. Come on in, come on in. You too, Ms. Tok." He motioned us forward and we entered his office, the door shutting behind us. We were directed toward a couple of chairs on the front side of a huge mahogany desk. A third chair was occupied by a slight dark-haired woman wearing a very formal black pant-suit (the really classy kind) and looking deferentially at us in that way that actually makes a person look more important by virtue of their humility. She made a seated bow as we entered, but did not stand up.

"This is president Ella Turner of the Milaun Essentialist Party" said the ambassador signaling her, "Dr. Turner, this is Edward Hill, and I'm sure you know Martha Tok—they're from Saf-T-Set, as I told you. Mr. Hill is here inspecting the plant, as I understand it, right, Hill?" I confirmed what I was up to. "I was contacted a while ago about you're coming out here," he explained, "we're always happy to serve American companies abroad."

"Very nice to meet you, Mr. Hill," said Turner in a soft and elegant voice. Martha bowed wordlessly to the president so deep that her forehead nearly touched the ground. Turner opened both her hands, palms up, and made a gesture which they both seemed to understand as the appropriate formal greeting for the context. Martha then sat down, and I followed suit.

"Right, I'm glad you could make it over so quickly, Hill," said Stryker, sitting down at his desk. "I really wanted you to have the chance to meet Dr. Turner and discuss a few things while she's still here. To begin with, I should welcome you to the island, of course—how are you liking Milau so far?"

"It's beautiful," I said, "really gorgeous."

"It sure is, isn't it?" Stryker seemed to take a certain pride in this statement, like maybe he had been on the island long enough to really consider it his own. "Well, we certainly do love to greet Americans here, and if you need anything, don't hesitate. We serve as the Consulate as well, as maybe you noticed, so we're here for you if there are any problems whatsoever." I thanked him. "Would you two like a cup of coffee?" He stood back up without waiting for our answer, walked across the room and opened the office door a crack, making the request politely to his wife.

"Thank you," Martha and I both said at the same time.

"Not at all," said Stryker, sitting back down. "Have you had a chance to try the island stuff, Hill? Really great stuff." We talked briefly about how good the coffee was before he settled a little deeper in his chair and appeared to go into business mode just as four cups floated through the door on a tray balanced above the long lovely fingers of Mrs. Stryker. She set them down and departed again.

"So, I know this probably seems a little bit unusual, since you're just here on business," Stryker began, "and I normally wouldn't bother you or anything. But, like I said, we've been in touch with your company for several months now about…well, about a number of different things that have been going on out here which have, or could have, a serious impact on you."

"Yes," I said, "I caught wind of that before we left."

"Right," said Stryker, "Did your management team tell you anything before you came, then?"

"No," I said, "nothing at all, really. They barely even explained what we're supposed to actually do out here."

"I see," he said, "then it's a good thing you came over here. I can fill you in. As for Mr. Bacon, you can just pass everything on to him whenever he manages to get out of bed. What do you know about Milau, Hill?"

"Well, just about nothing, sir," I said. "Got a little information on the internet before we left—nothing very deep. Martha has said just one or two things."

"Alright," he said, "what do you know about the current political situation then?"

"Um…not much. I just read this morning about the island sinking, if that's what you mean."

"Okay," he sat up straight and took a swig of his still scalding coffee the way a person might gulp down a glass of cold water. "The island isn't precisely sinking, of course," he said, "technically speaking sea levels are going up. But, yeah, it all amounts to the same thing. The bottom line is this little piece of land that we presently call home isn't going to be here for a hell of a lot longer at this rate. Are you aware of the history of this particular atoll?" I shook my head. "Well, let me give it to you short and sweet. This island, the one we're on now, is not the original island of Milau—not the native home of the Milauan people, I mean. That island, what do they call it?" he turned to the president.

"In my language we have no name for it but 'Milau,'" she said, "and this island we call Mamaoht—island of the ghosts. In English our former home is called 'Old Milau.'"

"Old Milau, right!" said Stryker, "I ought to be able to remember that, huh? Anyway, the Milauan people spent untold centuries on Old Milau until the second world war. Back then the whole archipelago was in American hands after an occupation by the Japs, and we needed to do some testing, you know, for the atom bomb—critical stuff—and the Milauans did their part, like real American patriots. They let us use their island for everything. We got everyone off, of course, and we were gonna rebuild their whole village and all even better than before. But when we figured out what radiation actually *does* to people—holy hell! You wouldn't believe it. I mean, nobody knew anything about it before…so, we can't really be blamed—it's all just a guessing game in life, right? But, it's a bad scene, and it takes a real mother of a long time for that kind of fallout to dissipate. So, anyway, it all meant that we had to move everybody here. This island wasn't inhabited for some reason—just sitting out here waiting, I guess."

The president chimed in. "My people tell an old story that the inhabitants of this island were devoured by the god of the lagoon when they failed to appease him. It is just a tale, of course."

Stryker nodded. "Yeah, so, anyway the Army corps came in here, built houses, the air strip, a harbor facility for shipping. Did it all in six weeks, in fact, and then everybody was happy again."

"Wow," I said, trying to pretend like even a single positive thought could be found in my mind after hearing something like that.

"Wow is right!" said Stryker, really pretty proud, "American ingenuity—that's why we're number one, let me tell you. But, none of that is the point now—that's all ancient history. The basic problem is that it turns out that this new island, Milau, is badly threatened by any change in sea levels—I mean, really badly—even worse than most of the islands out here, and that's saying something. So we're basically in deep water now, if you'll pardon the pun." I lied and said that I would pardon the pun. "And if you read the paper today, like you said, you know that we don't have much time at all to do something about the situation. In fact, the president and I were just discussing the new time-line here before you arrived. It puts some real pressure on us, of course, but I think we can still deal with it, as long as we can keep things under control politically."

"We have already developed a plan," said the president calmly, "and, in fact, we are well on our way to seeing it through to completion."

"Right," Stryker jumped back in, "us Americans have come back to rescue the Milauan people a second time, as is only fitting given all their service. We've already lobbied Congress and gotten a big old pool of money together to help out the island—close to a billion dollars. With that money, we believe we can do what's necessary to build flood barriers, provide some training for people, get more fresh water shipped in—all kinds of things—to buy us at least another few decades here on this island. "

"Sounds sensible," I said.

"Yeah, so now it's just a matter of making our plan happen. But, you obviously don't need to worry about that—not directly, I mean. The thing about it is, though, that we're not certain we can actually protect your operations here on the island for that much longer. See, the layout of your facility makes it extremely vulnerable—especially all those brining vats of yours that you put all along the shore on the ocean side. I still can't figure that one out, Hill, but I guess there's nowhere else to put them. Anyway…if the MEP wins the election, they're going to give it the old college try, preserving the plant, I mean, but it's quite possible you're not going to be able to continue making pickles out here, or at least you'll have to make a lot less of them."

"I see," I said. "Well, I've been instructed to look into shutting the place down anyway, so I guess we'll just keep all that in mind as we go."

"Yeah," said Stryker, "definitely. It's a bit odd that your company didn't tell you anything about this, though. They would have known, I believe…I mean, we told them. I'm surprised they wouldn't pass that on."

"I'm not," I said sardonically.

"Yeah, I get it," he winked at me, "one of those. Oh well—doesn't matter now. So, yeah, that's what's up with the sea levels and all, and, like I said, as long as the political situation stays stable here everything should be just fine. But that's the other thing that I did want to make sure that you are aware of both as a rep for your company, and personally…as an American citizen. There's a wrinkle in all the politics here…"

"The opposition," said Turner somewhat ominously. Martha shifted in her seat uncomfortably.

"Yes," said Stryker, "the opposition is starting to look like they're actually going to win. You probably read about that in the paper, too, right? The election and everything? Well, we're starting to get pretty worried because if they do win, it would be a really big problem…I mean, like, absolutely huge. The thing is, the billion dollars has already been transferred over…it's already in the hands of the government of Milau, and, to be totally honest, we biffed a little bit in that we sortuv assumed some things about who would be in charge over here…and, well, long story short, it turns out that the money now belongs to Milau and there's not a damn thing we can do, if the opposition wins, to prevent them from doing whatever they want with the funds. Well, revoking Milaun sovereignty, or other funny business aside, I mean."

"Just last week," Turner said, taking over the explanation, "we heard from the opposition that they have developed a new plan of their own for use of the funds. Their idea is to use the money for the relocation of our people back to our original home island, which is much less at risk from the rising sea levels than this island here. They say the funds will allow us to perform any clean-up necessary to reduce radiation levels below a safe threshold."

Martha, who was clearly getting pretty agitated at this point, set forth a nervous comment. "And they say that radiation levels are already low enough for us to return as long as we are careful."

"But that's all…well, let's just say it's unproven," Stryker said offering a patient but somehow impatient counterpoint to Martha, "We have no idea if it's safe to live there. There could be all kinds of radiation in the food, in the fish—who knows."

"We would only need…" Martha began in agitation, but stopped. She was silent for a moment and then appeared to gather herself. "I mean to say that the opposition *claims* that the island only needs the right kind of fertilizer and everything would be safe for us." There's a nota bene here, by the way, because after getting home I discovered that she was talking about high potassium fertilizer which, I guess, helps prevent plants from drinking in radioactive chemicals. So the idea, as it turns out, wasn't nutty at all, though it did sound a bit far-fetched at the time. Anyway, Martha went on. "They claim that it is very simple, and not expensive, and that with their plan there would still be plenty of money left for the transfer, for rebuilding our homes, and even perhaps for some other social projects if all goes well."

"Yeah, of course they do," said Stryker bitterly, though refraining from directing any anger to Martha in particular, "they'll say you can fix any goddamn thing with fertilizer if it'll win them an election. Anxiety disorders, a bad economy, restless leg syndrome—whatever you want, toss a little fertilizer on it! They know damn well what the story is. There's a whole mess of money they can get their hands on as long as they can con a bunch of people into thinking it's safe to move back home. All fairy tales. They just want to embezzle it for themselves like a pack of Chicagoans."

"That is our position," the president added calmly, clearly trying to diffuse the unspoken tension now bubbling between Stryker and Martha. "The opposition has many unproven theories, and we are in support of the safe plan to remain here. We are also deeply concerned about the connections between the NFMLA—forgive me, that is the acronym for the opposition party—and the terrorist group known as the Black

Salmon. We believe that any political party which would align itself, or seek support in, any terrorist organization is not to be entrusted with the leadership of our proud nation. The opposition is forwarding a candidate for president named Gavra Kis, a young man only in his twenties, and we have very good reason to believe that his grandmother, Mary Kis, who is a former colleague of mine from the university, occupies a particularly high-up position within the Black Salmon. I should not be so circumspect. She is their leader…in an absolute sense. Thus, the ties between the two groups run very deep. They intend to get their way, whether at the polls or by some other means. In fact, they have made certain somewhat threatening comments about the Air Force base and this very embassy in the past, though at present they continue to promise that they will await the results of the election before engaging in any violence."

"Yeah," said Stryker, "so, obviously, if the opposition wins, and all these people leave the island, you're not going to have anybody to work in your plant—and you need to know that. But on the personal level, you also need to stay on your guard…for your safety. We don't expect any real trouble…if we did, we'd get you out of here right now. But…there could be some danger down the line. We want you to know we're looking out for you."

"Well, thank you," I said.

"It's just our job," he replied, "But, let me also say that…just informally…just as an American…if it's possible, we would also like you to keep your ear to the ground. You know…if you hear anything or see anything unusual—just let us know. There are some dangerous people involved in all this—dangerous and potentially insane. Do you realize that they don't even have Salmon in this part of the Pacific? That's to say nothing about black salmon, which I'm not sure are even a real species. They're crazy people. So, we'd love to have your help in keeping an eye on them…just as a favor, like I said. Either way, we're here for you. The

MEP, Dr. Turner's party, I mean, has been a great friend of the plant and the United States since the beginning— so, for now, the Milauan authorities are on your side, too."

"We believe in progress—in growth," Turner said, "and in a bright future for our people. Our best days are still ahead of us. We are happy you are here on the island."

"So, any questions?" Stryker asked with a smile. I thought about it for a while, but everything seemed as clear as it was going to get. I told him if anything struck me, I'd be in touch. "Well, you know where to find us, obviously." I downed the last swig of my coffee, and stood up with Martha. With a round of handshakes, and another one of the bowing exchanges between Martha and the president, we departed, gave a wave to Linda sitting at the desk in the front room, and were out the door.

"Well," said Martha when we got outside, "now you are fully apprised of all the goings-on of the island and of your government's plan regarding my people." She snapped her eyes away from me as she said this in a gesture of harsh disinterest.

"Hey, look, I'm really sorry about all that," I said, "I mean…what we did to you. That's just…terrible." This comment seemed to warm her a little.

"Yes, well…it is a difficult situation, and I appreciate your government's interest in helping us with our problems. But there are many of us who…would prefer not to do things your way."

"I can understand that," I said. "I mean, this isn't really your home, huh? I didn't realize that. But, look, I really don't want to interfere with any of this, or get involved in it at all, frankly. I'm not here to represent the government or anything like that. I just want to do my job and head home, just like you."

Martha smiled. "Thank you for your sympathies," she said after a time.

"I am glad you can at least see things…from our point of view…a little."
I gave a nod, glad that we were on good terms again, apparently.

Now, as we were walking something happened that I didn't much notice
at the time, but that is worth telling you about. Outside a small house
in town two old men were seated, both smoking and talking with one
another. As we went past them we overheard their conversation.

"But Adou has been to see her," the first man said, "and he says she
claims there is another way…a third way!"

"Old nonesense…the little girl," said the second. "What other way? Hm?
Another way besides stay or go back? There could be no such thing."

"She does not say what it is," said the first man, "she says she will tell it
when the time is right."

"Yes, yes…always when the time is right, isn't it? She tells what she tells
when the time is right, and people like you listen to her! If she knows
something, she should say. It is all double mysteries with her."

"She knew of your leg…the injury, didn't she?"

"A guess!" said the second old man as we rounded the corner. "A lucky
guess."

That's all I heard from them before we arrived back at the hotel. Like
I said, at the time the conversation didn't seem notable at all, otherwise
I certainly would have asked Martha about it. I only recall it, in fact,
because I remember thinking that it was odd for them to be speaking
English…which it was.

Anyway, Martha and I headed back in the hotel both silently assuming
that we were looking for Doug. The girl at the desk reading a book
was—well, she was still reading a book. She smiled softly at us as if
she thought we made a cute couple. I figured that was well enough,

though Martha seemed to blush a little. We took a peek in the restaurant first, and indeed, we found Doug, looking barely conscious, and trying to drink some coffee. I greeted him.

"Where the hell have you been?" he asked, turning a little green as he looked up at us.

"Over at the embassy," I told him.

"Well isn't that just swell," Doug said sarcastically, "I'm half dead up in my hotel room and the two of you are jaunting off with diplomats. Thanks for the concern."

"It's just a hang over," I told him, "obviously you've got to go easy on that Aijee."

Martha laughed, the first time we had seen her do that. Her smile was broad and fantastically playful. It made her face look like a half-moon sinking slowly into a cup of tea, and inviting you to dive right in with it. "There are two kinds of people, gentlemen," she said in a teasing sort of way, "for the first kind, Aijee is like a life-giving moonbeam—ah, so invigorating. For the other…it is like drinking the urine of the grim reaper himself!" She burst out in another trill of beautiful laughter that rang around the room with the rich and hollow tone of a pocket full of seashells. "Doug, I think perhaps you are a man of the second variety!" Doug just shook his head in disgust as I joined Martha's mirth. "Don't worry, though," she said when she had calmed her jubilation a little, "the cure is very easy. Baked snails and breadfruit for lunch, and all will be well—you will feel alive again." The waiter, who was sitting in a corner paging through the newspaper, looked up at Martha for a moment, then stood up with a nod to put in the order. We sat down next to Doug, and I gave him the bullet points of the conversation at the embassy.

"Well, I'm glad that we've figured out what those feds were doing in the office," Doug said, rubbing his head a little, "I was really wondering."

"Me too," I said, "I'm not sure why they didn't just explain it all to us…doesn't seem like there needed to be big mystery about it."

"Plank probably just forgot," said Doug, "going on what we saw, we should count ourselves lucky that he even remembered to put on his pants that morning." Martha seemed to like that joke, I remember, which perked Doug up quite a bit. "So, you figure we're going to have to shut down for sure out here, then?" he asked.

"I don't know," I said, "but it sounds pretty likely. It won't be our decision anyway. We just have to get everything together, same as we were expecting."

The snails eventually came, and they really did seem to help Doug's hangover. I had another cup of coffee. Eventually Martha ordered some kind of pale yellow fish stew with coconut milk for us. It was pretty good. I don't really remember that afternoon very well.

# 6

In fact, the following several days are a bit muddled to me because noth-ing much really happened. I had been intending to ask Martha about what was going on with the plant, Baya's song and dance with us, and so forth. But there was something about Martha's reactions to Stryker that left me feeling ill at ease. So I decided that it might be better just to stay silent for a bit and see if I could figure anything else out on my own.

However, it ended up taking me about three days to get any more helpful information. For one thing, I wasn't particularly eager to work on the problem, and I'll admit that just playing chess with Doug at the *Conch and Dodo* quickly became much more appealing than doing any work, even though he beat me squarely every game. Between that and walks along the beach, the days felt pretty well packed. And, in my defense, I didn't much know where to begin my investigation anyway. As a result, when I did try to gather information, I mostly ended up just pawing through the same old files at the plant, or wandering aimlessly around the island like I was trying to case the joint or something. Finally, though, on the Wednesday after we arrived, I made a bit of headway. As I men-tioned before, Baya Vin had brought up a small shipping company that we apparently worked with, but had claimed not to know the company's name. After digging around, I managed to identify the outfit that must have been doing the work. They were called "Wide Pacific Shipping and

Unshipping." I could only hope that the concept of unshipping had some kind of meaning in Milauan that didn't translate into English. Instead of an address, they had a little paragraph describing the location of their "office," so to speak, on the beach next to the main dock near town. I decided to head down there and just start asking some questions. I remember that Doug decided that day to go back up to the plant and take some measurements for the drafting he needed to do, so he split off.

It was a bit of a busy morning on the dock when I got there. A handful of fishermen were getting ready to set off, tossing tackle and whatever else into their various water craft on the beach or off the pier. Most of the boats were old fashioned out-rigger type canoes, but with a few motor boats thrown into the mix. The fishermen didn't take much notice of me, though the ones that did all gave friendly smiles. The *Jed Red Sadie* was still there, quietly contemplating her surroundings and bobbing up and down. So, everything was normal except that when I got to the water there was a fairly sizable boat, which hadn't been there when we first arrived, tied off on the outermost portion of the pier. It was maybe a hundred feet long with the cabin area and pilot's booth set right in the middle, and what looked like a former gun mount sticking up from the aft. From the top of the pier I could make out a fairly rotund, mustachioed islander, fifty-something, in a white shirt. He was lying out on a deck chair perched precariously at the very front of the bow as if he liked the feeling that he might tumble into the water at any second. In a blue paint that seemed to want nothing better than to antagonize the red of the hull were written the words "Una," near the bow, and "Wide Pacific," near the stern. I figured I had found my man. I headed down the dock into shouting distance of him.

"Hey…are you the captain?" I hailed him as I arrived.

"Oh!" he practically leaped out of the deck chair, and it trembled as if it were about to fall into the water before setting back into its barely high-

and-dry position. "Yes, sir, yes, of course. Do you wish to sail? Are you ready to depart?"

"Uh…no," I said, "no…I'm not."

"Ah, we can leave whenever you like, sir—no shipments right now. Ticket to Hawaii, one hundred thousand Yen. I am sorry, sir, but it is so much because you are the only one. I can lower the price if you find another passenger to join us."

"No, I don't want to go to Hawaii right now…I'm sorry. I just wanted to talk to you."

"Ohhh!" He said letting out a breath. "Yes, I understand now. Please forgive me. Come aboard, most certainly, please be my guest." He rushed over from where he had been sitting and opened a little gate on the boat's side railing, signaling for me to get on.

"Ah, sir," he said when I was aboard, "come right this way, right this way. I see you are American, yes? Or Canadian? Australian?" I told him I was American. "Very good, sir, then let me tell you—I save this only for you, it cannot be for island people—I have been saving it for a very long time now, waiting and waiting—but right this way, I will show you." He practically dragged me by the shoulder over to the little pilot's booth, and, once inside, knelt down and opened up a bench seat there. After digging for some time through a tangled mess of lines, fishing tackle, a bilge pump, and some electrical wires, he pulled out a six-pack of pale golden Corona beer, the labels faded down with age. I don't care that much for Corona, but what can you do? He immediately cracked two of them open, using a hinge on the bench so deftly that you'd think it had really been designed for the purpose, and handed one to me.

"Oh…" I said, "well thank you very much—you're very kind."

"Yes, sir," he said, "I am fond of beer, I must admit, but we are not supposed to have it—not here on the island, except to serve to foreigners. A few years ago they banned imports of alcohol. Yes, with exception only for the resort and the hotel to give to the guests—it is only the Aijee that we may have now since it is made here. The president would have liked to ban even that—for she always says that water is enough for us—but she could not muster the votes to go quite so far. But you are a visitor, a foreigner—we may drink together these very fine drinks! Ah, I have been waiting a long time for such a moment to come again—we have all been waiting, it is like a resurrection, yes, like the old times when the sun himself brought prosperity drawn from our own sheer love of him? I am sure it is only my memory, but things seemed warmer then with people about, bustling." We toasted and each took a large swig of the not just warm but downright hot Corona. It was a bit hard to swallow at that temperature, though it was equally nice to taste a beer after several days.

"I used to love the tourists, sir," the captain said after loudly expressing his refreshment. "Many would come all the way by boat with me—the adventurous ones, and others by plane. So many smiles on their faces, money in their pockets. Ah, but now everything smells like pickles. They have long since gone. Long since." He turned to take stock of the island as if to confirm to himself what he was saying. "But, I am becoming an old man now, yes? Telling you stories you do not ask to hear like a gray-bearded fisherman tells you of his many illnesses in so much detail. Tell me, you are now a guest of my ship, tell me what it is you are here to discuss, yes?"

"Uh," I started—I had been a little taken in by what he was saying along with the unexpected hospitality, and had rather forgotten for a moment why I was there after all. "Right…yes. I'm with the company—the company that owns the pickle factory."

"Ah, yes, of course! You are the Saf-T-Set man—I heard that you were coming—they have finally sent someone once again. Yes, I used to look forward very much to visits from the company men—yes, and women, of course. Always free and happy, always glad to be away from home for a moment. It has been some time now…some time. Welcome back to Milau!"

"Thank you," I said, really feeling welcomed.

"So, what may I do for you, sir. Ah! I have not introduced myself—forgive me my haste to join you in this drink. I hope I have not offended you." He reached out for a handshake. "I am only Alexander—a man of no family name—my father was dead before I was born, sir, a fisherman who was taken in storm before the weather reports began. In our culture a son born without a father, as me, must await his own sons to bestow the family name once again. Ah, and I thought for many years, for you see my age plainly sir, that no such thing would come to be for me, for I had not a wife nor a hope of children." Alexander's voice had a really dramatic timbre to it, rising and falling with gusto as he spoke. "Oh how I wept over it night upon night rocking to sleep on this very boat, in the loneliness of the Pacific dark—oh it is piercingly lonely, sir, you cannot know. But, sir! Only a little more than one year ago a young woman, right here in Milau, my second cousin's daughter, though I am old and foolish as you can see, she took a shine to me, sir, though she could have had any a better man her age, and it is four months that we have welcomed him—my little boy, sir! Ah, the brightness of his eyes. A boy of two names he is, Alexander like his father and Vusu like his grandfather. Ah, and we are in love, and he—think upon him in your mind sir—the product of that love of a sailor of little account and a young woman of inexplicable kindness! What great fortune there is in the world, sir—what great joy!" A tremendous smile engulfed his face.

"Wow…uh…congratulations," I said—it was hard to follow up on a little speech like that, but I managed to shake his hand firmly. "Uh…yes…I'm Hill…just Hill…though that's my last name. Congratulations on your son. That's…really wonderful. May he grow up a good man like his father." I lifted my beer in a gesture of toast.

"Oh, Mr. Hill!" Alexander was gazing at me, his eyes enormous, like I had just said or done something really important. "Such very warm regards! I cannot thank you!" He reached out solemnly to take my hand again, so we shook a second time, this time slowly and thoughtfully. He gazed at me for a long moment before he continued. "Forgive me, sir. It is only that…to my people the blessings of a foreigner are sacred. It means a great deal, sir…a great deal." He stood there beaming at me for a long moment, while I tried to seem like I didn't much notice. "Do you have a son of your own, or a daughter?" he asked eventually.

"No," I said, "no kids. But maybe…maybe not too long. I'm thinking about getting engaged soon…when I get home, I mean."

"Oh, that is wonderful news, wonderful! And may you be blessed in good time as I have been. You will be, I know it! But, what may I do for you, Mr. Hill?"

"Well, yeah…so…I'm looking into some problems we're having up there at the plant, and your company—at least I think it's your company—was mentioned in some of our files. Have you been doing some shipping for us?"

"Yes…" said Alexander a bit quizzically, "A little bit—once in a while, sir. Not very much. We delivered some cucumbers there this morning…for the first time in, perhaps it is three months. That is normal now—a few deliveries here and there. It has been a very long time since I have done much work for the plant. It has been at least ten years, I believe, since we were working regularly. I can look at my records to confirm the exact date, if you wish. Now they order some cucumbers, one ton maybe, three times a year or four—a few other things."

"I see…" I said, frowning.

"Sir?" he asked, "please forgive me—have I said something to offend?"

"Oh no," I said, "no, not in the least. It's just that that's not exactly what the plant manager told me. He said you'd been doing a lot of work until eight months ago and that your boat has been out of commission because of the storm"

"Sir?" he asked again. "No, sir—I have had no problems with the boat. Indeed, I was very fortunate that in the storm I sustained no serious damage. We were not here, you see, but in port in Hawaii—a good distance sir, one week's sail—we merely had high winds there. I was happy at my good fortune, for I was able to remain in business and carry many supplies which were of great help to our people."

"So, you have had no impediment to your normal operations, then? There's no reason you can't ship supplies for the plant?"

"No, sir, no reason except that they do not order many supplies, and they never hire me to ship anything off the island."

"Are they using some different company, then?" I asked, "you're with Wide Pacific Shipping and…Unshipping, right? That was the only shipping company that I have any records of at the plant."

"Oh, yes, sir, that is us, as you can see looking at the side of the boat." He smiled proudly at this. "Yes, that is our company, and we certainly did work for the plant for a number of years, as I mentioned. Not shipping all the way to Hawaii, sir—you see how small my boat is. No, when the big container ships still came to Milau—here into the lagoon. You can see there the old harbor dock," he pointed to the crumbling concrete we had seen from the plane, "we do not even use it any more since the big ships do not come now. When they did, my company, we were contracted to run the harbor. We did many things…to help loading and unloading—everything, sir. Ah, we had four boats then, with a large supply boat and even a tug! Dozens of men worked for me, on boats and the dock—how strong we became! But I was forced to sell all but this boat for, as I say, ten years ago your orders all stopped, the big freighters stopped coming. We returned to the business the way my uncle ran it, with one boat and a few men—not dock work, but real sailing again. It was bitter-sweet, for my heart is the sailor's heart of my grandfather, but prosperity would have warmed that same heart indeed. Well, do not let me ramble on in such a way. I must answer your question and say that no, sir, I cannot imagine that your people are using another company, for, tiny as we are, we are the only boat capable of hauling cargo which has pulled in on the lagoon in many years. Yes, we are the only boat company here on Milau. Now we carry all supplies, all mail, all fuel, back and forth to Hawaii."

I wish I could say that what Alexander was telling me was shocking or something, but it really wasn't. "So, nothing's been coming out of the plant, then," I asked, "as far as you know?"

"No, sir, nothing that is leaving the island. You can buy pickles there on Mondays—but they do not ship anything off."

"Okay. So…what about ten years ago—back when you did work with us—what was going in and out then?"

"Oh, yes," said Alexander, "those were very good years. Many crates with pickles going out, many crates with cucumbers, other things, coming in. Let me see, wait now, just let me take a look. I can tell you precise numbers. I have kept logs because, as I have said, we coordinated everything in those days, our company I mean. Give me a moment—I will find my records." He gestured for me to sit down on the bench seat in the cockpit. "Oh, here, while you wait, please." He had me stand up again, pulled out another beer, cracked it open and handed it to me, though my first was only about half-way gone. "Yes, just a few moments and I will be back."

It took him about half an hour to emerge from the cabin space down below, so I ended up pretty glad that he had given me that second beer. I sat in the pilot's booth for a while, then walked up and down the deck. The boat seemed to be in pretty sturdy shape all-in-all, and a quick glance back at the "Jed Red Sadie" caused me to think that maybe it would be worth the hundred grand (in Yen, I mean) to travel with Alexander when we were all done on Milau. Seemed like he'd be good company, too. He showed back up as I was pondering whether to give his precarious deck chair a try.

"It is a wonderful boat, is it not, sir? We call her the *Una*—it is Milauan for the goddess of the front portion of the waves on open ocean—the part of them, I mean, where the foam begins to form," he made a crooked hand gesture to aid in his description, "she was the goddess of that part of the wave, and as such was considered a bringer of good fortune to those who sail the seas. Now it is just a name, of course, but it is a good name. Yes, the *Una* was a military boat, Australian—for patrols, but we have converted her into a good cargo boat, big enough for us living on such a small island, and with range just to Hawaii. She has always treated us well. And she is very fast, being a military boat once."

"I see," I said, "do you sail it all by yourself?"

"Oh no, sir," he said, "I have a crew of three men—very strong and hard working. It is not safe to sail alone such a distance. They are now at home with their families, sir—where else? We just made the island late last night, and they have hurried back. They are perhaps making love to their wives as we speak—I can only hope so. Good men, yes. I, however, must keep regular hours on the boat even in dock, for I must await any business that comes, even though I wish to spend all day with my son when I am here on the island. My crew, they have good fortune—they need only be present when we sail. I will see my family this evening, however—I must take comfort in such little hopes. It is perhaps a good thing that I have no orders for a time—perhaps I will not have to sail again for a few weeks. We Milauans take pride that we have all the necessities of life. Ah, but you cause me again to speak on and on! Here are the logs—I am sorry it took so long in finding them. They were very deep in a cabinet which I keep, but they have not been lost." He handed me three thick leather-bound ledger books. I flipped the top one open and had a glance. It was all beautifully kept in perfect clear hand-written pencil, quantities and types of cargo, shipping rates, dates of each shipment, the names of freighters and the companies that owned them—the works—starting roughly twenty years back, which is to say right at the time the plant went operational. Some of the entries were for long-haul type operations out to Hawaii carrying various and sundry items, mail and whatever. Most of them, though, were marked as going out on the big containers with *Wide Pacific* coordinating operations on the dock. "You may feel free to take the books for a few days if you like, sir," said Alexander. "I would prefer to receive them back, however, as I like to maintain this information for just such occasions when it might be useful."

"Alexander, you're something else," I said in astonishment.

"Sir?" he asked, puzzled.

"It just means you're…exceptionally helpful. Thank you so much."

"It is my pleasure, sir. It is because of your kind words of blessing to my son. Such words—they are invaluable! Yes. Oh, and let me tell you. These are all the logs which I possess for the ten years when I was working for your company…beginning twenty years ago. As you will see, at the peak we were loading and unloading for you once a week, at one time it was very regular—every Thursday—with maybe three-hundred-fifty, four-hundred tons in and out."

"So…what? About forty million pounds for the year, then, a bit less?" I asked, doing the math quickly in my head.

"If you say so, sir, I am not so quick with numbers."

"Well, that adds up about right—I mean for the capacity of the plant," I said, "when they were going full bore, that is. And that's probably about right for the supply of the brand state-side, too." He peered at me, obviously not having any clue what I was muttering about. "Never mind that…sorry. You say I can take these ledgers?"

"Please, be my guest."

"Alexander, I don't know how to thank you," I said.

"No need!" he said, exuberantly, "please, merely join me in one more drink—another beer, and simply cast your warm thoughts upon my family from time to time."

"Well, I can certainly do that for you," I said. After he fetched the beers, we stood on the deck drinking them for a while, talking a bit more about his wife and boy, how fast kids grow and all that. With some people that kind of conversation is insufferable, but he had such an energy about it all that it really sucked you in—you could have listened to him talk about his baby all afternoon. When I had drained my beer, and he had done the same, we shook hands and I made my way back down the ladder, clutching the log books under my arm and eager to start making a little progress into what was really going on with our factory.

Now, everything I've laid out so far about our trip has been pretty atypical, to say the least. But it was right after meeting Alexander that the first hint of the truly bizarre turned its twisted scowl on my three weeks in the North Pacific. I was coming off the dock and starting to make my way back toward the hotel when, out of the corner of my eye, I spotted an old woman sitting down beneath a palm tree near the road leading back into town. She was eating a large piece of what I can now tell you was raw bread-fruit, doing so messily and spitting little chunks of it out as she chewed. Her hair was a gray matted mess. She wore a garment which alluded to having once been one of those flowing white gowns that Martha liked to wear, but which was now close to black with filth, and ragged. I gave her a polite wave, which seemed the natural thing to do at the time, and as soon as I acknowledged her, she leaped to her feet and came running at me with the kind of frenzy that only a clinical lunatic can cultivate. She charged up so fast, in fact, that I found myself holding up my arms and cowering as if to prevent her from flat-out attacking me. She did not do so, however, and, once she reached me, she stopped dead in her tracks, hunched down and stared up at me from below like she was sizing up a dead animal hanging in a tree, and maybe contemplating the thought of actually eating the thing.

Look, what the hell else could I do? "Uh," I said, "can I help you?" Stupid, yes, fine—but really, this kind of thing doesn't happen much in Grand Rapids. It does happen…but not much.

"Aayeeee," she said, a bizarre noise approximating some of the more notable shrieks common among the Striped-Footed Boobies. She was bobbing her head up and down and tilting her weight back and forth on her legs.

"I'm sorry, ma'am, I don't understand." I was trying not to escalate the situation.

"You…you…aayeee," she said again, still not making any sense. "I know you…I know you, you been here now, now five days, now. You been here, aayee!"

"Uh, yes," I said, "five days…something like that…"

"We seen you, seen you—we seen you five days now, you been here, your friend here, your friend WANT TO FUCK MARTHA TOK!!" She absolutely screamed that bit so that the whole island could probably hear her. I mean literally the whole island. "Ya, ya—the Tok daughter, he want to make twins if he can with her—aayeee, I seen you both."

"Ma'am, I'm sorry—I don't understand." I was looking around in some of the profoundest embarrassment I'd ever experienced. There was no one in sight, so at least I didn't have to face anyone's gaze.

"Aayee, you no need ta unnastand. Listen now, you listen now. We know you—you Americans—we know you, we see you in the firelight, ya, in the darkness? We see you, lookin' in at you, watchin'. The little girl, she know you, she know you and see what you here for, she see it all, all! She see where you come from. Your pretty *girl*friend at home, white white *girl*friend, she see it. You not bad—maybe not good, she don't know—but she see you not bad, she know—she lovva man not bad. You meanin' no harm, you not wanna *get in* that way. But not you, no, no, not you the point—everybody else! They can call you Ishmael!" I believe she was making a reference to Moby Dick there, "Ya! You just watchin' everthin'. You okay to do that. But you stay outta anybody's way. You let 'em what they will, the people. You *afraid* American not-bad man? Ya? If you *afraid*, you come down to us, then. We know, we see—we wanna protect you. You not gonna go wit' anyone else, you alright, we make sure, we watch for you. We see your pretty *girl*friend, little boy you have, like the shipman, ya? Same kinda little boy you have—oh, no, no, no, not yet, is it? Ya, you gonna have to stay around, ya, no dying yet, for your *girl*friend, your little boy you gonna have. Your friends, maybe they stay, too, maybe if they want, but maybe they don't want. We watch your friends for you." At this moment, and I remember this very vividly, she stopped all her crazy gyrations completely, stood up almost straight enough to look me in the eye and said, as if punctuating the mad paragraph she had just spewed out: "But we gonna go!" Then she fell silent just looking hard into my eyes, and I sure as hell didn't say anything. After a little while she smiled wide and then spit a little piece of breadfruit in my face, like she was blowing me a kiss or something. She turned around and disappeared quickly down the road into some palm trees.

Well, at the time I had no idea what she meant, and though I've got a better sense of it now, I don't think that it's any of your business, so I'm going to drop it. But it is important that I met her that day, so I wanted to make mention of it. I stood there looking like an idiot for quite a while—which was probably appropriate. Eventually, I guess, I made it back to the hotel. I was basically dazed and decided to skip dinner and just stay in my room. I took a shower, and paced around until I was feeling a bit better. She was just a crazy lady, after all—you find them anywhere you go in the world. Nothing to give a second thought to. Why should she leave me feeling haunted?

When I felt up to it later in the evening, I took a glance at the ledgers I'd gotten from Alexander. As I already said, they were beautifully kept in every way. He had misled me just a bit on one thing, though. He had made it sound like these were the books just for the years that he was working for Saf-T-Set a lot, but as it turned out he had given me the records for his peak period of business with us, and for a couple of years after that. The picture that the ledgers painted was just as he had made it out to be. During the first ten year's of the plant's life, Alexander's company had been involved in operations for a whole mess of big ships, pulling in a large quantity of pickle-making supplies, and ferrying out a large quantity of pickles, to the tune about thirty-eight million pounds per year, right about where I had guessed. So, that could only mean one thing. We were, in fact, making North Pacific brand pickles on the island of Milau for about a decade, as absolutely ludicrous as it was to do so, and shipping them off to somewhere (probably Toledo).

But here's the thing. After about ten years of working for us, Alexander's logs just flat dropped off a cliff. From regular weekly shipments he went to absolutely nothing over-night with just a single warning sign showing up on the ledgers. The anomaly was this: on his very last full job loading up one of the big freighters, he had logged absolutely nothing coming in for that week. That meant that we finished up production at the plant, sent off a last shipment as you obviously would, didn't resupply, and then we were done. And that shut-down of our major shipments on and off the island happened almost exactly ten years before I stepped off the *Jet Red Sadie*, not eight months, not one year, but *ten full years*—way before whatever problems were causing our current difficulty in supplying pickles to Michigan and Canada's finest retailers. In short, the records that Baya had showed us up at the plant all *began* more or less exactly at the time when we *stopped* shipping pickles off the island according to Alexander's books.

Now, here's where the couple extra years that were recorded in the logs really got me curious. Following the sudden end of our shipments, Alexander himself, on his own boat, started hauling a limited quantity of supplies for us direct from Hawaii. Just like the logs at the plant showed, he was bringing in what added up to a few thousand pounds of cucumbers a year. The only place where there seemed to be a gap was with the polysorbate-80 and yellow-5, which I assumed were what he meant by "food coloring" and "other" in his book. He did carry some, it seemed, but only a little bit—basically the amount you'd need to make a few thousand pounds of pickles a year. Delivery of all those items was to Saf-T-Set, written there loud and clear, with the plant's address right in the books. That address was "5 Factory Way," if you're curious, but don't ask me why the hell we were number 5 being the only building on the street. So, our intake of supplies dropped to virtually nothing, but did not, in fact, stop completely at the time that the big freighters quit showing up.

There's one more thing about the logs I need to mention to you, and that is the fact that late in one of the final books I noticed that Alexander had started shipping in a huge quantity of fertilizer, along with some other chemicals that he hadn't been moving before. He also began carrying a substantially larger quantity of gasoline, and some stocks of "hunting ammunition" for the first time. So, unless a massive corn farm had briefly been opened on the island that just so happened to need a whole lot of gas and bullets, somebody was making bombs and loading guns. And, lest one have even the slightest doubt, the organization receiving all those items was listed right there in logs like it was no big deal to anyone: the Black Salmon.

# 7

It was probably somewhere around midnight that I started feeling like getting out of the room a bit before going to bed. I headed down the stairs. The girl reading a book looked up at me with a gentle smile. I glanced into the restaurant which was dark—definitely closed for the night. I nodded back at the girl, and without handing over my key, I headed out the door. The sign on the *Conch and Dodo* was brightly illuminated.

I had actually made it all the way to the bar, sat down, signaled for a drink, and received it before I even noticed that Doug and Martha were sitting there at a table together staring over at me. I must have looked awful, I guess, because their mouths were a little bit agape.

"Hey!" Doug said finally, which is about when I realized they were there, "Hey, Hill! Where you been, man? We were knocking on your door for about ten minutes. The girl in the lobby said you were up there—you alright?"

"Uh…" I said, turning around. "Yeah—yeah, I'm alright. I was just feeling a little sick—sorry—I didn't hear you knocking." I really hadn't heard them.

"Well, did you get anything to eat? Come on over here, sit down with us." I smiled weakly but it's not like I could pretend I was meeting some-one or that I had something else to do, so I got up and went over to their table. "Did you eat anything?" Doug asked again. I shook my head. "They do have food here—I had one of the goat burgers for lunch, if you're hungry." I was indeed pretty hungry, so I mustered up some ver-bal agreement and the bartender headed back into the kitchen without a word, evidently to put in an order for one goat burger.

"So, I haven't seen you since breakfast, what have you been up to all day?" Doug asked. I told him vaguely what I had been doing, though I neglected to go into much detail about the boat logs, or to mention any-thing about the crazy old woman. That wasn't really on purpose, though. I was just a bit frazzled still.

"Huh," said Doug, "well, that's productive, I guess."

"How 'bout you?" I asked.

"Well, we've been having a really lovely evening here, haven't we?" he looked over to Martha who gave me a friendly, but poker-faced look. "Without you around, not that I mean we didn't want you around, but anyway you weren't—so, we had a really nice dinner, and we've just been chatting here. You know, about life, and the island…art…love," he looked back at her again, "The…uh…the usual stuff. Just a really nice evening. We were just talking about Martha's garden, actually—the flowers—you were describing them so beautifully…" he looked at her as if she should repeat what she had said.

"Well," she looked away from me as people do when they're prompted like that, "yes…just…the blues and violets. I was only saying…I wonder how they can strike the eye like that—it is nearly a taste that they have—very vibrant."

Doug nodded and took a deep breath, seeming to drift away for a moment. Then he looked back up to me. "But, yeah…let's see, during the day…well, I made some real progress on drafting out the plant. Got a whole bunch of measurements—basically everything I need to get down to actually drawing the thing. I was thinking maybe I'll just do it by hand—I don't have a lot else to do, right? And it's been a long time since I've actually gotten out the old pencils."

"Was there anybody up there?" I asked, the first few sips of Aijee beginning to energize me.

"Yeah, a few people," Doug turned to Martha as if for confirmation. "Baya was there—sends his greetings to you. Some other employees. Looked like they were cutting cucumbers or something. They had the machines in that front room running, whatever that means."

"Yes, they are the cutting and washing machines," said Martha.

"That confirms it, then," I said with a puzzled sigh, "they really are making pickles here."

"By all accounts, at least some," said Doug. Martha shifted in her chair somewhat. I looked over at her as the shadows of suspicion began to darken in my mind. I thought it over. She knew something that she wasn't saying, and the time had come to ask her point blank what was going on. But, as I opened my mouth to politely flip the lid on that Pandora's box, two things suddenly happened that drew my attention away from her. The first is that my burger showed up, and I admit it actually looked delicious. The second, which is more to the point, is that Tom, the pilot, burst through the door looking like some kind of bat trying to get out of a butterfly net.

"You two!" he shouted, as soon as he saw us, "I'm glad you're here! Look, I gotta go—I gotta get outta here. Right now. Night license be damned—I'm flyin'!"

"What's going on, man?" Doug asked as we all turned to stare at Tom.

Tom ignored the question. "Two glasses of Aijee—right now!" he shouted at the bar tender. "I gotta double-fist these things for the road—I gotta get outta here!" He jammed his hand into his pocket and literally threw a fistful of money onto the bar, several bills tossing about in the slight breeze of a ceiling fan before they hit the counter. The bartender hopped to and mixed the drinks like he was a field medic dressing the wound of a man near death. We watched him in stunned silence until he set the first drink on the bar. Tom was literally panting as it arrive.

"Tom!" I said this time, and very insistently, "what is it?"

Now he turned to us, grabbing the drink and chugging about half of it in a single go. "That bastard, that son of a bitch—he was serious! That bastard! That son of a bitch!" He slammed the remainder of the drink, and then slid the glass down the bar, throwing it so hard that it glided right off the edge like a suicide jumper, and crashed to the floor with an over-dramatic shattering sound. Tom took only a passing notice of this, and waved his hand toward the pile of money that he had thrown on the bar as though to indicate, quite rightly I'll note, that he had already more than paid for the damage.

"You gotta slow down, man," said Doug, looking about ready to stand up and give Tom a couple of Hollywood-style slaps across the face.

"Shit…shit!" Tom was saying, appearing to settle at least a little bit, and picking up his second drink. "Shit…I'm sorry. It's just. Nothing like that has ever happened to me."

"Tom…" I said slowly. "What…happened?"

"Look, I was here earlier, y'know, like usual, an' I had a couple drinks before I saw this pritty little island girl—sixteen maybe—caught a glimpse of her through the window, y'know, and decided to go after her. Sweetest little thing, just a doll, and she and I were just takin' a stroll down the way of the beach headin' north, right? Just lookin' around maybe for a little spot where we could be alone, you know—just the sweetest thing, she was. But that bastard, that son of a bitch, he comes right up—like, outta nowhere, right up to me with a *knife* dammit! Right in my face, just here, like this." Tom craned his neck and made one of those throat-slashing gestures, then took a sip of his second drink, now ready on the bar. "He says to me 'you get off the island now, if you wanna live!' And I'm saying, 'what the hell?' and 'who are you?' and 'caint' you see I'm onna date here, fella?' I mean, I just thought it was some bastard mugger or somethin', I mean, I couldn't see his face right off. But he tells me again, and then he turns me around an' it's that son of a bitch Dominic—Dominic Vin, the fella who sold me the gas, like I told you boys. An' boy let me tell ye, he had fire in his eyes like he really coulda killed me right there and then! No messin' around, no sir—and I'm a customer, am I right? He treats a customer like *that*. That bastard! That son of a bitch!"

"Jeez, Tom," said Doug, "what, was it his sister or something?"

"The girl?" Tom finished his second drink, and now much settled, signaled for one more. "The girl? I don't know. On this island she was probably at least his cousin. But he didn't say nothin' about her—didn't care a lick from what I could tell. She just rushed off as soon as she saw him anyway. It wasn't that, he said somethin's about to go down, I don't know what, didn't say anything about it—just said he thought I was gettin' off the island when he sold me all that gas for damn near nothin'. Didn't think I was gonna be hangin' around, is what he said—he wanted me gone, that's why he sold me cheap. Said he had to make sure I was leavin' right away—tonight—no delay. I told him I ain't got a night license to fly, and he said he didn't give two shits about that, didn't matter to him—he said get out now, I can fly without a license or get stabbed to death tonight in my bed. That bastard! That son of a bitch! He just said to grab my things and get out, and that he's gonna be watchin' me the whole way outta town. He's watchin' us right now, I'm sure of it!"

"What the hell…" said Doug, suddenly looking out the window with low-level panic in his eyes. "So now you've roped us into this somehow? Thanks a million, Tom."

"No, I didn't mean to…" Tom's eyes got big and watery in an earnest repentance. "No…I didn't know you'd be here…I just needed a couple 'a drinks to cool my nerves so I could fly outta here. I didn't mean…"

"It's alright," I said, trying to diffuse things, "I'm sure it won't cause any trouble…I mean, if you are leaving and all."

"You're damn right!" Tom basically shouted, grabbing his final drink and chugging it back in a gulp. He slid this glass across the bar like the first one and it teetered right on the edge, taunting its own fate, as the bartender watched with worried eyes. The glass, so it would seem, decided to keep living, and settled down, just barely, on the bar.

"That's it, that's everythin'. You got my bag, Sam?" he looked at the bartender, whose name we were just learning. Sam nodded and grabbed an old leather back-pack from behind the bar and handed it over to Tom. "Then that's it, I got it all. I'm gone."

"What about us?" Doug asked hurriedly.

"Aw, dammit…" said Tom, obviously not having thought about the problem already. He stopped mid-stride halfway to the door and looked over at us sympathetically. "Look," he said, glancing around a couple of times, "I'll come back for you two. On schedule—three weeks from last Thursday—8:00 AM—you be there at the dock—just be there waitin'. I won't come lookin' for you, so if you two don't show up, I'm heading back home no questions asked, okay?"

"But, shit," said Doug, "I mean.."

I held up my hand to him, and looked squarely at Tom. "We understand, Tom. We'll be there. Thanks."

"You boys're alright," Tom said, smiling mostly at me. "Now, I gotta get the hell outta here right now! See ye!" and he was out the door so fast that the little bell on the hinge didn't have a chance to ring.

The first thing I did was look over at Martha. The color was drained right out of her face, and her hand was quivering a little bit as she tried to take a sip of her drink. She didn't manage to even raise the glass, in fact. Something about what had happened had disturbed her way beyond what you'd expect. Doug looked first at me, and then followed my gaze over to her, appearing suddenly even more nervous than she was, though with a look on his face that said he didn't actually know why he should be uncomfortable. So, basically, we were both staring right at her, and now we had an obvious question on our minds.

"Martha…" I said slowly, "do you…know what that was about?" And that's when she dropped her head to the table like she was about to cry her eyes out. Doug pulled his chair over to her and set his hand gently on her back, in a startlingly intimate gesture.

"It's alright," he practically cooed, "it'll be alright. You can tell us…it's alright."

"No," she said as if in a panic, but without lifting her head, "none of you should have been threatened like that." Doug kept trying to soothe her quietly. Then, quite suddenly, she bolted up in her chair. "I must go now, I must go home," she said, "I cannot tell you anything more—it would only put you in danger. I don't want you to know anything."

"Look, Martha…" I began.

"No," she said firmly and frantically, "no, that is all for tonight. Good night. Sam," she said, turning to the bartender, "please, for them—they are my friends—please, don't say anything." Sam nodded and gave a very solemn smile of the sort that makes you really trust a man. "I will pay their bill tomorrow. Please, let them stay as long as they like." Sam nodded sternly again, and as if signing a covenant that his lips would be sealed, he quietly picked up a broom from the corner and started in on cleaning up the broken glass. "Goodnight to both of you," said Martha, and she reached for the door.

"Wait, just stay…I mean…" Doug sputtered, still hopeful.

"We will speak later—not now. I cannot tell you anything," she said, and with short tears welling suddenly in her eyes, she bowed and walked out. The bell jangled, the metallic thud warmed the room, and then there was nothing but the grating emptiness which is the sound of a broom sweeping hopelessly across dirty linoleum.

Doug set his hands down on the table and let his forehead drop into his palms. "What the hell is going on, here, Hill? I mean…what the hell?"

I didn't say anything in response for quite a while. In fact, as I recall, I eventually just ate my burger in silence with Doug not even looking up. When that was done, I answered him. "Look, I don't know what any of that was about—especially not with Martha—but I'm going to guess we'll probably find out soon enough."

"I'm not even sure I want to," said Doug, finally sitting back up.

Just as he did, Sam strolled over to our table holding two little glasses filled half way with a pale golden liquid. "Here," he said with a friendly smile. "You'll be alright. Nobody wants to hurt you—not you. It's not about you." He set down the glasses. "American whiskey," he said, "Bourbon. I only got one half a bottle. But if not now, when?"

I gotta say, Sam's gesture there really did make me feel a lot better. Doug seemed a bit warmed by the whiskey, too—and it turned out to be pretty decent stuff, though I'm not sure the brand. We both sat and drank a few sips, a needed sense of home flowing down our throats. Sam returned behind the bar. That's when it hit me that I hadn't told Doug anything at all about the boat logs, or the crazy old woman I had met during the day.

Figuring it was probably not the best idea for him to be in the dark, I laid it all out for him.

"So that's why you didn't want to come down for dinner, then," said Doug after I had finished.

"Yeah…that's right. I just don't really know what to make of any of that."

"We probably should have made Tom take us back to Hawaii with him just now…" Doug said, looking out into the darkness beyond the window.

"Maybe," I said, "but, I don't know. I don't think it's all bad, here. We've tripped over a hornet's nest, maybe, but who knows what that means."

"Look, let's just talk to Martha again tomorrow," Doug said, finally seeming to calm down completely. "She obviously knows a lot about something."

"Yeah, and I want to find Baya, too," I said. "I need to see what he says about the boat logs."

"Those numbers from the first day," Doug asked, "I mean—the supply numbers and all that…how old are they?"

"Ten years, and not a single record from before that…at least not that I found. And the plant's been operating here for twenty." Doug nodded, and I took another sip of whiskey.

We finished off our drinks slowly. Doug suggested that we play a game of chess, just to clear our minds, so we did. I actually won that time—just about my only victory, I think. After maybe an hour and half, we headed up to bed. Sam gave us a friendly smile as we left. We passed by the girl reading in the lobby once again. Back in my room, I just tossed myself down on top of the covers, figuring I might be able to keep my head clear that way. Funny enough, I slept pretty well.

# 8

I practically pissed my sheets when I woke up in the morning, I was so startled. In the chair just across from my bed, directly in my line of sight, sat a fat sixty-something woman in a jet-black dress. It was some kind of sari from what I could tell, but with big poofy ruffles on the shoulders. She was absently twirling a massive hunting knife in her fingers and she had a couple of striking streaks of silver in her hair which were honestly a little bit sexy. Her black eyes stared at me through little baubles of fat resting just on the tops of her cheek bones.

"What the hell?!" I shouted, sitting bolt upright. She held up a finger calmly as if to bid me silence.

"Never mind any of your questions," she said, "I am not here to harm you so long as you do not force me to do so. Don't get up, and don't try to run. Let me introduce myself. My name is Mary Kis. Do not bother to reply—I already know everything I need to know about you, Mr. Hill. Just relax, sit back."

"Right…" I said loudly and sarcastically, "sure…I'll just do that then."

She straightened up slightly and sniffed at the air several times, her nostrils flaring out. "You smell like a clean enough man, Mr. Hill? Your hygiene—you take good care of yourself, yes? No filth hiding in the depths? Nothing unwashed?"

"What the hell kind of question?…" I said.

"Never mind, Mr. Hill, I can smell my answer. Now, let us speak. Mr. Hill, I am only visiting you for a simple reason. We understand that you have obtained some documents from Alexander the boat captain. These documents may contain some information that we would prefer to remain out of your hands. Our membership are outraged by the incident, quite frankly, but we have determined not to pursue the execution of you, or Alexander, or Mr. Bacon, so long as you hand everything over immediately."

"Holy shit, lady," I managed, "take them—jeez—take them, they're over there." I pointed to where I had set them down on the dresser next to her. "I was only curious about company shipments—shit! I had no idea!"

"But you did inspect them, yes? You understand why I am concerned?" "Yes…" I said, more quietly now, "I understand. Just take them, alright? I don't care about what you're buying. None of this is my business."

"Thank you, Mr. Hill, we appreciate your cooperation, and I assure you that in light of your help you are in no danger. A simple mistake. We understand such things." She picked up the logs as though she had honestly been waiting for my permission to do so. I mean, she had to have recognized them just sitting there out in the open, and she could have taken them while I slept if she had wanted. "Mr. Hill," she went on, turning back to me. "We have discussed the situation at length, and we are no longer concerned with regard to your investigation of the Saf-T-Set facility here. A few of our members wished to demand that you halt all further inquiry, but we have concluded that we are close enough now to our primary objectives that it is of no consequence. Your facility is quite probably not long for this world anyway. In fact, I urge you not to spend very much time there in the near future, for your own safety," now she actually pointed the knife at me "but involvement with anything beyond your work on this island could have serious risks—and that includes revoking the privilege of your continued existence, Mr. Hill…if you will forgive the circumlocution."

"You've got to be kidding me…" I said practically under my breath, then raised my voice back to her, "what the hell is this?! I told you—I don't care about your island politics!"

"Don't be alarmed, Mr. Hill," she said in an almost soothing tone, "I do not expect you will find yourself in any serious danger—I most truly do not. But, we know you have met with your ambassador already, and that you are, as everyone is, a man of your people. We simply do not wish you to run afoul of anything—we want to be certain that you remain safe."

"Jeez, okay—I read you, alright?" I said, "I won't stick my nose into anything. I wouldn't have anyway."

"You know whom I represent, do you not, Mr. Hill?"

"Yes…yes, they told me who you are."

"The Black Salmon, Mr. Hill, are not what your government would have you think. Our interests do not lie in chaos. They do not even lie in power. Control is forever out of the hands of any man—I use the term 'man' in its old sense, Mr. Hill. No, we seek only our homeland. Do not misunderstand, Mr. Hill—we have no hatred for you, nor even for your people. We understand your machinations—your ignorance of everything which you do. In fact, we rely on your people's ignorance, Mr. Hill—it is our lifeblood. You are those who seek to justify the world by claiming that you have purchased yourselves and your freedom like a man purchases the love of a whore; it is natural for you to treat us as you do. We all have our ways, adrift in the dark of the Pacific, Mr. Hill—even you have your ways. Our way is to guide our people home—back to the place where our old gods still reside. It is not so sinister an ambition, is it?"

"I…" I began, but came up short. "No…" I said finally, and sincerely, "it's not."

"There are plenty of people here, and you know most of them already, I think, who want other things. They are *your* people, even though they have skin like mine. But we give them no ground, Mr. Hill. We pity Turner and her ilk. Yet, we know well that they can speak as persuasively as we do—for rhetoric which is born of true belief has a power which no other speech can capture. All I ask is for you to find yourself between two such rhetorics, Mr. Hill, not to choose one. We will take care of the rest. If you do no more than your job requires, we will be satisfied."

I just stared at her. Something about her comment did make sense. She was being sincere. Maybe that's why she hadn't just stolen the boat logs, if that was the main thing she had come for.

"Okay…" I said calmly after a deliberative pause. "I understand. For the tenth time, I don't care about your politics."

"Good," she said. She paused, then stood up and quickly slid her knife under the collar of her dress, apparently into her cleavage, from what I could tell. "Thank you for the logs, Mr. Hill. I am very glad to see your possession of them was nothing more than a misunderstanding. Please, have a pleasant stay on Milau. And if you are in need of any help while you are on the island, you may consider the Black Salmon your allies. We are friends to all, Mr. Hill, who are neutral at a minimum." With that she walked up to my balcony door, opened it up, and effortlessly, without looking back, jumped right over the rail and out of sight. Not kidding.

Well, what would you do after something like that? I sat in my bed for a few minutes, tossing things about in my mind, and then I just got up, took a shower, and went down to the restaurant. The fish roe actually tasted a little fresher than usual that morning, so if you tally up the over-weight terrorist making some sense, and add a nice breakfast, then, on median averages, it was already a pretty good day on Milau. I decided not to bother with the newspaper. It seemed more soothing to engross myself in my caviar and stare out the window. Doug showed up a little bit later, and I greeted him as usual, making the executive decision not to tell him anything this time.

I was finishing my third cup of coffee when, to my astonishment, the heretofore unmoving girl from the lobby walked in, her book gently folded around her finger to save her place.

"Sir," she said, looking at me. "I've a message for you from ambassador Stryker. Have you finished your breakfast?" I told her I had. "Then the ambassador would like to meet with you. He says it is urgent."

"Well," I said, looking over at Doug, "sure, are you ready to go?"

"No, sir," said the girl, "he was quite clear—just you."

"Odd…" I said, giving Doug an apologetic look. "Well, alright then." Doug just shrugged and ate some more roe while I stood up and followed the girl out of the restaurant. She, as you probably would have guessed, just sat back down and returned to her book, apparently assuming that I knew the way to the embassy.

I'm not sure if I've said this already, but it's basically always sunny on Milau, which was swift becoming just about the only perk to being there. Walking down the street, I looked out past the beach and toward the lagoon, watching the light crackle on the still water. There was some-thing going on there, down on the widest part of the beach near town. A bunch of shirtless guys looked to be setting up some sort of big tent, moving about like little fingers of flame along the sand. I paused to watch them for a moment, then turned the corner away from the lagoon, and arrived at the embassy.

I decided to just open the door without knocking. Linda smiled and stood up from her desk when she saw me. "Welcome back," she said, "glad that you're here. Go straight in, no reason to wait." She opened the door to Stryker's office and ushered me through.

The ambassador was sitting alone at his desk inside, with the curtains drawn so that only a rectangular outline of sun could be seen cutting into the dark room. "Hill—good to see you. Sit down," he said, not looking up from some papers he had in front of him. His demeanor was nothing like the first time I met him. He looked worried and over-focused. "Look, I'm sorry about leaving your friend in the lurch there, but I didn't want to meet him for the first time under these circumstances. You I already know. I'm afraid to say it, Hill, but we've got a really big mess on our hands. Really big. Did you read the paper today?"

"No, as a matter of fact, I didn't think to look at it," I said, taking a chair.

"Well you should have," he continued. He looked up at me, pausing a beat before he spoke again. "The Black Salmon have made an open and public declaration claiming that we intend to rig the election against the opposition."

"I see…" I said, mulling it over. Stryker, still hunched over his papers, stared at me in silence. "So…are you?" I asked after a moment, not really knowing what I was supposed to say.

"Am I what?"

"Are you planning to rig the election?"

Stryker dropped his pen and looked around. "Of course," he said flatly, finally sitting up in his chair to devote all his attention to me. "The opposition will take just under half the seats, and Turner keeps the presidency. On Milau it's as simple as a pre-stuffed ballot box at one poll location. Two inspectors just have to look the other way, pretty much literally. We'd rather not have to do it, but we have no choice. Hill…if they win they're actually going to do it—they're actually going to try to go back to Old Milau. People will die. They'll be growing cancer all over every single part of their body before they can even eat their second morning's breakfast. Do you have any idea what kind of radiation our reports actually show out there?"

"Well, no, ambassador, I don't…" I said.

"The bomb might as well have been dropped yesterday. Not even that, actually…it' gotten *worse* since everybody left."

"I don't think that's possible, is it, sir?" I said.

"Yes, it is," said Stryker, running a hand through his slightly disheveled hair. He trailed off and took a deep breath, and a very long pause. "Look, Hill…I shouldn't tell you this, but the fact is we didn't stop using Milau after the initial tests. Once we got everybody off and the whole place was clear we started using it to store nuclear waste. I mean, the place was already a waste-land; it made sense. Bottom line is that the NFMLA can paint as rosy a picture as they want based on projections, but they're assuming that the contamination was a one time thing. They don't know what they're talking about, Hill—this isn't just political. There are a lot of lives at stake here, and that's a hell of a lot more important than a democratic election."

I actually agreed with him on that last point in a certain sense.

"And…" I began to ask after a long pause, "you can't just…tell everyone that?"

"The truth about the waste? That's a government secret. And the MEP has been saying for months that the opposition's projections are way too low and the old island isn't safe to live on, so that's a…form of the truth. But, people hear what they want to hear—you know that. What they want to hear is that they can go back home and it will all be okay if they just take a little care—but they can't. The only solution is the MEP solution.

Hell, the next best idea is to just jump into the ocean and see if we can all grow gills before we die. Anything is better than trying to go back. We tried to win fair and square, but now we have to cheat. That's just how it goes sometimes."

I just shrugged at him—what could I say? "Look," he went on after a moment "I didn't bring you here to talk about any of this. I brought you here because with word out about the election the Black Salmon are threatening real action. They've demanded that all US personnel on the island, which basically means me, Linda and the air-base, and maybe you and Bacon—I don't know what they think you are—anyway, that we all evacuate within 48 hours. If that demand isn't met, so they say, they intend to destroy your pickle factory at precisely 8:00 AM Saturday morning. Woulda done it tomorrow, I guess, but it's a holiday."

"Oh…" I said, the seriousness of the situation now hitting me, "well, that *is* a bit of a problem, isn't it."

"Yeah," said Stryker with a sigh.

We sat in silence for a moment while I thought over the new information. "So…" I said finally, "is there anything we can do? Can we guard the facility somehow?"

"Hill, I've got no security personnel here. All we've got is the Air Force installment over the way—have you been up there—have you met the Captain?"

"No, ambassador, I haven't had a reason."

"Well, you should meet him. But, no, the base is a small facility, no good for providing protection. In fact, it's just one man. Fella by the name of Paul Pickett, rank of Captain, like I said."

"One man, sir?" I asked.

"Drone strikes, I guess—he flies from a computer screen or something like that. They do the tricky ones out here for the privacy, apparently. But, anyway, the answer is no, we don't have any security at all."

"Are there any police on the island?" I asked.

"Police?" Stryker seemed almost surprised at the question, "well...they have a little volunteer force, if that's what you mean. Five or six guys on call. Nothing ever happens here, Hill—people deal with their problems on their own most of the time. Anyway, the 'police', such as they are, don't have any training for this kind of thing, and probably most of them are in the Black Salmon themselves." He made a little grimace at this thought.

"And...what about the Milauan military—I mean, is there one?"

"None," Stryker said, "none at all. Being a US territory, they don't need one."

"I thought it was a sovereign nation, sir..."

"Are you getting on my case about foreign affairs, Hill? Don't expect me to know anything about that. Just let me do my job. Listen, there's no military, and no security, and no police – nothing. So, unless the Black Salmon are blowing smoke (and they're not) we're in some deep shit. And I have no intention of evacuating yet. Not until we're in serious danger."

"Isn't that...right now?" I asked.

"No. Not yet. They've only talked about your plant."

"And you just trust them not to go after anything else?"

"Trust them?" Stryker asked with a sarcastic laugh, "Of course I trust them! This is the Black Salmon. They never deviate. If they said they would watch your dog for the weekend, and then burn down your house, you'd come home to the happiest damn Schnauzer you've ever met diligently protected from the blazing inferno of all your possessions. They say exactly what they're going to do. That's what makes them so damn scary. But I do want you to understand that *if* they say we're in danger, then we are—so you need to keep an eye out. We'll work on contingency plans if that happens, and it is my consular duty to consider you and Doug Bacon when making those plans. For now, just remember to be sure as hell *not* to be at the plant Saturday morning unless you want to die."

"Alright," I said, "I think I can manage that."

"Good," said Stryker, appearing to settle down a little. "There was one more thing. I wanted to ask you if there are any important files—documents and that kind of thing—up at the plant…that you want protected. I'm sorry I can't offer anything more than that, but if you want to move some things over…I can ask a favor from Captain Pickett. We can house whatever you want up there at the base—I'm sure he won't refuse."

"Is it safe up there right now? At the plant, to go get files, I mean?" I asked.

"Yes—until Saturday. They won't jump the gun. They're honestly hoping we'll just leave the island so they don't have to bother with the plant. Only terrorist organization in the world that really seems to dislike violence. They use it as a last resort—like that gives them some kind of moral credibility." He scowled sardonically. "Anyway, yeah, it's safe until they say it isn't."

"Okay…" I said, taking a breath. "Well, yeah, then. I guess it probably does make sense to move some stuff over."

"Right," said Stryker with a nod, "I'm sorry that that's all I can offer—I really am. I'll send a note up to Paul, then, right away. You can meet him up there in an hour and get things moved. He's a good guy, Paul…a bit…frazzled, you might say. But don't let it get to you."

"Should I take Doug up there with me?"

"Whatever you want."

"Alright then, ambassador," I said, "thanks for all that."

"It's my job, Hill," he said, with a quiet humility. "Hey—hold on a second. I wanted to ask you…have you heard anything or seen anything going on that you think I ought to know about?"

Well, the obvious answer to that question was "yes." The threat to Tom and my encounter with Mary Kis less than an hour before were certainly pretty relevant. But Mary's words about staying out of things were still ringing in my ears. I gave Stryker a long, hard look. As far as I could tell, he really was just trying to protect as many people as possible, albeit in a somewhat convoluted and morally ambiguous way. I didn't distrust him or anything like that, but, I guess I just wanted to keep hedging my bets. Better to avoid making an enemy than to go out of my way to gain an ally. That's what I was thinking, anyway.

"No," I said, after the long look. "It's been a boring trip so far, really. Well, until everything you told me just now."

Stryker looked back at me equally long and hard. Probably he was suspicious that I was holding something back, which, of course, I was. But, after a few moments he just said, "Alright. If anything comes up…let me know. We need to stick by each other out here."

"You got it, ambassador," I said, not certain myself if I was lying. I stood up and headed out. He gave me a friendly nod as I walked through the door, then he looked back at his papers.

"Nice to see you again," said Linda as I emerged.

"Thanks, Linda," I said. I had that feeling that I should say something else before leaving, so I stopped for a moment. "Uh…what are they up to out there, on the beach, do you know?"

"Oh—they're setting up for the festival—the independence day celebration tonight. It's a big public party—lots of fun. Maybe you could take a break from your work and come down for a while."

"Oh that's what it is?" I said, then paused to think about it for a moment. "Yeah, that sounds really good—music and dancing and everything?"

"Oh, yes, and fireworks over the lagoon right at midnight. The holiday is actually tomorrow—the Milauans always celebrated *into* their holidays…like we do on New Year's. Anyway, it's really great, you should come for sure."

"Yeah—I'll be there, then," I said, "See you there?" She nodded. I headed out the door with a wave.

# 9

I went back to the hotel restaurant where I found Doug engrossed in the four pages which were that day's paper.

"Hill, did you see this?!" he said excitedly as I came in.

"No, but I was just talking to Stryker about it. The threat to the plant, right?"

"Yeah—holy smokes! This is getting out of control."

"You're not kidding," I said, sitting down. "But Stryker says we're not in any danger just yet—not unless we're threatened. And…I heard that from somebody else, too…" I trailed off.

"Who?" said Doug with interest.

"Oh, sorry…uh…nobody. Just Linda is all I meant." Doug gave me a puzzled look, but then shrugged. "Hey," I said, "I've got to go up to the plant right now. Stryker offered to let us move some files. I've got to meet the guy from the Air Force base up there."

"What?" asked Doug, "What guy from the Air Force base?"

"I guess the base here just has one person on it," I said. Doug gave me a cock-eyed, questioning stare. "They do drone strikes or something.

Stryker said they…or he, I guess…can hold on to our files up there, and I figured that was probably a good idea."

"I don't want to go up there," Doug said, with a touch of fear in his voice, "they're going to blow it up."

"I know," I said, "but not until Saturday. Stryker says we can trust it until then. Look, you can stay if you want, but I'm sure we could really use your help." I made pleading eyes.

Doug grumbled for a moment. "Alright," he said, "but I'm going to bolt at the first sign of anything dangerous, okay?" I told him that that was fine, and I'd bolt right along with him if need be. I explained that we had about an hour to kill, and excused myself back to my room for the duration. I actually got a quick nap in, as I recall. After that I found Doug back down in the restaurant, staring out the window and waiting. He stood up when I entered, and we headed off.

When we got to the plant there was a tall, shirtless, rail-thin man, about forty, wearing one of those Australian-style leather hats standing at the door. He was fiddling with what looked like a set of keys. He had enormous glasses, tied back around his neck with a neon green band, and a pair of khaki cargo shorts flapping slightly in the breeze. He skin was so pale you could practically see it getting sun burned as you watched, and his muscles had that special skinny-guy flab of lost hope. He was surrounded by about half a dozen little kids from the island, all of whom were looking eagerly up at the door like a pack of Wal-Mart shoppers at 4:00 AM on Black Friday. We walked right up to him, stopped, and were standing practically over his shoulder before he even noticed us coming.

"Gah!" he shouted, jumping about three feet to the side. I mean, really, about three feet—he actually knocked over one of the kids, who thankfully was not injured. "What the hell?" he said, looking at us and then looking all around. "Who are you?!"

"Edward Hill and Doug Bacon," I said, "we work for the company that owns this plant. Can I ask what you're doing here?"

"Trying to open the door…" he said, his voice dropping down to a near whisper. His hands were shaking in tweaked-out agitation, and one of his eye-lids seemed like it was trembling slightly.

"And can I ask why?" I responded.

"To move the files in there—they've all got to go up to the base, and there isn't much time." He shook his head as if he were sad about something. "Did Stryker send you two up? Do you have keys to this place—I can't find the right one…"

"Uh…do you mean to say," I asked, sizing him up a second time, "sir, are you Captain Pickett?"

"Yes!" he said, quite loudly all the sudden, "who else would I be?" He looked at me in wild-eyed confusion as if he were really concerned that he might be someone else.

"Oh," I said, feeling a bit embarrassed, "I'm sorry, sir. I didn't realize. I assumed you would be in uniform."

"Uniform—right…to impress all my superior officers," he looked back at his keys and shook his head in resignation, "because let me tell you, Major Lamp-Stand and Lieutenant-Colonel Coffee-Maker really get on my case if I don't wear my fatigues all day." He looked back up with some pleading in his eyes. "Kid, I cut my uniform up into strips for toilet paper three years ago. Hell, I fly half my missions naked, and I mean that literally. Now, can you open this door for me or what?"

Doug stepped up and pulled out his huge key ring, deftly selecting the one for the door and opening it. The kids scurried like a bunch of barn mice right into the half-light within, and we lost sight of them immediately.

"Kids!" Pickett tried to shout, though it was clear he had no idea what to do with them. "Sorry...dammit...I just hired them to help carry the files. They'll work for almost nothing, and I don't have any staff, so what can I do? Kids?! KIDS!" They didn't respond.

"It's alright, Captain," I said, "they won't hurt anything in there."

Doug reached inside the door and hit the big switch on the wall that turned on all the power in the place. The lights came on with a loud echoing click. The kids were still nowhere to be seen, so we just walked over to the office door, and opened it up with another key. As soon as the door swung inside the children all appeared practically out of nowhere as if the door hinges had just played an old ditty from Hamlin. It actually gave me a bit of a shiver...really strange.

Anyway, I had wondered as we were coming up to the plant whether we would even find anything inside the office when we got there. I figured that if the Black Salmon had wanted to, they could probably have gutted the place of anything valuable at any time, and I'm sure I was right about that. But everything was there, untouched, just like we had left it a few days before.

"Alright," barked the Captain, coming pretty close to a proper military commander's attitude. "You want all these moved? Every one of them?" I nodded, figuring there was no point leaving anything there. "Right!" he barked at the kids, "Hop to—all the files out—keep them in order—everything to the base—leave the cabinets."

The kids got to it right away, each taking hand-fulls of files. It was quickly evident that they didn't understand or didn't care what Pickett has just asked. They grabbed documents seemingly at random.

"Dammit!" he started to shout at the kids.

"It's alright, Captain," I said, "we'll just sort them back out when we get to the base." He grumbled, but gave in to the inevitability of that plan.

Thankfully we discovered a few cardboard banker's boxes folded up in a corner, or else we probably would have needed to make about eight trips back and forth instead of two. We each packed up as much as we could carry and got ready to go. The Captain, it turns out, was a lot stronger than he looked, and he managed to pick up four full banker's boxes, stacking them so high he couldn't seem to see, though he appeared to have no trouble moving around. Some kind of Air Force training, maybe, that lets you look through solid objects—I don't know.

When we were all carrying what we could handle, Pickett led us out duckling-style up to the base. I realized as we were departing that I should have asked how long we were going to have to walk, and maybe taken a leak, but, then again, on Milau nothing is ever very far away. We headed down toward the outer shore, which is to say the ocean side of the island, and walked along the beach for maybe a quarter mile before turning back up through some palm trees and stepping out into full view of the little denuded grassy field which was the air strip that we had seen on our inbound flight. While it was completely over-grown and unkempt, you could still vaguely see that there had once been an actual tarmac there, and a pretty big one at that. There was a little radio tower which looked to be made out of rust, a few signal lights fully collapsed on the ground, and two worn out old planes sitting on their own flat tires off to the side of the "runway." Not military planes, mind you—they were little ten or twelve passenger things with prop engines—the kind you usually see used for private flights, or maybe one of those really tiny air-lines. They were both painted silver with red, white and blue stripes—like they had belonged to American Airlines several decades ago, which maybe they did.

"Do those things fly?" Doug asked the Captain.

"Probably," Pickett said, "I mean…they're supposed to. Landing gear looks a little flat, though, doesn't it? I think I'm supposed to take care of that—but what's the difference to me, huh? I never have a reason to use them."

On the north end of the area there stood the remains of a pretty large concrete building, now totally collapsed, with what was probably an air-control tower, also collapsed. The complex looked like it had once been a small but functional airport, with maybe a dozen or so rooms in it. Now it was rubble. Not far from this there was a crappy little ranch style house with a sagging roof. It was a split level, and it had a two car garage—like they had built it off the plans for some old subdivision without modifying a single thing. There was a tiny front porch with a white plastic chair sitting on it, around which were strewn probably six hundred styrofoam cups and several piles of cigarette butts so massive that you could make them out clearly all the way from the water. That house, as we would come to discover, was the current "base." The only thing military-looking about it was a big array of satellite dishes, maybe eight in all, and a couple of spinning radar receivers attached to a mast and boom rig sitting on top of the garage. These, in turn, were the only things in sight that looked like they were in decent repair.

"Alright, let's put all these boxes in the garage," said Pickett, like this little image of a sci-fi, white-trash suburbia was completely normal. He walked up to the garage door, set his boxes down, and opened it. About half the garage was empty, while the other half was full of computer equipment, apparently attached to the satellite dishes above. "All operations are from the house now," the Captain said, "used to go from the main base, right near the airport there, but now that it's just me, I moved everything right in here. It's a better commute!" He laughed hoarsely. "It's the commanding officer's residence. Guess they wanted to make me feel at home." He laughed again, which caused him to go into a really horrible rumble of a cough—one of the worst smoker's coughs I've ever heard.

We put our initial loads down, then made another trip back and forth with the rest of the files. Once all of these were safely in the garage, the kids immediately scurried out into the runway area to start playing some kind of game, the rules of which they all clearly knew, and which involved literally kicking one another in the ass…hard.

"Hey—kids!" Pickett shouted to them. "That's a live runway—do you want to die? Huh? Get off there. Come get your pay and go home." The kids came back, and Pickett handed them each a one hundred yen coin. Then they hurried out of sight happily.

"Alright," said the Captain. His voice had lost the authority he had had a few moments earlier. It now fell back into the soft and grasping tone of a man who has given up on everything. "Let's sort through these and get them put away," he said, looking at us mournfully. "You boys want a coffee while we work?"

"Uh…sure…why not?" said Doug, turning to me.

"Hold on." Pickett passed through the door between the attached garage and into the house, opening it wide enough for us to catch a glimpse inside. All the curtains were drawn tight so that the place was almost completely black but for a blue computer-screen light which was twisting about the room like a nauseous ghost or something. Pickett headed over to the galley kitchen as the door fell shut, and emerged a minute later with three foam cups full of blazing hot coffee—not the good stuff from the island, unfortunately, but some awful crap which we had to assume was military issue. As he came back out, I caught a second glimpse inside and noticed another old Milauan statue, this one in a dark wood of some kind, depicting a voluptuous nude female with an inviting smile on her face.

"One of the Milauan gods?" I asked as he stepped back into the garage.

"What?" he said, turning around, "Oh yeah. You're not supposed to look in there. But, yeah, they gave that to us when we first got here—some kind of token of friendship or something, I don't know. Kept it over in the entry-hall to the base for years, and I decided to hold on to it when I moved everything over. I guess she's the goddess of cumulus clouds, or something like that. Not other kinds of clouds…just cumulus, they said. I don't know. Nice statue, though."

"Yes," I said, "I keep seeing them around. They're really interesting."

"Yeah," Pickett said, obviously without any interest. "So, anyway, this is the base." He waved an arm and handed us our joe, "Your tax dollars at work, kicking ass somewhere else in the world."

"So…the ambassador said you fly drones from here, then?"

"You bet," said the Captain, perking up a little as he offered an impotent coffee-toast to nothing.

"Thanks," I said, tapping my cup on his for some reason. "So…where do you fly?"

"Ha!" said Pickett after taking a gulp, "that's top secret. But you wanna know something? I'd tell you if I even knew. Point of being out here is that nobody knows where I'm actually flying, not even me. They give me some coded coordinates, a target, and I get the *kill*—and that's *that*." He was getting a little agitated there at the end, which made me and Doug nervous. "Boys, I've *killed* more people in my life than you've ever *met*, and I'll bet you a thousand Yen that you've gone to *bed* with more people than I've *met* in the last five years. Ain't that just the way?"

I nodded and said something like, "Yeah…that's just the way." He wasn't really listening.

"You can't see what you kill anymore, boys—not with your own two eyes. And you can't kill what you see. You ever read Homer? You ever read the *Iliad*? Probably not—they probably don't let you touch that stuff in school any more. They *shouldn't* let you touch it. I wouldn't. It'll make you mad with blood-lust. But pick it up some time if you want to know how it used to be—face to face, intimate—feeling the black blood of your enemy with your own hands—dragging a corpse behind your chariot—looking into the pale blue dead eyes of your victim and knowing what you've done. Those were the days." He paused and drank his coffee as if it were likely to calm him down. "But, it's easier like this—it's easier now. Safer!" He shouted all the sudden. "Safer for me, that is. Not for them—I'm the lethalist bastard you've ever met…literally. SAFETY, boys—that's what it is. Isn't it dandy…huh? To be safe?" There was a real rancor poured into the resignation in his voice.

"I don't know, Captain," Doug said, looking down. We were all silent for a good while. "Uh…how long have you been assigned out here?" Doug tried, foolishly, to change the subject.

"I've been here fifteen YEARS!" Pickett nearly shouted. "But I've only been here solo for five." He calmed down again quite suddenly. "Used to have a Lieutenant and two airmen out here with me, but they've all been sent home."

"Why?" Doug and I both asked at the same time.

"Are you asking *me*, sailor?" he looked at me, his voice lifting back up into his drill-sergeant register.

"Yes…I guess so," I said meekly.

"Oh," it seemed like he hadn't expected me to say that, and he cooled off yet again. "Oh, well, I've always thought that it was because it's easier to eliminate just one man than four if something were to go wrong out here and they had to take us out." He seemed completely serious about that assessment, like the idea of the Air Force putting a hit on its own people was as natural as the threat of getting fired from your job at Starbuck's. "On the books it was just run of the mill downsizing. Budget cuts, you know how it goes. But out here, you can't know what anybody else is really doing—you can't even know what *you're* really doing. Boys, I may well be picking off dime-bags of Swedish school teachers every day, and I'd never even be able to ask, even if I wanted to know. That's the point. They took the other men off, and I don't need to know a damn thing more than that."

"It's gotta drive you half nuts being out here all alone, huh?" Doug really should not have said that, I think.

"Who you callin' NUTS, sailor?!" came the Captain's response with a glare. Then he broke into a wide and pleasant smile, speaking calmly. "Little old me? You sure do know how to make a boy blush, doncha? Yeah, I'm nuts as hell, sailor." He smiled warmly again. "It's better that way." He took a sip of his coffee. It seemed clear that he was genuinely warming up to us. "Listen, you little shits," he said in a jocular tone after a moment, "we gotta get to these files, alright, and I don't have all day. Gotta fly tonight. So, let's go."

"Hey, so why are you helping us anyway?" I asked out of curiosity. "What do you care about our files?"

"Nothing!" the Captain proudly declared, "Air Force…this is the Air Force, you got that? Your fruity little company can kiss my pasty ass." He paused. "But, I guess Stryker cares, or wanted to help you—I don't know…you're the one who would know that. So, he just asked a favor. We do this kind of thing from time to time for each other. Nobody else on the island, right? And I'll be damn sure I get my money's worth out of it, too! Last time he owed me one I got him to send up a whole case of Cuban cigars, and Linda baked me three dozen brownies. You get that? Homemade brownies, sailor. The real stuff. I'd go a lot further than moving your junk for that." I nodded. It really did make sense when I thought about it.

We flipped over three of our boxes and set down our coffee. The Captain lit a cigarette and offered one to each of us, which we both declined.

Basically all we needed to do was get the files back into a reasonable order in case we did need to look at them again. We decided to just stack them on the floor in big piles since there weren't any file cabinets available, and we weren't going to go move the ones from the plant. The job didn't, in fact, take all that long, though the Captain managed to get through a pack and a half of cigarettes and five cups of coffee during the hour or so that we were there. We didn't talk much. It was all pretty boring.

But there's a reason I'm even mentioning the whole thing with moving the files, and it's not just because that's the day we met the Captain. It's because as we were pawing through the various folders I made the big discovery that finally allowed me to piece together what was going on with our plant. Slipped into one of the many manila folders that we opened up over the course of sorting everything, I discovered a small yellow envelope stuck between some HR records. The records in question, by the way, documented the progressive discipline of an employee who kept stealing pickle juice to drink with his lunch. Anyway, the envelope had clearly been opened, then re-sealed with tape, and was addressed as a CC to Baya Vin care of the plant, dated ten and a half years previous. What I found inside was a very straightforward memo on old fashioned carbon paper addressed to Baya and someone named Lilly Gardeau, who, I could only assume, was a former manager no longer working for us. The memo was informing them that the plant was to be down-graded to a local supply facility, and that production of all North Pacific Pickles for the American and Canadian markets was to be transferred within six months to a facility in…drum roll, if you will…Zeeland, Michigan, about thirty minutes from Grand Rapids.

The memo was clear, however, that operations at the plant were not being shut down completely. The facility was to continue to supply the market on the island of Milau itself, which the memo kept describing as "lucrative" and "as yet not fully capitalized." The absurdity of such statements was not lost on me. I found myself imagining a small band of lonely goat-herds sitting on a cold beach; ten men who had not yet heard of North Pacific Pickles. How would we reach them with our brand and message?! Well, that little bemused fantasy aside, the instruction to continue operating the plant at very low capacity made sense of nearly the whole situation.

I actually jumped off of my box in excitement when I first realized what it meant, but I decided not to tell Doug about it with the Captain sitting right there. So, after my little leap, I shuffled my feet and told them I had been bitten by some kind of bug, which caused all of us to look around hopelessly for the culprit for about ten minutes. After that, to hide the memo, I asked where I could take a leak. Pickett told me I was not supposed to go inside the house, so he directed me to just go against the outside wall on the other side of the garage, which I did, after tucking the letter into my pocket for safe keeping. When I returned, Pickett was just finishing up a final once-over of the stacks of files we had created.

"So, they should all be fine there," he said, "but take any of them that you want right now. Don't leave anything here that you're going to need in a hurry." He stood there and gave me a look which made me feel obliged to grab at least something.

"Okay," I said, and walked over to the stack. I considered for a moment how fortunate it was that I didn't actually need anything from the middle of the piles. I grabbed the top folder from each instead, "these three have summaries of everything I'll need." I flipped through them as if to double check. The first one was full of unused computer paper, and the other two were just plain empty.

"Well, if you need anything else out of there, you'll have to come up and find me—and I may not be easily available if I'm flying a mission. I can't come to the door in those situations—you understand that FULLY?"

"I really don't think I'll need anything more," I said, "but I understand."

"Alright…you two get the hell off my base, then," he gave us a really furious glare, and just as we were about to run in fear, he burst out laughing and opened his arms wide for a hug. "I'm just givin' you a hard time, come here." A real roller-coaster, this guy, but by all accounts we had passed muster in his view…somehow. We both had no choice but to hug him, so we did. Anyway, we were happy to be leaving on a high note.

After that, Doug and I headed back to the hotel.

"Man, what a life," Doug said when we were well out of hearing, "all the way out here all on his own? That would mess anybody up."

"No kidding," I said, "worse than a death sentence, really."

"Or they end up being the same thing," said Doug, with dark seriousness, "I mean…people have limits. Frankly, he's doing pretty well, all things considered."

I agreed. I then explained to Doug about the company document that I had found.

"That's fantastic!" Doug said. "That explains everything then—it's all really simple. Low production, small shipments in from Hawaii, just like you said, and nothing going off the island. Case closed!"

"Well, not completely," I said. Doug asked what I meant. "I mean, why would anyone at corporate—Josh Plank, mainly—why would they think we were still sourcing pickles from way out here when they're actually just coming from frickin' Zeeland? On a clear day you can practically see Zeeland from the board room at headquarters. You can probably see the real pickle plant. And then what about Baya? When we got here he wanted us to think that the shipments coming off the island were still happening. Then he tried to blame a shipping company that turns out to be operating just fine, and can only carry a few tons of supplies anyway. So, he was just plain lying to us twice over. And not only is what he said untrue—it hasn't been true for a *decade*. What the hell is going on with that?"

"Well," Doug smiled, "I can't speak to why corporate wouldn't know—not now at least. But as for Baya there's only one way to find out, I guess. We'll have to go find him."

"Have you got a clue where he lives?"

"Nope—but I'll bet I know someone who does."

"No, I don't want to ask Martha about this. Not right now," I said.

"Well, she would probably know, too," said Doug, "but I wasn't thinking of her. I was thinking of the girl at the front desk."

# 10

"Yes, of course," the girl said, standing up and pointing out the window as she gave us the directions. "Just down the main road, towards the dock. You will see a little white house with a blue mail box. Look for the blue mail box especially. A very nice home, not a shack." She smiled sweetly and asked if there was anything else.

"Hey, I'm just curious," I asked her on a lark, "what are you reading anyway?"

"Right now?" she asked, a little puzzled, "now I am reading Dr. Turner's newest translation. The copies have just come, on the last boat, from the printers. She is very happy with it. You can purchase a copy from her. Oh! You probably do not read Milauan, do you? I am sorry."

"Translation of what?" I asked.

"*Ecce Homo*, sir," she said.

I paused. "By…Nietzsche?" I asked in disbelief.

"Yes, sir, by Dr. Nietzsche. A good summary—the Professor speaks of himself—a man of very much irony. My people are lovers of irony. It is very good."

"The president of Milau translates Nietzsche in her spare time?"

"Oh, yes, indeed. She is a very great philosopher. She is a very good translator, and she gives many notes which I like. She is much better than Mary Kis."

"Better at what?" Doug asked.

"With the…language," said the girl, thinking deeply about the question and failing to notice our surprise, "she uses Milauan in a way that is more clear than Mary Kis—Mary Kis is very wooden, and many things she leaves in German, and I do not prefer that. Mary Kis says that one must know some German to understand Dr. Nietzsche—but I do not have the time to learn German, for I work here, as you see—and so it makes me despair! But Dr. Turner says we may understand him even in translation. And her notes are happier. I do not like things so dark, like Mary Kis says they are."

"Uh…" said Doug, "let me just get this straight. They…both…translate Nietzsche…into Milauan."

"Oh, yes, of course!" said the girl with a smile, "they were very great friends once—at the university—they studied together. But I suppose they are no longer so friendly now. Yes, they are both famous translators, yes." The girl smiled happily at us both. Doug and I stood there, not really knowing what we should say next.

"Thanks for the directions," I finally said after a long silence, and with a quick look between us, we headed out the door.

"At least it's not too long a walk," said Doug in obvious exasperation about what had just been discussed. We began the two block march down the main road to the house where Baya apparently lived. It was tucked away behind a few palm trees, and, just as promised, it had a bright blue stand-alone mailbox in the front that made it easy to recognize. Doug and I both stopped at the path leading up from the road like you do when you're testing to see if the other person is willing to go first. Well, it was really my job that had brought us, so I assented to get in front. We walked up and knocked politely on the door. After a few moments, someone opened up.

"Oh, sirs!" it was Baya. "Very good to see you both! Please, come in, come in." He opened the door and invited us through. The place was just three rooms in what you might call a "semi-western" lay-out. It had a sitting room in which we could see bed mats folded along the wall, a little dining room of sorts with a table just big enough for three people, and a large traditional-looking kitchen in back. It was without any furniture beyond one chair, and didn't have a stove or fridge or anything of the sort. It did, however, have a hearth, some bowls and buckets, all clean and inviting. A woman about Baya's age was sitting on the floor in there, weaving a basket it seemed. She smiled at us but didn't rise. In a corner of the living room stood yet another tall statue carved in heavy wood and painted green. It was a figure of a man, hands outstretched but looking toward the ground, his expression approaching a combination of scorn and depression.

"Ah," said Baya when I noticed it, "another one of the old statues, like the one from the plant you saw. This one I have made a special point to keep—it relates to you, too, in fact. On the old island of Milau there was a very particular kind of vegetation—a vine that grew only there—nowhere else in the world, not even here on the new island. It grew close to the ground and bore delicious fruits from yellow flowers—they were green and fragrant and very nutritious—very much like cucumbers, they were. The old people who remember them often pine for the taste, but there is nothing quite like it, they say. This god was the god of the vine from which they grew—the cucumber vine. I made a special point to take him here because of my work. It seemed a serendipity. And it is a beautiful statue."

"Indeed," I said, "one of the finest I've seen." That was true, in fact.

"Please, come and sit," Baya ushered us toward the small table. "This is my wife, Malinn." She smiled again. "I have told you—I have mentioned that we do not have any children. I only tell you because it would be traditional to present them now. We asked the little girl when she first arrived. Do you know of her?"

"No…" I said slowly, not understanding at all what he meant.

"Ah—she lives here on the island. She is…a seer, you would say. We asked her, but she said it was not to be for us to have children. I have never known her to be wrong. It is certain now that she was right, for we are growing old. Ah, but let me bring you some refreshment." He passed back into the kitchen and exchanged some words in Milauan with his wife who stood up and helped him lay out a plate of breadfruit and three cups of some kind of tea.

"You Americans drink coffee, I know," said Baya apologetically as he came back to the table, "but we Milauans cannot stand the taste. This is only humble island tea." He set it down, and after thanking him we tried a sip. It tasted like chamomile or something—pretty good.

"What brings you here?" said Baya, pulling a chair out from the kitchen and sitting down next to us.

"Uh…well," I said. It was a bit difficult to decide how to begin. "Listen, Baya…I just wanted to talk to you about things with the plant. I've got some questions."

"Oh, yes sir!" he said, excitedly, "yes! Everything is going very well. I spoke with the boat company only today—everything has been repaired—perhaps you saw the little boat in the lagoon already? Everything is fixed—nothing to worry about."

"Baya," I said frankly, "I know the boat never had any problems, alright? And there's no way in the world that that thing would be big enough to do our shipping anyway. You can drop it. I spoke to Alexander yesterday—I know you've been feeding me a line."

"A line, sir?" said Baya, obviously unfamiliar with the idiom, "I do not know such a dish, please forgive me, I have lived on the island all my life."

"No…" I said, feeling a bit ashamed in the face of his innocency, "no, it means you've been lying to us."

Baya's eyes got big as we sat in a long silence. He gulped hard, took off his glasses, rubbed his eyes, and then looked back at us. "More tea?" he asked finally, just buying a little more time, I guess.

"Yes, please!" said Doug, holding up his empty cup eagerly, "this stuff is great!"

Baya got back up and prepared Doug's second cup of tea, bringing it back solemnly and sitting down once again. "Yes, sir," he said finally, not looking at me, "it is true. There have been no problems with shipping. And just as you say, the little boat in the lagoon is much too small. I only thought there was a very slight…a very very slight chance you would not notice."

"Notice what, Baya?" I asked.

"That…we are not sending anything back to the United States," he said, and fell silent.

"Well, that much is clear," I said. "Look, I want to show you something." I pulled the carbon paper memo out of my pocket and unfolded it on the table. "Do you know what this is?" Baya leaned in to look at it, then nodded his head.

"Yes…" he said, "we received that notice, what is it now? Ten years ago, it must be."

"And after that, the plant was shut down, is that right?"

"Well, no, sir, not quite. We were to begin supplying the island only. We have complied sir. We continue to make pickles for Milau. It is perhaps a larger market than you would expect—many tons of pickles every year." Here he perked up just a little bit, as if the thought gave him some comfort. "And all up to protocol…" he said, pointing a finger in an absent, hopeless gesture of remembered triumph, but still not looking up at me.

"Right, I did notice that it was only a reduction. And, you're really doing what you were told? Just level with me now."

"Yes," said Baya in a tone that convinced me he was telling the truth.

"Okay," I said, "so then why have you been lying—I mean, why did you want to pretend you were still shipping pickles out to us, Baya? You're doing what you're supposed to be doing."

"Well, sir…" he took a sip of his tea and cleared his throat, "there is no reason now not to simply explain everything. When we received that notice, we were very disappointed, and also quite confused. Milau is very very small, sir, and the facility here was so large. The company—they did not seem to understand what they were asking—they were unclear about what we produced, what we shipped…they did not seem to know anything at all about our facility. When the company said we should continue with only pickles for Milau, we could not comprehend what that should mean in a facility so large. So many vats—so much capacity—but not to be used? We had to fire almost all employees—several hundred people, sir, and there was great despair on the island—great hopelessness. The workers protested, they picketed for many months outside the door of the plant—but what good is a strike, sir, when there is no work to be done? What could I say to them? Ms. Gardeau, who is mentioned in that letter—she left the island at that time. It was darkness…all darkness." He fell silent.

"I'm sorry, Baya," I said in genuine sympathy, "I'm really sorry to hear all that. But that still doesn't explain…"

"Oh, no…" he said, looking up. He was clearly on the verge of tears. "No, sir, it does not. It was during that time that we were formed. The workers sought out leaders, and the leaders sought out a flock—Mary Kis gave speeches—many rousing speeches—oh how she spoke, I wish you could have heard! You would have joined us yourself, sir! Even I—still with a job—even I joined the cause! We believed her, Mr. Hill—we did. We still do."

"The Black Salmon," I said, "you mean the Black Salmon."

Baya nodded sadly. "Yes. And soon after that is when I realized it, sir. The banker, another member—he noticed it first and brought it to my attention. It was the company; they had not altered our budget—they had even raised it slightly as they had been intending the previous year. We were still receiving all the funds. I am so sorry, sir…I should not have. I should never have done it. It is theft, that is all it is! I should have called the company—I should have reported the mistake. But, sir, forgive me…there was much pain here, then. My people were afraid. And so, I said nothing."

A cold silence fell over the little room. Doug drank another sip of tea while I just gave a long hard stare at Baya. Finally, I asked. "And what did you do with the money, Baya?"

"I took none for myself, sir! Nothing!" he sat up straight and looked at me. "Only my usual salary, nothing more! But—oh sir—I called together the workers to the plant, and I promised to keep paying them all. It is a promise I have kept. Ah, there were cheers that day—I can hear them still ringing across the island—rattling over the walls of the plant—turning the brining vats into bells—so sweet a sound it was! They would live, there would be joy! I spoke with the bankers to keep everything under wraps. We have been paying the workers in cash, once a month, through the bank. I am sorry…"

"And what about the rest of the budget? Everything you had been spending to supply the plant?"

"Some of it, sir, we still use. As you say, we proceeded just as we were told—supplying the market here—and the supplies are much more expensive in small quantities. But the rest of it…you will not be pleased to hear, I am afraid. That…I have been providing to the Black Salmon. It is our only source of funding. We survive on it—without it, we would have no hope. Without it we could not pay for the plan to salvage our home and to return."

Baya fell silent and slumped so deep in his chair that he practically fell out. Doug's mood had become pretty morose, and I just leaned back against the wall and drank my tea in silence for a few minutes, looking over at the statue of the god in the corner.

"Well," I said when my cup was empty. "I guess that's my answer then." Baya looked up with tears in his eyes. "Baya…" I said slowly, trying to be careful with my words. "I…don't really have any loyalty to Saf-T-Set…and Doug doesn't either. To be honest, I don't really care that you've been stealing from them. I don't. But, I don't know how I can avoid telling them what's been happening out here."

"Oh sir!" said Baya, finally bursting out into stifled sobs. "Sir, you are so kind to even think of keeping silent! But, no! No! You may tell them anything you wish, sir. We have known from the very beginning that the time would come—that this could not go on forever. We have watched each and every month, only waiting for the moment when we would be found out. I have been waiting these years—these ten years—to be taken away by the company, by your government—perhaps by your gods themselves—as a thief and a liar. When you arrived, we knew—we all knew that it must almost certainly mean the end. I tested to see what you knew—just a little—in case there was a chance even you would not notice. The last man to come here for the company never discovered…so I thought…perhaps. But I had very little hope, once you came. Ten years was far far longer than we could have imagined. Perhaps it was even too long! Ah, we thought the error might buy us a few months—but a decade? It became hard to live this way for a while, but soon it was merely routine—accepted. But, sir, we knew when you arrived that you would find what you have found, that you were to us a god of the closing door. Some even spoke, sir…we spoke of perhaps trying to stop you. Oh, sir!" he exclaimed, really starting to cry now, "There were a few who would have killed you to protect us a little while longer. But she stood up to them—Martha Tok, she decried them—convinced us all that we were now too far along, that we could no longer be stopped. She spared your lives! I would have spoken the same, but I do not have her…eloquence, isn't that the word?"

"Yes…" I said. My stomach felt like I had eaten a traffic signal and washed it down with eight glasses of Aijee. Doug just looked dazed.

"Yes, so it is, sir—we knew that your coming here was the end of the money for all of us—and we have been in silent worry since we received the letter portending your arrival. But it is of no matter—no real conse-quence, for now, sir…now our life here as it is, living whether as thieves or honest men, must come to an end regardless. We can no longer remain on this island, and it is now not a question of your company, but of the sea which hungers to swallow what it granted us. It does not matter if you catch us now. You may tell the company anything you wish. Yes, tell them the truth—it is finally time for such a thing. And I thank you, sir…I thank you for what you have said, for you have spoken the words of a man who knows what it feels to have the blood of other men flow-ing in his veins. If you, at least, have forgiven…then…well, sir…it is of some meaning."

"Thanks, Baya" I said quietly, "I will tell them…about the error—and I don't know what that will mean…legally or anything. But I won't point the finger at you. They might catch you anyway, though. I'm not going to stick my neck out for you either."

"Yes, sir…" said Baya, "it is already far more than I could ask."

"So, Martha knows all this, too, obviously?" I asked.

"Yes, of course, sir." The topic seemed to calm Baya down a little. "For a few years it was only me. The woman before Martha…Ms. Gardeau…she was an American like you, only living here for her work. She departed the company just after we received that letter there—the natural choice, for the island was much too small for her already. For many years—five years—it was only me. Then the company contacted me to hire someone new—I do not know for certain why. Perhaps it was only after several years that they noticed the vacancy left by Ms. Gardeau? I suggested Ms. Tok. She was a member of the Black Salmon already then…but she was very truly qualified for the position, too, I assure you! She was the last graduate from our university, sir, before it closed. We only hoped they would hire her, and not send another American, so we would not be found out. The company agreed most easily. They sent someone to meet her…Mr…Plank, I think it was—it was the last time anyone came here before you. He did not examine our records—ah, but that is obvious, forgive me. He hired Ms. Tok right away. I do remember, sir—we drank ten toasts that night—to a new lease on life!"

I nodded solemnly. "Alright, Baya," I said, "I think that explains everything. Thanks for admitting it all…finally."

"Sir…it is I who must thank you," he said sincerely. Doug nodded his head slowly and sadly. We were all pretty low, in fact, but it was also one of those moments where you feel like you've had some kind of psychological scrub-down—you're depressed, but you're clean at least—you feel like you'll be okay in the end.

We sat for a few more minutes. I recall listening to the sound of Mrs. Vin turning the basket she was making around and around on the kitchen floor. She was eyeing us in silence the whole time—obviously well aware of everything we were being told, and long-ago accepting of the fact that we would come to know it. After an uncomfortable wait, we bucked up our courage, and got up politely to leave.

"Thank you, sirs…" said Baya as he was letting us out there door. "I cannot express my gratefulness for your kindness."

"We haven't done anything, Baya," I said sadly.

"But you have, sirs," said Baya, "you have. It is enough."

"I guess I'm glad you feel that way, at least," I said, starting to turn away, but then stopping suddenly. "Hey, Baya. I almost forgot one last question."

"Sir?"

"The records from the plant…there's just one funny thing though I guess I can figure the answer. You say you've been buying, like, half the world's supply of yellow-5 or something? Food coloring, I mean."

"Oh, sir…" Baya said, chuckling a little, though still looking repentant, "it is…what do you call it normally…money cleaning, you say? Money…laundering, yes, that is the phrase. Yes…to make our expenses match our budget…that is what we have been doing."

"Right," I said, "Thanks, Baya…thanks for your help."

Baya smiled, thanked us one more time, and shut the door gently. We walked back down to the main road.

"Time for a drink…" said Doug seriously when we were past Baya's gate, and we set off on a bee-line for the Conch and Dodo. "At least you've got all your answers."

"Yeah," I said, "only thing I can't figure out now is what happened eight months ago that got us sent out here in the first place."

Doug mulled over this for a bit as we were walking. "Who knows. With this level of incompetence involved, it could be anything. Might have to wait until we get back to figure it out…if you ever do."

"Yeah," I said, "I guess so."

"At least we know enough for the moment."

We made our way into the bar and signaled for our drinks. I sat down slowly, already mulling over what I would say in my eventual memo to the company. I did submit one when I got home, by the way. I'm sure you can get a copy of it from them if you want. Anyway, as I sat down with Doug and the first taste of liquor shivered over my lips in a welcome wave, I let my forehead drop all the way to the bar and closed my eyes for a little moment's peace. Doug patted me on the back in a friendly way.

"It'll be alright, buddy," he said. I nodded with my forehead still planted to the cold formica.

# 11

We hung around the Conch and Dodo for a couple of hours—nothing much else to do, really. I don't think we actually had more than maybe two drinks in that time, mind you. Doug seemed like he wanted to take it easy, given what Aijee apparently did to his system. At some point Sam asked us if we'd like to play chess and we agreed. It was getting on toward evening, and we were starting to debate whether to eat at the bar or the restaurant when Sam overheard us.

"Oh no, sirs," he said, "we will not be serving food here tonight. The restaurant will be much the same, I believe. The cook is not here at all today, and, in fact, I was just going to begin closing the bar very soon."

"What?" said Doug, "why?"

"The festival, sirs…" said Sam. "If you would have preferred to stay here, I am very sorry. But you are most welcome to come to the festival yourselves. Very much food and drinks."

"Right!" I said. I'd forgotten all about it since that morning. "Yeah, it's independence day here tomorrow, Doug. There's a big party on the beach—Linda Stryker was telling me about it. Sounds like a good time, actually. We should go."

"Well why didn't you say so?" said Doug with a grin. Our moods had improved quite a bit, I should note. "Wouldn't miss it," he said, turning to Sam, "sorry if we kept you here late…"

"Not to worry, sirs," said Sam with a smile, and started busying himself to clean up. Doug and I decided to head back to the hotel and hit the shower before going over to the beach.

We met up again in the hallway and headed down. The girl from the lobby, along with her book, were conspicuously absent. We made our way out the door into the street. The moon was in the dead center of the sky overhead, and we could hear the soft strains of some smooth electric guitar and the driving beat of a snare drum not far away. As we turned in the direction of the sound, we were startled by the noise of an engine behind us, and shortly thereafter the honk of a car horn. A big white Toyota Land-Cruiser, the first car we'd seen on the island, rumbled by along the rough pavement, filled to bursting with smiling islanders already making a ruckus inside. I couldn't make out who was in the front seats, but the back row had three nice looking young women in it. They waved as they passed, and one of them winked at us in a way that seemed rather seductive at the time.

Anyway, we followed the car down the road and toward the lagoon, the guitar growing louder in our ears with some horns starting to mix in until we could make out "Love Man" by Otis Redding cutting through the peaceful whiteness of moon-soaked water. I don't know why, but I guess I had expected some kind of traditional dancing or something. But, old American soul—well why not? Anyway, it could have been a hell of a lot worse, and the mood was pretty irresistible after a while.

There was a big tent set up on the beach, brightly lit inside with a bunch of tables and chairs spread out and all kinds of people sitting around eating, drinking and laughing with each other. There were dozens of Milauan flags (the purple ones) hanging all over the place, flying from poles, and pinned up into the top of the tent, and there was purple bunting everywhere too. Inside the tent they had a bar all set up, with a few bartenders behind, and some waiters hurrying about. Next to the bar stood a tall wooden statue I didn't recognize of a male god spreading his hands out and giving a look of profound largesse. The DJ was in a little booth out closer to the lagoon in front of a big open area on the beach. There wasn't a whole lot of dancing going on when we first got there, but the few people who had gotten started were just going right out on the sand. It looked pretty hard on the ankles to me, but that's the way they did it. A few couples or groups scattered themselves near the water or trees for a little more quiet, as you'd expect. In short, it looked pretty much like a beach wedding missing only an over-dressed couple hopelessly trying to mingle with everyone.

We figured we'd make our way toward the big tent first and scrounge up some chow. As we entered the soft glow of the electric light within, we were spotted by Linda Stryker who greeted us happily.

"You made it!" she said, tipping her glass of Aijee towards us like it was maybe her third on the night already, "very glad you're here." She walked right up to me and gave me a friendly hug—nothing suggestive, I mean, but surprisingly familiar. "Come on over here—have you eaten anything? There's lots and lots of goat—as much as you like—all free to anyone. And drinks—it's an open bar." She shuffled us all the way into the big dining tent and over to the bar in the back. "You get some food and sit down, let me find Reg." She hurried off while somebody behind the counter handed us two heaping plates of stewed goat and a drink each. We signaled our thanks and sat down in some open chairs nearby.

"Americans!" said Stryker, appearing with Linda and sitting down next to us. "Happy independence day!" Doug smiled and shook his hand, and I followed suit. "So, Pickett says everything went fine today, huh?"

"Yeah," I said, "no problems. Got the files we needed, and everything else is safely stashed."

"Good, good," said Stryker. "Pickett said he's coming down later, actually. He hasn't been out to one of these in years. Said he's got the time tonight, though."

"Oh," I said, surprised, "sounds good."

"Look, I was wondering," Stryker continued a little more quietly. "Has anyone…spoken to you…anyone from…uh…" he dropped his voice all the way into a low murmur, "the Black Salmon?"

This was the second time he had asked me that basic question, and as such I figured he had probably gotten wind of my encounter with Mary Kis somehow. But, I determined the die was cast, and I wasn't going to change course now. So, I lied. "No," I said, "why would you ask?"

"No reason…no reason," he said, sitting back up straight, "just wondering—because…some things have been said—some rumors. But nothing concrete. I'm just trying to gather information."

"Well, good luck," I said with a shrug.

"Yes, yes," said Stryker, now standing up from the table, "we'll tell you if there's anything you need to know. We're making preparations—you don't need to worry about anything. Hey, listen, you two enjoy your dinner, okay? I've got to make the social round a little bit here, you know. Diplomatic thing…or whatever. Come find me later." We told him we would, and he and Linda trotted away quickly.

"Huh," said Doug when they were gone, "What's he on about?"

I paused. "I'm not sure." Now I was basically lying to Doug, too.

"Maybe they've threatened the embassy or something," he said with obvious worry.

"Could be," I said.

We ate our food and had another drink. I've always enjoyed people watching at these kinds of things—I'm not much of a dancer, and that seems to be the main thing to really do, if you like *doing* anything. Doug kept looking around impatiently—hoping to spot Martha, no doubt in order to put a little fuel to the fire of whatever was going on between them now. But, as is so often the case, it's the fella just digging a well who strikes gold first. So it went with us because, all the sudden, I felt a tap on my shoulder, and turned around to see a beautiful young woman standing behind me smiling. It was one of the girls from the Toyota. She was wearing a gorgeous purple muumuu—really pulling it off, I must say, which is hard to do with a muumuu.

"I'm sorry, sir," she said a little bashfully. I could make out several of her friends sitting over at another table giggling to one another, among whom sat the girl from the hotel lobby. "But I wondered…would you like to dance with me?" Doug gave me a surprised and rather jealous look, while I sputtered about for a moment looking for an answer. Honestly, I think I would have liked to say "no," a fact which she probably noticed. "Oh, no, sir—it is only a dance. It is a friendly thing in our culture to dance—just to pass a little time together in such a way." She seemed pretty sincere, so what could I tell her—that I didn't want to make friends? I agreed awkwardly, and she took my hand, leading me out onto the coral sand.

"Oh, your shoes!" she said with a giggle, "you cannot wear shoes and dance on the beach!" She smiled like I was just the nicest kind of moron. Those are the real compliments—when a person realizes what an idiot you are and still seems to like you. I took off my shoes and set them down over by Doug who said dismissively that he would watch them.

I returned to the girl and we started to dance. She insisted on holding me extremely close, locking her arms tightly around my back so we were right up against one another. The whole scene was uncomfortably romantic at first blush. But in all truth, as we began to actually move a bit to the music, there really was something about her demeanor that escaped sexuality…at least of the traditional sort that ends with two people sleeping together. There was an earnest compassion in her touch…I wish I could describe it a little better. It felt like I was dancing with a long lost sister maybe. The girl seemed content, like that, to just be two people dancing, like dancing could be a thing of its own—like the mind didn't need to race away to all the dark corners of the beach where the fleeting desires of a given moment could be stupidly consummated, the consequences left to destroy our lives on another day. We just…danced, is what I guess I'm trying to say.

"Have you enjoyed your time on Milau?" she asked me with a pretty smile.

"Yes," I said, starting to feel relaxed with her, "It's a beautiful island. And you're all so friendly—we've really been impressed by everyone here."

"Ah—yes, I am glad," she smiled again. "It is important…in our culture…it is important to welcome the stranger. Ages ago, to visit the island meant that a man had traveled to us for weeks or months. Such a visitor was a sacred thing. That is why I asked you to dance—you must feel welcome and not sit all alone during a festival such as this! Your friend, he is waiting for someone, or else my girlfriends would have asked him, as well. Such a someone is more important than simple hospitality."

"Well, thank you," I said, "you're very kind. I'm Ed, by the way." Somehow my first name felt right in that context.

"Lanya," she said, guiding us into a little spin on the sand. I nearly lost my footing, and she giggled again joyfully. She held me up—surprisingly strong, she was—and started leading us both as we went along. A wise move. I felt most of the tension and absurdity of the day flow out through my feet, massaged in the rough sand, and let my arms curl snug around the beautiful girl. In time the song faded out. Lanya dropped her arms from my waist, and made a little curtsy. I smiled with a nod.

"Your friend has found her," she said, pointing over to the table. Indeed, Martha, looking really stunning in a flowing dress of purple and blue, was sitting across from Doug, talking softly with him about something serious. "Do they wish to be alone? You are welcome to sit with me and my girlfriends, and my husband. I am sure he would be happy to meet you."

"Oh…you're married?" I asked her in some surprise.

"Oh, yes sir," she said happily, "I am not sure where he has gone off to. He is somewhere nearby." She looked around for a moment trying to find her man. "Ah, yes, there he is—just there. Alexander!" She waved high above her head to call him over.

Indeed, it was the boat captain, tightly clutching an absolutely adorable little baby boy wrapped up in a thick blanket in his arms. "Mr. Hill!" he said joyfully as he bounded over to us, "It is so good to see you here!"

"Oh, you have met, then?" Lanya asked, apparently quite pleased.

"Oh yes, yes," said Alexander, "We met just yesterday—Mr. Hill came by the boat with some questions. Mr. Hill—this is him—my baby boy of whom we spoke." He practically shoved the child into my arms, and I carefully accepted to hold him. The little guy looked up at me with a bright smile. That was a relief because babies usually burst into tears with me.

"And you have met my wife, then," said Alexander, embracing her sideways. "Isn't she beautiful?" He smiled and kissed her square on the lips. "Ah, I have so often wondered—I have wondered how it could be," he went on, looking at first into her eyes and then at me, then into the pale white lagoon, "but I think, perhaps, it is that ocean itself, Mr. Hill. Out in the darkness a man is alone. I wonder to myself—I wonder, perhaps could it be that it is only in such a place as that that one can become new? Perhaps I am not clear…what I mean. I mean to say that…one feels like he is dead, and only thus is alive. One prays black prayers—dark prayers—prayers for the right kind of wave that takes us home. Perhaps it is that only those prayers in that darkness, do you suppose, perhaps only they can bring one such a woman as Lanya?" He looked back at her. I really wasn't sure exactly what he meant by all that, so I didn't say anything. He seemed not to be expecting a response—it was more of a soliloquy, I guess.

"We were just dancing," said Lanya after a moment, starting to giggle, "Mr. Hill is not much of a dancer."

"Ah, well neither am I, and yet you dance with me night after night," said Alexander, "so perhaps it is only you who are not very discerning!" They both laughed. The baby looked up at me and then reached out to touch my chin.

"He likes you!" smiled Lanya, "it is a great blessing for you both." We stood together in silence for a little while. I glanced up at where I had been sitting with Doug. He and Martha had disappeared. Lanya noticed me looking at my empty seat. "Your friend is off with Martha," she said, "you must come sit with us, then! Come!" She and Alexander led me back to their table where the other giggling girls were sitting. They cooed like a bunch of city pigeons at the sight of me with a baby.

I sat while the others chatted away for some time about some local island gossip involving people I didn't know. It was one of those situations where you're just as happy not to be the center of people's attention—just to be near other human beings without having to really talk with them in a particular way. Eventually the baby did start getting fussy, so I passed him back to his mom. At some point, while the girls were engrossed in their conversation, Alexander turned to me with a serious look.

"Mr. Hill," he said quietly, "I did not want to make any big mention of it to anyone. My logs—did…Mary Kis take them from you?"

"Yeah," I said, making sure no one was listening, "yeah. She showed up this morning—I didn't know what to do. She basically threatened both of us if I didn't hand them over."

"Ah," he said, appearing unsurprised, "then you did the right thing—I cannot thank you." Here he paused and his whole body seemed to shrink before my eyes. "I am so sorry, Mr. Hill…for the mistake. I should have known—of course they would not want you to see such things. I had forgotten, that is all. I did not wish to endanger anyone—only to help you with your work after your kind words. They were very angry when they came to see me last night. I was worried for you—that I had put you in danger. I am so sorry."

"That's alright," I said, "I understand—and nothing bad came of it." On hearing that, Alexander perked up right away.

"You are a true friend, Mr. Hill. I wanted you to know, also…I do not…I do not support them, necessarily…nor oppose them. It is not that I am a member—I only ship for everyone on the island, no matter who it is. It is not for me to decide—I ship for everyone what they want so long as it is legal. And everything they order…it is legal…everything by itself, I mean. I know what they intend for it—but the things they buy—there is nothing wrong with them on their own. I cannot refuse. It would be an accusation."

"Don't worry about that either, Alexander," I said, "I understand. I'm not here to judge anybody, least of all you." He smiled warmly, tears welling just a little in his eyes, then patted me on the shoulder gently.

It was about that time, as I recall, that everyone's attention was turned to the DJ who was now stepping out from his little booth with a microphone. He gave it a few loud test taps, and then turned to face everyone sitting in the big tent.

"Yes, welcome everryboddy!" he shouted. He seemed to be affecting some kind of Jamaican accent or something. It wasn't natural, whatever it was. "Yes, yes, yes—an' welcome to everrboddy in Milau! Now. Now, we've got for you—for the annual address—our president—Ella Turner—everybody give her a hand now!" I was a little bit surprised, given what I'd been hearing about island politics of late, that the president indeed received a warm round of applause before the DJ handed her the microphone. She was dressed in another stylish black pant-suit, and appeared to be wearing high-heels even as she stood on the sand. She held a glass in her hand which must have been water, as it lacked the pale green hue of Aijee and didn't have any ice in it.

"Good evening everyone," she began in practiced fashion. "Welcome to the independence festival. I wish you all a happy independence day!" A burst of applause rose up from the crowd, along with a few loud shouts and some whistling. "Yes! Today we celebrate the birth of our country. We are a small nation—but we are a proud nation!" She pumped her fist up in the air to more applause. "Now I know," she said, the crowd beginning to settle in for the speech, "that this is one of our most difficult independence celebrations. It has been a trying time for our people these months. Never have we faced such times since the goddess of coral gave birth to our first ancestors on our old island home many thousands of years ago. But as she promised to her children then, no island is safe from the sea forever. The sea is a jealous thing—it feeds us only at a price, and it has come to our generation to pay ten thousand years of debt." A couple of light boos came from somewhere. Turner waved her hand in acknowledgment. "Yes, many of you would prefer to deny such a hard reality. I myself would prefer to deny it—yes, if I only could. But I cannot, and we Milauans cannot. We do not have the luxury to dismiss what we would rather not see." As a counterpoint to the boos, a few scattered claps rang across the beach. "But seeing what we see, we must also know that it is not the end of ourselves as a people that we face—it is not a true death. Far from it, it is a birth of its own—it is in this chance that we may be born posthumously as all great ones must.

"Now, it is not the time for me to make a political speech—I speak now only as your president. You all know our party's plan—you all know that our only hope of safety as a people is in the refuge offered us by this plan. And, indeed, you all know well the spirit of our American friends." Here she pointed straight at me which I had neither anticipated nor by any means desired. "You see that they are a friendly people—a good people—very much like us. Like us, they are a people of hospitality—they are a people who welcome strangers. They are our friends, and they offer to us salvation once again, as they did decades ago." Here sprang up a mixed cacophony of cheers and boos. "But, as I have said, it is not the time for a political speech. Tonight I wish only to rally us together—to call us to think upon these festivities, the song and poetry which we witness as a reminder of the strength of our people—to remember that it is not an island that makes us who we are, but ourselves, our ancestry, our language, our society. Have faith in these things, my dear Milauans, and let them calm your fears as we accept the only path which lies open to us now.

"Yes. And with all this in mind, let me offer you my regards on this independence day—the day when we were granted our sovereignty by the American government. Today we are an independent people—a free people! Today we embrace the spirit of life which is here for us on this island—in the good things we have here—our jobs, our food, our festivals, our families. Today we affirm this life—and we affirm the freedom to buy a new lease on our existence and so continue to call this place home. Lift your glasses with me to a free and proud Milau for decades to come!" She let the hand holding the microphone drop and raised her water in the air as a toast. A loud mixture of all manner of human emanations poured forth from the crowd. The boos probably stuck around the longest, in the end, and were most of what you could hear as Turner handed back the microphone to the DJ and made her way into the tent near where we were sitting.

"Now," the DJ was saying, "now we don' wanna have no accusations. You know, you all know there was a big debate. But the parliament—they've spoke. So, we gonna have Gavra Kis come up now—Mr. Kis, from the opposition—we wanna have him speak, come on up."

"That is the presidential candidate," Alexander said to me in a loud whisper, "from the opposition party. He was very agitated earlier today and saying it would be unfair for only the president to speak. Many angry words, I am told, and so they allowed him."

From somewhere along the beach a man in his late twenties emerged, dressed in a simple white shirt and khakis—looking calm and effortlessly stylish. He, too, had a glass of water in his hand, which struck me as surprising, though I guess it's just as well if all the island's politicians didn't drink. He took the microphone from the DJ. "Hello people of Milau," he said exuberantly, sounding something like a motivational speaker, albeit with a vague accent. There was loud and really sustained applause after his greeting. "I do not wish to say very much here today, but I wish to thank the members of parliament who were so kind as to grant me the right to address you." He nodded over to a group of people sitting at one of the tables near us who were, I guess, the parliament. "Now, I wish to say just a few words. It is with great respect to our president, who has led us well for many years, that I wish to agree with her on something most fundamental. I wish to raise my voice along with hers to say that this is indeed not the time for political speeches. No, our good president is right about what this evening represents for us—for all Milauans. It represents our freedom, our culture—our nation. This we all know—it could not be in debate. But the president raises a question that we must address. She raises for us a question of our innermost being—of what we are as a people. For her, for the president, we are a people of this island. For her, we have drunk it in and eaten it up so that it has become us. For her, this is our home—and it is right in her mind that we should seek to remain here as long as we can. Now, my fellow Milauans, I merely ask you a simple question. Do you agree? I, for one, do not." There was a small murmur from the crowd. "Our people, we well know, were born on another island—on the real island of Milau—a thousand miles away from here! Our people were born of the coral goddess, and we came to live upon her back as her beloved children when she died upon the ocean, sacrificing her very life so that we should have a place to grow and thrive! We are Milauans—a people of the coral, not a people of the ghosts on Mamaoht!" he shouted this last phrase and most of the crowd stood up and cheered.

"Now," he went on, after they had calmed down a bit, "the president is right about something, at least. She is right that now, this time in which we are living, is the most important time in the history of our people. But it is not important for the reason she says. It is not important because we are faced with the crisis of staving off the ocean for a few more years. No—we are far, far from the kind of disaster which she describes. Oh, the sea is rising, to be sure—but disaster does not await us. Milauans, my people, now is the great time in our history because it is now that we make our return—back to our home—back to where we can live in peace upon the back of our ancestral mother herself, who will provide for us as she once did—who will free our people from the bonds in which we are held—the stink of the death which is the foundation of this place that we are living. Today is a day of return—let this be the last great festival of independence ever celebrated on this unholy earth—this place which is a mere imagining! Let us return to our gods, where they are waiting for us, and once again be truly free as we have always been, and are destined to remain—one people, the people who alone in the world have before them the opportunity to exist unbounded by anything but the gods of the trees and rivers and streams of their true home—gods who demand from us and take from us and in so doing dance with us, make music with us, make love with us, give birth to us! These did not follow us here to the island, as we all know well. Their likenesses here are empty—only statues of memories. No, they are not here with us, but are waiting back at home—waiting to rise up once again in the face of the idols these 'friendly' Americans brought down for us: their factories, their bases, their resorts," he actually got a couple of boos here. "No, we will return to our old island home. We will taste those waters again, dear friends—we will give our yes to life, I assure you—beginning this night. So let me, then, offer a toast to our independence—to Milau, our real island—our home!"

Well, the crowd basically went ape with excitement, and I have to admit even I was pretty roused by the whole speech. The guy's tone, while certainly polished, was so genuine that you just couldn't help being drawn in. I recalled what Mary Kis had told me when she broke into my hotel room earlier, I mean about honest rhetoric and who to believe. I guess she had gotten what she hoped for; sitting there listening to someone whose plan was evidently equivalent (according to what Stryker had told me) to certain horrific doom, I think I may well have jumped up and supported him anyway.

After the crowd calmed down a bit, the DJ got the music back up and the whole party returned to its previous state. I looked over to Alexander, who had kept a straight face during both of the speeches, probably to avoid showing his hand politically in front of a guest. "Would you like another drink?" I asked, my glass empty. Alexander declined for the moment, so I got up and made for the bar on my own. There was a decent sized line of people who had waited until after the speeches for a refill, so I got in it.

As I was getting close to the bar myself, a flabby hand landed on my shoulder. I turned around, and there stood Mary Kis, smiling at me like she knew something I didn't. "Mr. Hill," she said in a friendly tone, "might you have a moment to speak? Please—get your drink. Very good. Now, come this way, where it is a little more private, so we will not be overheard." I glanced over at Alexander who was now absorbed in bouncing his baby on his knee and laughing about something with his wife. Mary dragged me by the elbow out onto the beach away from the tent and all the dancers, directly past the large statue of the god looming over the whole scene in the tent. "Ah," she said, pausing a moment in front of it, "the most revered of all the old gods. The god of the moonlight on the lagoon. Come, come with me." She dragged me to a couple of palm tree stumps to the north of all the activity, and we sat down.

"I'm sorry for intruding upon you, Mr. Hill," Mary said. "I simply wanted to speak with you—about today…and the events soon to unfold."

"You mean you and your little mafia blowing up our plant?" I asked with obvious bitterness.

"Yes," she said flatly, ignoring my tone. "Precisely. We are aware that you removed most of the documents which were stored there. That is perfectly sensible—we would have done the same. We are also aware that you have spoken to Baya Vin, the plant manager, is that correct? You have confronted him?"

"Yeah, I guess so," I said, "he told me what you've been up to. Frankly, I really don't care personally speaking. If it were up to me, I'd let you steal from Saf-T-Set 'til Kingdom Come."

"But," she said, as if scolding me gently, "you have told Baya that you intend to report our activities to your company, have you not?"

"Yes," I said, looking out onto the pale lagoon, "he said it didn't matter anyway. Lady, I've got no skin in this game—I'm not going to take any risks for you or your gang, alright?"

"Oh, of course not!" said Mary. "Of course not! We would never ask you to. And Baya is quite correct—it won't matter what you tell the company now. We knew when you arrived that this would happen. Please,

Mr. Hill, I am only confirming the situation with you—I am not here to threaten you. In fact, just the opposite. Just the opposite."

"And what is that supposed to mean?"

"Well, Mr. Hill," she said, "we have been pleasantly surprised at your…consideration…your sympathy toward us, I mean. Everyone has spoken to it, Baya and Martha in particular. And it seems that your friend is becoming very close with Martha which can only mean he, too, is…at least not hostile to our cause. I only wished to tell you again that…in light of all you have done, whatever happens on this island in the coming days, you need not have any worry for your safety."

"You mean when you destroy the plant?" I asked.

"Yes, certainly then," she said, now looking out into the darkness as if deep in thought. "We have no intention of hurting anyone at that time, least of all you. That is why we have advertised our plan—so that every-one may stay away. The explosion will be controlled. We have been very thorough in that regard. But…" She paused and looked back at me again like she was trying to figure me out, and, evidently satisfied, she began to speak like a person does when they've decided to really trust you. "Mr. Hill, we are very concerned that there will be more violence. Your embassy seems to be taking no heed for our warnings about the election, and we may have no other choice. I only wish you to know that you will not be targeted. You are not an enemy of our organization."

I stared at her for a long moment. Honestly, it seemed a little bit shocking that she would tell me that. To go out of her way to hand over that kind of information just to reassure me—there was no real reason for it, no strategic gain. I could only believe that she was just doing it…because she thought it was the right thing to do, or something…like she really did just care about me even outside the scope of whatever role I had to play in her politics.

"Well…thank you," I said finally.

She smiled wide, wrinkling the fat on her cheeks and showing her teeth. "You are most welcome, Mr. Hill." We sat in silence for another moment. "And what did you think of the speeches? I ask only from curiosity."

"Uh…" I said, trying to decide if I should really answer the question. "Your son, is it? Gavra?"

"Grandson," she said proudly.

"Yeah…well, he can really speak, that much is for sure. He really drew me in. Honestly, you'd probably even get my vote—even knowing what I know."

"And what do you know, Mr. Hill?"

"That your plan is completely bogus. You'll all die if you go back home."

"Ah…" she said, with a nod of understanding, "and you presume that we and our supporters are all simply *unaware* of this? Perhaps we have a difference of opinion about the facts, Mr. Hill—we do have our own studies and figures—but perhaps we also have our own views on what is important between the waves of the ocean—not so rigid an understanding as you have. Or are you, maybe, a follower of that little girl? A believer that there are simply ways around things in the end—ways to do neither one thing nor the other? It is sad nonsense, Mr. Hill. One faces things or does not." She stopped dead and stared sharply into my eyes again, as if checking to see whether I understood her. I'm not sure what she determined. Either way, after a long hard pause, she stood up, ready to leave. "Please, enjoy the rest of the festival," she said, "I must depart now, but I see you have made enough friends on the island—I will entrust you to their care. Remember—you are in no danger, even if there are others here who are." She smiled at me again, and disappeared off somewhere in the darkness.

# 12

I sat there on the stump by myself for a pretty long time, enjoying the chance to sit and have a drink on my own and try not to think. The moon was starting to come lower over the lagoon, cutting an identifiable streak of blue-white across it in place of the diffuse and transcendent glow from before. I glanced over at all the dancing and lo, I caught sight of them, Doug and Martha together. They were swaying to a quick beat, holding each other close and not speaking a word. Maybe Alexander was right about the dark of the Pacific night. Maybe it was the moonlit water itself that was dancing in them, and the same water speaking to me through Mary, like the light on the lagoon was the thing that wanted me to know something, a truth or a lie, her voice merely its instrument. I must have had a lot to drink to be thinking things like that, huh?

Well, I was just going to start wandering back to the table where all Lanya's girlfriends were sitting with the baby (Lanya and Alexander had gotten up to dance themselves) when the whole thing broke out. At first I could just make out a couple of loud voices, then I spotted the scuffle, and then there it was, Gavra Kis falling right over one of the big tables in the tent, collapsing it and tumbling down into all the somber people who had been previously identified as members of parliament. The requisite female shrieks bounced off the water and over the sand. Standing there, still shirtless, and with blood on his fist, was the man himself: Captain Paul Pickett.

I stood up and trotted over to the scene. The Strykers had appeared, and the ambassador was holding Pickett back by the shoulders while Linda held her hands up to her face and started sobbing.

"Captain…dammit…what are you doing?" Stryker was shouting at him.

"That son of a bitch!" Pickett shouted back, trying to toss off Stryker's grip, "that son of a bitch! Did you hear what he said? Huh? Called us liars! Called all of us Americans—you too!" he pointed a finger right at me as he noticed me arrive. "Called us all liars and cheats and then he cursed us—some kind of incantation!"

I stopped short of helping Stryker hold the Captain back as the latter made another attempted lunge at his victim. Gavra, for his part, was still lying on the collapsed table, with a bloody nose that looked like it was probably broken. The parliament were all completely drop-jawed. Oh, and the DJ had just kept playing music like nothing had happened.

"Dammit, Paul, calm the hell down," Stryker shouted again, and this time it seemed to take. "Have you been drinking already? Huh? You just got here!" Pickett glared at the ambassador but didn't say anything.

"Well," said Gavra, finally trying to get up from the ground and dabbing at his nose. "I suppose you can see for yourselves, then. You can all see for yourselves." He gestured around the whole festival. Everyone, of course, was watching the scene. "Here is your American military man, yes? And your ambassador? The company man? Here are the benevolent governors that your president trusts to secure this island. What is the cost, then, gentlemen?" he turned to Stryker and Pickett, "of that security? Will it cost my people their dignity just as you have tried to strip me of mine? Hmm? How many more of our noses will be broken?"

I turned around to see if I could spot the president. She was sitting alone at a long table now, staring into her glass of water as if there might be an answer in there. In the corner of my eye I could see that Alexander was beet red with embarrassment. Lanya was trying to keep the baby calm while the erstwhile giggling girls were all holding their hands up to their mouths. From out on the beach, Doug stared directly in at me, like I should have some kind of clue what to do. Everybody else was just looking at Gavra.

"Alright, pal," said Pickett, apparently calm enough not to take another swing, "you can say what you want. Say whatever you want about us, or about me, or about my mother if you want to. I don't care. But if you think…if you think all these people…if you think *I* am here to fuck with you…you…then you got another thing coming. Go ahead, play your little games, get me worked up. I see what it is—I see it all. Just watch yourself."

"Oh, no, Captain," said Gavra, a sparkle of pride in his eye, "it is you who will need to be on guard. For we have grown tired of your presence here, and all your antics, as you have just displayed them for all to see. Be very careful, Captain—and if you see any signs of danger…I urge you…heed them." He delivered this last bit in a deep and ominous tone. Then he stepped away from the scene and headed up to the bar where he was given some clean towels to wipe his face and staunch his bleeding.

"Paul, go back to the base," said Stryker in resignation, "just go."

"Shut up Stryker," said the Captain angrily.

"Paul, you were here for five minutes and you already got into a fight. You're on edge, alright—don't tempt fate."

"You listen here," Pickett snapped back, "if anyone is going to tell anyone what to do on this damn island it's going to be me telling you. I'm a goddamn Air Force captain, you got that, Mr. Diplomat? And you already owe me a favor from this morning, too. You don't give the orders to me around here."

"Captain," I said, butting in perhaps stupidly, "it's not an order. But, maybe it's a good idea."

Pickett turned to me like he figured he'd punch me first and ask questions later. But then, like he saw something he hadn't expected in my face, or maybe just fully recognized me at all, his anger suddenly dropped. "Yeah," he said after a long pause, "alright. I'll just go, then. But it's on my own damn volition—alright? And you watch that little prick," he was now addressing everyone in the place and pointing at Gavra. "You can all paint me the crazy bastard around here if you want—but you didn't hear what he said—you didn't hear him…he actually believes it…and you think I'm far gone? He doesn't give a shit if he kills anybody—not just us—even all of you! I'm doing it on orders, you understand that? You think I just drop bombs around for fun? I do it on orders. These people…they think it's…what? Justice…or something…some kind of courage? Bullshit! Not behind a button—no—you're all cowards—everyone behind every button…just masturbating—me, and you…and them! You've never seen the black blood. None of you know a damn thing about it! None of you! And all for a woman made out of coral? A thousand ships for that?! All of you!" He flung his hands wildly around at the crowd.

I suspect that to most everyone there that night, that all just seemed like the ramblings of a drunken loon (though I'm definitely not sure he had had anything to drink at all), but it gave me, at least, some pause. For one thing, he had ruined his own night for the sake of whatever Gavra had said, and I actually don't think even Pickett would have made that choice lightly. I was convinced, and I am even more so now, that there was someone in him…somewhere…that at least remembered what self control looks like on paper. But, even regardless of that, as he stood there, now staring at me like I was his only friend in the world (though we had barely met once) there seemed to be something in what he was say-ing that must have made sense. No…there was something that did make sense…or it did to me. At the very least, it left me feeling that Gavra almost certainly deserved to get socked in the face.

"We'll walk back with you," said Linda Stryker very sweetly, wiping away her tears. The ambassador didn't seem to like that idea, and gave me a glance like he had wanted to talk to me about something, but he resigned himself to going with his wife. And it's not like anyone else wanted him there right then, either. I wasn't even sure if I should stick around. Anyway, the Captain sadly agreed to the offer of an escort, and the three quietly headed out from the tent and into the darkness.

It took a little time, but the party did settle back in eventually. A couple of people from behind the bar managed to fix the table, and Gavra got shuffled off, presumably to see a doctor or something. The members of parliament seemed less than shocked, and quickly returned to their own conversation. The music just kept on rolling, and the dancing found its feet again. I sat back down with Alexander.

"Oh, sir," he said very sadly, "I am so sorry…for what Mr. Kis said—please, it is not all of us who feel that way. It is only a very few."

"It's okay, Alexander," I said, "Pickett made a complete ass of himself there, no matter what Gavra said. Looks like everybody got what they deserved."

"Ah—you are indeed a good and patient man." He smiled.

Doug and Martha hurried over and sat down next to us. I introduced them to Alexander, in whom they didn't seem interested (well, Martha already knew him, of course).

"Are you okay, Hill?" Martha asked me sympathetically.

"Yeah, why wouldn't I be okay?"

"I don't know," she said, "I just…saw you there near Gavra—I wanted to make sure you were alright."

"I wasn't involved," I said, "I'm just fine. Where have you two been?"

Martha blushed, and Doug tried to play it cool. "Oh, just chatting for a while down the beach—you know, away from so much noise. And then we were dancing for a bit. Just enjoying the festival. The usual."

I smirked and gave him a wink which I don't think Martha could see. "Well, it sure has been eventful, I'll say that much." We all sat in silence for a little while.

"Hill…" Martha began after she had shaken off her embarrassment, "I…saw you with Mary Kis a little while ago—talking with her, I mean. I wanted…" she paused and looked around. Alexander wasn't paying much attention to us right then, and neither was anyone else. "I wanted to…to just ask after you. I mean…has she said anything to worry you?"

"No," I said. "No, just the opposite, in fact."

"Good," said Martha. "I have already talked…to Doug about all this. But, by now it is no secret that…I am a member of the organization. I was worried that perhaps you would look at me differently."

"Hey," I said, "like I told Mary, I don't have any skin in this game."

"Thank you," she said, glancing at Doug, "Doug has said much the same. I wanted to tell you also, however…about Tom, the pilot…what happened to him. I want you to understand. They did not want to injure him. Dominic was only surprised to see that he was still on the island. Dominic was trying to protect him. He sold him all the fuel he needed—right away—he assumed that that would mean he would leave. When he did not, Mary became worried. She did not want him to get hurt. So Dominic threatened him…he would never have hurt him, no matter what he said. It was the only way they could be sure he would go back home, where he will be safe from everything." Doug nodded his head eagerly in confirmation, as though he had any way of really backing up what she was saying. Not that I didn't believe her. I did.

"I see," I said, "well, that's good to know."

"Hill…" she said, a bit sadly, "I am so sorry for misleading you…for helping to steal from the company. I was a member of the Black Salmon first…and…we didn't think you Americans would…even notice the loss. Since you two came here, I have been in great pain for what I have done. You have been nothing but kind to me…I am so sorry. I don't know what is right anymore." She fell silent.

"Well, look," I said, "you were stealing, that's for sure…but you weren't stealing from us. I mean, me and Doug. And you're right, the company never missed any of it. If they had, they would have looked into it years ago. Fools and their money, you know…"

"Yes, perhaps…" she said slowly, "perhaps this is fair. But things are no longer clear to me. Doug has been telling me all about your home—all about America. People—just like my people. Is it right to take from them?" She was visibly shaken up at the thought.

"Well, don't worry about that right now," Doug said with a soothing air of intimacy. "We don't have to make those decisions here…not tonight. Let's just enjoy the rest of all this, huh? Chin up." He reached across the table and touched her arm. She, in turn, set a hand on his wrist and accepted the comfort.

After a moment, Doug got up and got us another round of drinks. Just as he was sitting back down, Alexander, still next to me, gave me a nudge. "Look, sir, out over the lagoon. They're starting!" The music faded out and everyone turned to face the water. Three or four practically naked guys were bounding about on a flat raft of some sort with enormous torches, shouting to each other in Milauan. Then, up they went. The fireworks.

It was really a pretty dazzling show—not just amateur stuff—real big professional bursts, mostly purple and white, dripping down out of the dark sky like flowers somehow happy to be dying. Doug and Martha held each other's hand tight while Alexander rested his on my shoulder in a friendly gesture. The baby stared at the fire in the sky with the wonder of a person who has never really seen much of anything before—taking it all in. It was one of those really peaceful scenes, smiles spreading all about the place. After the finale, which was about five minutes of totally disorganized but unrelenting colored flame, wild applause rose from everyone. Couples (including Doug and Martha) kissed each other, friends lifted glasses and dished out hugs. The mood was pretty damn good, all in all. Pretty damn good.

Martha and Doug got up and said they were going to turn in for the night. We agreed to meet up again in the morning for breakfast, and they headed off, hand in hand. I stuck around to finish my drink, gazing out into the water. It was then, as I was looking across the lagoon, after the fireworks were over, that I noticed it. Way up on the northern end of the island, as I've mentioned before, was the derelict old resort. Just as the fireworks were over, one of the windows up there lit up like someone had flipped on a lamp inside.

"Alexander," I said quietly, leaning over, "there's a light on up at the resort."

"Oh," said Alexander, "yes. Probably the professor likes to watch the fireworks. Perhaps he is just going off to bed now that they are over."

"Professor?"

"Yes, Mr. Hill," Alexander smiled, "Dr….oh, what is it…wait one moment. Dr. Gibson, yes…yes, that is it. He has lived there since the university closed. That is…fifteen years ago at least. He keeps to him-self—I have not seen him in town in a long time now."

"You're telling me a university professor lives up in the resort…cur-rently?"

Alexander just nodded like that was a perfectly natural thing. He paused a moment as if he were thinking about something, then said, "you know, you should meet him! He is a good man. You would like one another. He is American like you. Ah, and he knows everything one can know of Milauan history, so I am told—if you are curious, he can tell you any-thing you would want. Even the president used to see him sometimes for advice, I think…though perhaps not so much anymore. She was his stu-dent, and Mary Kis, too."

"Huh," I said, mulling it over, "yeah…maybe I should." In fact, I had already given some thought to exploring the old resort anyway. Like everybody, I'm fond of abandoned buildings. Alexander smiled in agree-ment.

Just then our heads snapped out to where the DJ's voice was coming over the speakers once again in the soothing tones of a man drawing a party to a close. "Alright, alright, alright everybody," he said, "last call for every-body, and now we gonna play it out like we always do, with the mas-ter, Mr. Otis Redding—like we always do—happy independence day!" There was a loud cheer as "Dock of the Bay" came on over the speakers, the second Redding tune of the night, you'll notice.

Just when Otis started in to whistling, everybody seemed to stand up almost at once and make their way back up from the beach. As the crowd was thinning out, Alexander turned to me with a smile.

"Happy independence day," he said.

"You too," I replied, offering my hand for a shake. He took it.

"Thank you so much, Mr. Hill," he said. "It is a special day for me—for all my people, of course—but for me in particular. It was on this day, two years ago, that she told me—the little girl—she promised me that it would come to be. I always remember—I did not believe her at first."

"Alexander..." I said, looking at him quizzically, "who is she? Baya mentioned the little girl, too."

"Oh, Mr. Hill," he said with a slightly sheepish smile, "I am sorry to have mentioned it. It is for islanders. It is perhaps a little superstitious, but she is often right—what she tells us. As I said, she was right about Lanya, and my son. And I am not the only one—very many people have experienced much the same. So, we listen. We are never certain, but we listen."

"I really don't understand..." I said.

"Mr. Hill, please," Alexander really didn't want me to press the issue, "do not worry about these things. She lives on the southern part of the island. She came here, perhaps it was twenty years ago—very strange, on a boat alone. She went to live there, where she lives now. We have come to revere her advice. Most of us have sought her out in a time of need. She is a seer, Mr. Hill, it is all I can say." I shook my head, still not really getting it. "It has been a fine evening," Alexander said, "we have enjoyed your company very much. I am sorry again to have brought it up. Please, just return home and enjoy your sleep."

I reluctantly agreed and stood up, as did Alexander. Our little group gathered up its things for a moment, and then we headed toward town. Alexander and the rest of them waved goodbye, while Lanya, still holding her baby, trotted up to me and gave me a big, joyful kiss right on the lips. It was long and passionate in the same elusive way our dance had been—beautiful while alluding to nothing more than itself. Alexander stood there smiling.

"Thank you for the dance!" she said happily, and returned to her husband, the baby nodding off in her arms. He put a hand on her waist and they headed back to their car with their friends. While the bar tenders ran about closing everything up and collecting the final glasses and plates off the tables, I made my way back toward the hotel. But just as I was about to reach the main road, and the dark shadow of a palm tree enveloped me, I was suddenly stopped by a wrinkled hand reaching out and grabbing my arm.

I probably should have screamed, but for some reason (maybe I was drunk) I just turned silently toward her. She stood, practically blending in to the trunk of the tree, and staring at me with eyes that looked like they were glowing with their own sickly yellow light. It was the old woman I had met down by the dock. She was hunched again, looking up at me from below.

"You gonna come, then? Come see the little girl, then?" she asked me, appearing fairly calm in comparison to our last meeting.

"What?" I asked, perplexed but somehow not shocked to see her. "I don't know what any of you are talking about with this…this little girl thing."

"You come down. It's time for you to see her. We gonna go soon—all of us. We gonna go from here. They comin' for us already. They almost here. All the people gonna come down to the little girl—they got nowhere else to come to soon. Then we all gonna go—go away, you never see us no more. You come see her first—before…otherwise—too late. You come soon."

I wrenched my hand out from her grip. "I can't understand you," I said in frustration.

"We *know* it—ya? We know we can't…can't go back. They think so—but we go back, we gonna die. She seen us eatin' of the breadfruit, an' our babies dead next day—seen death growin' in us like a vine, she say, like the vine of the old cucumber fruits, growin'! We know it, and soon we gonna tell everyone—when they come—when they don' have no choice. You know it, too. They told you—you know it. The little girl see it in you. She wanna tell you why. She wanna tell you so somebody know—somebody still here. She seen it all. You come down to her."

I looked at her long and hard. Those eyes—those glowing eyes were persuasive somehow—honest, I guess. There was a warmth about her now that steeped her madness into something softer. She was most certainly crazy, but not *just* that. I looked around to see if anyone was watching us. Virtually nobody was left on the beach, and nobody had taken any notice of me standing there. I looked back at the woman, but couldn't find anything to say to her.

"Go on," she said, gesturing away from me, "you go on now. Sleep now. But you come soon." And with that, she turned and made her way toward the water. I watched as she walked down the beach. She pulled up her filthy dress and waded partway into the lagoon, heading south along the shore, until she was out of sight. I turned back around and after running a hand through my hair and taking a deep breath, I made for my bed.

# 13

Doug woke me up the next morning by knocking on my door.

"Hill," he said as I answered, a bit bleary eyed, "what a night! You wouldn't believe it. She was here for hours afterwards, Hill—just talking, hours and hours—walking on the beach again, too! Hill, I'm crazy about her!"

"Can you slow down for a second?" I said, "I haven't had any coffee yet."

"Sorry," he said, despite not really slowing down at all. "It's like what you said—you remember? About being a…what did you call it…beauty addict? It's like that—it's like we can talk or not talk—just be, you know? It's not that she's cold—she's just…who she is, that's all—no matter what. She makes you chase that smile of hers—but it's worth it. She doesn't want it to come cheap, you know? But that means it's real. That's what I want…I just want it to be real."

"Doug…" I said again, rubbing my eyes and trying to get him to take it easy, "I just got up."

"I know, I know," he said. "I'm sorry. Look, we're meeting up this morning. I mean…she slept at her place…she doesn't want anything to move too fast, she said. It's good—you don't want to ruin things. But she said she'd like to introduce me to her family even!"

"Okay," I said with a yawn, "that's just great. Good for you two."

"Sorry," he said again, this time with a bit more sincerity. He paused and started back in a good bit slower. "Hey, listen, there's no breakfast downstairs because of the holiday…that's why we're meeting. We're gonna go pick some breadfruit and eat it on the beach. She said she can show me how—you wanna come?"

I rolled the idea around in my mind slowly, and then agreed to come down with them if they waited for me to make a cup of coffee in my room first. The rooms had those little coffee-makers…don't know if I mentioned that. Anyway, I made my coffee and got dressed, and carried the mug with me outside. Doug led me over to Martha's house, which was just across the road from the hotel. He knocked on the door, and she appeared, wearing another flowing white gown, with a flower in her hair. She smiled at Doug and stepped outside, with a friendly nod to me.

Martha led us up the road and away from the beach, northward towards the Air Force base. She guided us over to some tall lush trees and directed Doug to pull down a big green fruit all covered in bumps. He just managed to get it without falling over, and she smiled as he nearly lost his balance, which made him blush happily all over.

"You see how lush the tree is?" she asked, "It is a good fruit because it is the only tree that can grow like that here. It is a mild taste, but that is why it is the fruit of life. Here—we have to cook it first. Someone will have a fire already on the beach—come." She led us back toward the water, further north than we had been before, until we spotted some grizzled fishermen cooking their breakfast. Martha spoke to them in Milauan, and they gestured that we could toss our fruit onto their fire if we wanted. She took care of the rest, roasting the thing for a while, cutting it up, and putting the slices on some leaves for us. The taste was pretty unremarkable—but, it was something to eat, and I rather enjoyed spending the morning by the shore of the lagoon.

When we had all finished, Martha spoke. "Hill," she said, "I promised Doug that I would show him the ocean side of the island today. Would you like to come with us?"

Doug gave me a wide-eyed look that made it clear my answer was to be "no," which it probably would have been anyway. "Oh," I said, "I don't think so. I was thinking I might go up to the old resort this afternoon and poke around. You two have a good time."

"I see," she said simply, "very well." We sat looking at the water for a little while longer. "I also wanted to say, Hill…again, to say that I am sorry. About last night, and about everything."

"Don't worry about it," I said. She smiled and nodded, looking at me deeply for a moment before she let the point go once and for all.

When we had finished, and they were gone, I got up and decided to head straight north along the beach. We had already come close to half way to the resort on our walk, so I figured it made sense just to complete the journey. I passed a few more groups of fishermen along the way, evidently all hanging out for the holiday rather than fishing for anything. They greeted me with friendly smiles. I recognized some of their faces from the night before.

The resort was way up on the northern corner of the atoll. It perched there like a decrepit bird of prey over the lagoon, too tired for another strike, waiting to die. As you got up closer to it, you could see wide gaps in the stucco walls, rotting red shingles designed, poorly, to evoke the ceramic roofs of an older world, a dock jutting out into the water now half fallen in, and a single forlorn looking sailboat still tethered. It was a haggard thing, a miserable thing, as are all things cheaply built when they become blighted. There is a certain sense of nobility in a proper ruin—in something that was built to last but failed. Slap-dash suburban things are what become truly ugly when they begin their collapse. I guess it's because theirs is the death of something that never lived in the first place. Seeing the resort standing there broken brought to my mind memories of a heyday worse than the blight itself, when people ran about seeking to escape the lagoon's beauty through cheap drinks and mad unbridled fucking. Well, I'm sure you don't care about any of those impressions…but it was a piercing sight like that—it would have left you feeling the same if you saw it, at least if you really opened your eyes and looked at it, I mean.

It was easy to get into the place. Some old fencing paid homage to the idea of blocking off the private section of the beach from undesirables, but it was broken down enough that I just stepped through it. The area beyond the fence was eerie and quiet. You could see an empty Olympic swimming pool in the center of a big courtyard built up in yellow brick. Some old lounge chairs were still spread around, and a pathetic banner advertising martinis on Thursday dangled by one thread over a poolside bar. There was a tattered Milauan flag next to that. Surrounding the area were several small buildings of uncertain purpose, and one big one—the old hotel, four stories tall and built in a U-shape. There were some tennis courts near the beach on one end, the furthest one of which was half flooded, the waves lapping it gently. It was a good thing I hadn't come at night—it would have been creepy as hell.

As I stepped into the pool area, I heard a muffled male voice coming out from an open window on the first floor. "Hey, American," it said, "what are you doing up here?" I couldn't see a face behind the window, which made it a little awkward to respond.

"Uh…sorry, sir," I said, trying to seem surprised that someone was living there, "I was just looking around."

"Why?" came the voice back again with mild indignation.

"Just…exploring the island a bit. Wondered what was up here."

"Huh," said the voice, then paused. "Well…you want a cup of coffee or something? Wanna see the inside of the place?"

I was pretty taken aback by the sudden invitation. I mean, I had expected to meet him up there, but I guess I'd assumed that anyone living in a place like that would be hostile to visitors. But, there you go—he wasn't. "Well…" I said, not really knowing how to answer. "Sure…I guess."

"Alright," came the voice, "let me get dressed a second." In maybe three minute's time I heard the big main entry door from the pool into the hotel open up and watched as a figure emerged. He was a white guy, maybe six foot, probably sixty-five years old, skinny, with a full head of hair gone about half silver, not long but badly cut, three day stubble and a pair of thick black-framed glasses. His clothes, noticeably dirty, consisted of a simple white t-shirt and a pair of worn-out chinos hovering over bare feet. "Well," he said looking at me a bit impatiently, "come on in then. Just put a fresh pot on anyway, so you're not putting me out." He waved a hand summoning me through the door.

Inside was the big atrium area of the hotel, the ceiling cutting up two stories, with glass windows back out onto the pool and a double glass door leading to the same. Everything was bright in the sunshine. Up two little steps from us was the main entry. An old marble fountain sat in the middle near the front door, and a wide formica check-in desk was starting to give up the ghost nearby. There were two elevators, some cheap white tile, simple blinds on the windows—about what you'd expect. We were standing in the lounge, I gathered. There was a bar sitting in the middle, to which my new acquaintance made his way immediately, and there were a whole bunch of worn but still serviceable white couches and chairs tossed around the room, most of them lined up near the windows to look out.

"You take any sugar?" the guy asked, "I don't have cream. Pain in the ass to get that, and it's goat cream anyway."

"Black is fine," I said. He rummaged through some things behind the bar and came forward with two white coffee mugs, wisps of steam rising pleasantly from each.

"I never go up above this floor," he said, pointing, "Nothing interesting up there—just rooms. Down the hallways from here it's the same. You can take a look if you want. Mostly stripped—a few beds here and there—you wouldn't be surprised at anything. My library's down there," he pointed, "and I can show you that if you want. And this here is my living room," he motioned around us, "pretty grand, isn't it?" He smiled sarcastically.

"Very nice," I said, being pretty serious. Well, when you thought of it as a living room, it really was in a way. I reached out my hand. "So, you're professor…"

"Heard of me then?" he asked in mock suspicion. "Gibson," he extended his hand, "but that can be the last time you call me professor anything. I'll tolerate 'Doc' if you feel the need for some kind of title. Who are you?"

"Hill," I said, trying to give as firm a handshake as I could. He was one of those guys who came close to damaging your hand when he shook it and made you feel like a ninny for not being able to give him as good as you got. "It's nice to meet you…Doc."

"So, are you really just into urban exploration, or did you come up here to see me? You know who I am, obviously."

"Well," I said, "both, I guess."

"That's fine either way. I couldn't care less what you're up to. I'll show you around if that's what you want, or talk the rest of the day. Up to you. But if you do want to talk, I don't know a damn thing about sports anymore, so let that be known."

"Duly noted, Doc," I said.

"Yeah, well…welcome, then. Nice to see somebody. Especially an American. Milauans are good people, Hill, but you know how it is. You just miss your own after a while. Can't stand 'em when you get back home though—I remind myself of that a lot. We love our contradictions, don't we? Where you from, Hill?"

"Grand Rapids," I said.

"Never been," he answered, taking a seat in one of the easy chairs near the window. "What's it like?"

"It's nice enough," I said, "not too small…not too big. Mostly quiet—the river downtown is pretty—economy's okay, I guess."

"Sounds good," he said, "I was born and raised in Buffalo, myself. Same kind of thing. People look at you like they're sorry for you, but I've never minded it out there. I don't get what a giant goddamn difference it makes anyway, do you? I mean—we can't just be wherever the hell we are? Gotta run off to some hot-shit place like we think it'll rub off on us? Worst thing is it usually does." He invited me to sit down on another chair next to him. "So, what brought you to Milau, Hill?" I explained to him what I was doing there for the company and all that. "Saf-T-Set, eh? Conniving little bastards, you are. Pretty clever, though. I must admit, I admire clever kinds of evil. They've got some substance at least."

"Well, clever might be a bit of an overstatement," I said, and proceeded to briefly explain about our never cutting the budget for the facility. After listening, the Doc burst out in a guffaw.

"That's rich, Hill! But, not shocking, is it?" I shook my head. "Oh well, sounds like you've had a bit of fun out here, then. What brought you up to my beautiful abode today? You're not here on business, obviously."

"Well," I said, "I noticed your lights on last night, and somebody mentioned that you lived up here and suggested that I come and find you."

"Oh, right!" he said, "yeah, I was up watching the fireworks. Fireworks never get old, Hill. They might be the one thing that doesn't. You can get jaded beyond all comprehension and you'll still like watching fireworks."

I laughed. "I've always suspected that," I said. There was a long pause. "But, yeah…I guess I was just wondering…what kind of person would be living up in a place like this…and, why, I guess."

"You're a slippery fella, you are," he said, standing up and wagging a finger at me. "You've got it all wrong, Hill, just like a lot of people. You don't know what, or who, is actually interesting in this world. If you're wondering about me, you're just wasting your time. I'll tell you anyway, if you want, but let's take a look around the place first so you know what you're even asking about." I nodded my head and stood up with him. He poured himself a second cup of coffee, not offering me another, and gestured for me to follow him as he stepped outside.

For the next two hours or so he snaked me through the old resort, showing me some of the rooms (which he called "caves of debauchery from the orgiastic halcyon days") some of the old utility areas, a bunch of outdated exercise equipment and things like that. Really the place was too new to be all that interesting. The only very striking thing we saw was the library he had mentioned.

Down one of the wings of the first floor he pulled me through a door marked "117" and switched on a light. All the shades were drawn and the electricity took a moment to flicker on, but when it did it was a sight to behold. Right in front of us stood a massive steel shelf completely loaded with books. And while that would have been interesting, what was really amazing was that someone, presumably the Doc, had knocked gaping holes in the walls between this and the next room, then again through the next, and so on, producing a make-shift hallway. Scraps of wall studs stuck out in places and crushed fragments of dry-wall wept themselves to sleep around the corners. As you looked down through all the holes, you could see that every room was loaded to capacity with books on the same steel shelves—rows and rows of them, thousands of volumes, at least. The jagged holes seemed natural somehow, but all the books belied a different world of straight lines and erudition. It really left an impression on me.

"All from the university," the Doc said, "took as much as I could. Classics, philosophy, history, theology, psychology. I even grabbed most of mathematics near the end, not that we had a very good collection there. It wasn't easy getting it all here, either—I genuinely had to steal these puppies. They were going to take 'em all back to the States. Took me three months to get everything in here, just a few at a time. Lots of walking—I mean *lots*. Made Aristotle proud, I would think."

"How far did you have to come?" I asked.

"On a straight line, I guess it was about three miles or so," he said. "It's completely gone now, the university I mean. It was just one building—a big old ugly white box like all the rest of 'em, but with two stories and a little garden in front to make it more 'unique'. It was down on the south end of the island. After we closed it, they reclaimed most of the building for scrap. Not sure what they did with it."

"So…when was that?"

"Interested in that are you?" he asked in cock-eyed surprise. "Well, suit yourself. Come get another coffee and I'll tell you about it if you really want to know." He led me back into the atrium and refilled our mugs. We sat back down on the chairs by the window.

"Yeah, so, let's see," he said, taking a sip, "…the University of the North Pacific quit admitting new students thirteen years ago, and shut doors the year after that. This place here—the resort—had been closed about three years previous to that.”

“And our plant shut down ten years ago,” I said to myself, trying to piece the time-line together in my mind.

“Right,” said the Doc, “all within a few years of each other. It was a real bad scene, let me tell you.” He laughed to himself a little, “real bad indeed.”

“So…” I said, just a little worried I might offend him. “Why…was there a university here to begin with?”

He laughed sharply. “You think I don’t ask myself that question every morning?” He laughed again and sat way back in his chair. “Honestly, it was just a weird little experiment, basically. It was a government program they started thirty years ago. I guess the Milauans decided it was something they really wanted—and it certainly is unique—nobody puts a university out on these islands. Anyway, they scraped up the cash somehow and just went for it. We started off with undergraduate degrees in…what did we have…history, literature…math…and philosophy. I think that was it. Got some more later on, like business near the end. We had some classes in the hard sciences too, but we couldn’t really put much together for real program way out here. Anyway, you basically had yourself a liberal arts college out in the middle of the damn Pacific ocean. Strangest thing I’d ever heard of…or any of us had. And I think that the five of us—or maybe it was four right at first—who actually came out here to run the place decided to come out and give it a try mostly because it was so damn absurd.”

“So, you were here from the beginning?”

“Oh, yeah,” he said, waving a hand dismissively in the air, “yeah, from the very first. Went right from my PhD—Columbia, if you’re curious—straight out into nothing—out here. I mean really—it was really pretty much that direct. I think I got my flight out to the island about three days after my dissertation defense. Funny to think about that now."

"So what happened?"

"What do you mean, 'what happened?'" he shot back, "we ran a damn college in the middle of the ocean for twenty years is what happened. The place was free to all Milauans, so right at first our enrollment was actually great. I think just about everybody over the age of eighteen took classes with us at some point. A few years in we hired some more faculty, and really started digging in to try and grow. We managed to get a few international students to come and pay tuition. About the ten year mark we were frickin' crazy enough to start a doctoral program. Can you imagine? Only ever had one student finish."

"Ella Turner," I murmured audibly.

"Yeah, that's right," he said, "she's the president now."

"Well, so…"

"Why isn't the place still here?" he caught my drift, "yeah. Well, what can I tell you about that? Like I said, we were a government program, almost completely on the dole. We faculty got paid next to nothing by American standards, but, then again, it cost almost nothing to live here, so we tolerated it. Everything was stripped down—no technology, no computers, just terminal degrees and chalk boards. We actually liked it that way—the people who came out here, I mean. But even so, we amounted to an absolutely massive expenditure for this island. There are fifty thousand people here, Hill—fifty thousand people, and no economy at all—especially not then. All in, we were chowing down, like, forty or fifty percent of the entire national budget, and even if we had started paying ourselves in bread fruit and fish tails, we still would have been pushing the absolute limits of what this place could really fund. The plan had always been to become revenue independent—get more and more international students—send our graduates to good jobs in the States and have them donate money back to us here. And we really were making a little bit of progress doing that—maybe we actually could have pulled it off if we had had another decade or two."

"But, you didn't."

"Well, no," said the Doc, finishing off his last swig of coffee, "because you assholes showed up." He laughed in a friendly way. "I mean, at first it seemed great…great for everyone…the plant, that is. Your company trots into town kissing babies and shaking hands, the American ambassador behind them the whole way—jobs, money, tax-revenue (which we figured would mean a pay raise for us)—sure, everyone was all for it. First it was a construction boom just building the place, then it was jobs all over the dock when the freighters started coming in, and jobs at the plant itself. We got electricity twenty-four hours a day in a steady supply, phones, computers. The president got so popular that his party took every seat in parliament within three years. That hotel in town got built, the Conch and Dodo opened. It was all high times, like living back in the States practically." He stopped and chuckled to himself. "Man, you could get cigars, lamb-chops, candy bars, we even had a Toyota dealership for a little while. We had twenty-two kinds of cigarettes and eight different brands of nicotine gum. Xanadu." He laughed yet again.

"But that kind of thing doesn't last, Hill," he went on, "no matter what you and I were always taught. That plant and the docks and ships together needed to hire almost every working age man on this island just to keep running. That had been the whole idea in the first place when the Americans came up with the plan. 'Get people working'—that was the mantra. But it's all a zero-sum game. Pretty quickly, this resort found they couldn't get a soul to work for them. The first or second year after the plant showed up, the resort ended up canceling every single booking. They had literally no one on staff—not one person. They couldn't jump to fly a hundred temporary people onto the island every high season, they couldn't pay the new wages, so they just shut the doors.

"Now, that seemed like no problem at the time. I mean, the islanders had better jobs, so the tourism industry wasn't exactly missed. Not until later, I mean, when everyone started getting fired. Woulda taken the resort back, then, naturally—but too damn late. Once the resort was gone, the airline flight out here got canceled, too. No tourists to ride the planes, and no one to work at the airport. So, there went all that.

"As for the university, it was the same kind of thing for us. The third year after the plant was built we had something like five students enrolled, two of them in our brand new doctoral program studying ancient philosophy, of all the awful things, with *me*! We had a faculty of ten people here by that time—ten professors, can you imagine, for an island of fifty thousand? But, like I said, we had had really good enrollment at our peak—back when there was nothing else to do out here but take free classes and bask in the sun. Jobs, though—jobs trump everything. There were forty really lucrative hours a week for anyone who wanted them, so that was it—just not very much point in getting an education any more, and no time either. International students weren't interested in a ghost university, and couldn't get here and back without a flight. We had problems hiring support staff, too. So, after seven years of trying to find a way to survive, the only two students left were an undergraduate named Martha Tok in business, I think it was, and Ella Turner, who was finishing up her dissertation with me; so, we shut everything down. A couple of us hung around pro bono for a year just to let the two students complete, and then we all left for wherever home was—except me, as you can see." He paused and gazed into his empty coffee cup for a moment, then brightened up suddenly. "Hey, what time is it?" he asked, "you got a watch on your wrist there?"

"Yeah," I said, "it's four thirty." The day had really gotten away from me between cooking a bread fruit for breakfast, walking up to the resort, and touring around with the Doc.

"Close enough," he said. "Have a scotch with me?"

"Oh," I said with some surprise, "sure. Sounds great."

"Got myself a lifetime supply of Chivas shipped in just before I came up here," he said, "Spent literally half my savings, and I would have rather had something better. But Chivas will do. At this point, I don't remember what anything else tastes like anyway. And you can't get anything on the island anymore except for that gin." He walked up to the bar and started pouring a couple of drinks. He didn't ask how I took it, and just handed it to me neat in a coffee mug. "No glasses," he said, "but it doesn't matter."

"Thanks," I said, taking a sip as he sat back down. I gave him a minute to settle in, but I really did want to ask, so I didn't let it go too long. "So, why did you stay, then?"

"Huh?" he said, as if his mind had entirely wandered from the previous topic, "oh…yeah. Well, I think about that a lot. No clear answer, really. Cost me a marriage too, did I mention that? Yeah, I was married. Never had any kids. She was happy to come with me out to Milau, and live here for those years. But I guess she had always assumed that we'd go home one day. So, she did. Just not with me."

"Well, so why didn't you go, too?"

"Oh, I don't know," he said, shaking his head, "I don't know. I guess the big thing was that I really wouldn't be doing anything different back in Buffalo, or wherever the hell we went. I'd be sitting in my living room there, just the same. I haven't published since the second year I got to this island, Hill. Nobody cared out here whether I was writing anything. They were just happy I was willing to live here and teach classes. That's one of the things I loved about the place, in fact—never felt any pressure. So I just read a lot of books, and lectured—why bother with anything else? But, anyway, I doubt I could have found anything State-side after a couple of decades without an article, no connections, and the most bizarre teaching experience available on the planet. Couldn't very well have lived there on my minuscule Milauan savings, either, so I don't know exactly what we would have done…or what my wife *is* doing, come to think of it. I guess I figured if I was just going to sit around all day and stare into the distance, I might as well do that right here. Ha," he chuckled, "I guess that means that I like this view more than my ex-wife. Yeah…that's probably right. Anyway, I don't need hardly any money this way. The breadfruit's free, and what's left in the bank will buy me coffee and fish until I'm ninety. If I make it that far, I'll just have to starve to death with a raging caffeine headache. But, oh well." He smiled, then paused a moment. "Look, what the hell do you care about any of this anyway? Not that I mind."

"Well," I said, "I guess I've just gotten curious being out here. It's been…an interesting week to say the least."

"What's that supposed to mean?" he quipped.

"Just a lot of…stuff swirling around, is all. I mean…do you get the news…up here?"

"No," he said flatly, "once in a while I still show up at the Conch to scope things out. Haven't done that in a long time, though."

"I see," I said, "well…you've missed a lot lately, then." In retrospect, it probably would have been more prudent not to discuss the whole situation. But, he was such a comfortable person to be around. So, I told him the whole crazy saga of the threat to the plant, everything with Stryker, Baya, Martha and Doug, Pickett and finally my run-ins with Mary Kis. He sat and listened with interest, seeming to find the whole thing engaging if unsurprising. But when I mentioned Mary, he perked up a bit.

"So you met *her* did you," he said, "the woman herself. I'll be damned."

"Yeah," I said with a solemn nod.

"Well if that's the case, I feel like I owe you an apology," he said, and without asking he stood up, walked to the bar, and pulled an entire bottle of scotch off the shelf, bringing it back to where we were sitting. "Have another drink. Hell, let's finish the bottle—for my sake. It'll make me feel less guilty." I agreed with some reluctance and let him pour a full mug of whiskey for me as he sat back and started in.

"Yeah, so Mary was my other doctoral student—the one who never finished. She and Ella studied together, right at the same time. They're not much younger than me, as you know. They were just living as wives on the island when we first showed up, raising kids and that. They took a few free classes with us in the early days, and it turned out they had some pretty serious chops. They got degrees and were pressing to keep going just as we were thinking about having doctoral students. So…we stupidly talked ourselves into taking the plunge, started the program, and they enrolled. Probably the only thing in my life that I'd take back in a heart-beat. But, they were working on the right stuff back then. Philological projects…solid…you know, foundational. And they were both good. And then, over time, they started just…going down hill. I don't know how else to say it. They'd be rambling on in my office, or arguing with each other. I mean, to them it was all bright ideas—revolution or some shit, and a future for their people, and who knows what all. Eventually Mary just quit altogether. Couldn't be bothered with the grind anymore, just to get some letters on her name. I didn't blame her, of course—not on that account, I mean. Funny enough, Hill, I had opposed the whole PhD program idea in the first place, and here I was supervising its only two students. But, you do your job—can't always love it. So, yeah, Mary quit, and Ella kept at it out of sheer force of will, but she was pretty well gone herself. When she finished she set her work aside completely and headed off into politics on the island just like Mary. And you obviously know the end of the story on that."

"Yes," I said, "I guess I do. But I don't think I know what you mean…about revolution or whatever you said."

"Yeah," he took a big drink, "Sorry…it's all just so clear and so murky in my mind. Well…I just mean that out here, cut off from everything, the two of them, both…just went off like month old milk. It doesn't just turn into yogurt when it sits out, you know—you have to make yogurt on purpose. No, milk in the sun just plain spoils. That's what happened to them. They wanted to get into the heavy shit, and now they're just a pair of codependent junkies. That road always leads the same place. They didn't listen to me. Seneca—Seneca is what you need. A man of a silver age, that's what you need. Somebody not deluded by the profundity of himself. A man with the guts to say one true thing and live a completely different way. Teach honesty and defraud everybody to hell, teach simplicity and let your slaves do the chores. There's a man! The courage to just embrace your own hypocrisy. Only a silver age can give you that. Anything else has to make you disbelieve that you're a hypocrite in the first place, or, if you just won't, it has to send you all the way to the loony bin in some kind of quest to actually practice what you preach. Good options, huh? You can stuff your golden ages, and your bronze ages, and your iron ages—you can stuff your damn stone ages, even. A silver age knows itself." All I could do was nod. I didn't have the foggiest what he really meant by that.

"Anyway, I told them all that, Ella and Mary, but most people think that it sounds…well, maybe not crazy but just weird. Hypocrisy doesn't play well, Hill. It doesn't get a very good rap. They were going to make Milau into this or that—embrace life or something. Milau was ripe, they just kept telling me—it's isolated out here, culturally, not just geographically—and that's true. So, to them, this was the place where it was all going to be born. They were singing ancient Greek poetry together out in the front garden, trying to get everybody else on the island to sing with them. They were spray-painting the church. They were dancing naked on the beach in the middle of the night. It was a bunch of whacked out bull-shit, like it still is, though maybe a little more fun in the early days—at least for them. Anyway, that was their dream. And now, I guess, from what you're telling me, you've found yourself mixed up in it. That's the part…well, Mr. Hill…let me say again that I'm sincerely sorry."

"Don't be," I said, pausing for a moment. "They were close at first though?"

"Yeah," he said bitterly, "inseparable. But, you know, they each grew up a little bit—started to think more concretely about it all. It wasn't just a big naked dance after a while—they had to start working on what to actu-ally *do*. Turner ran for president, and she won, as you know. Mary ran for parliament, and she won too—she's not in anymore, but she was—and they started thinking about policy and law and all the rest. That's back when they would still talk to me now and then—Ella especially would come up here pretty often. But, yeah, when they got into the nitty-gritty, Ella started really thinking that the Americans and all their ideas, the base, your plant—that they were all really good things. Mary decided they were the ultimate impediment, and got on about returning to the old island. And there you go. Now they're the bitterest of enemies, and they don't even give me the time of day. Which I could use. I don't have a clock up here." He laughed a little at his own joke. "Yeah, so that was that. And there's one last thing—one last piece of advice I gave them both, near the end, before they quit talking to me. Do you know…have you heard anything about what they all just call the 'little girl?'"

"Yes…" I said slowly, "yes, I have." I didn't know if I should say any-thing more or mention the old woman.

"Well, that's good then. You know what I'm talking about. Yeah, she's been down there for something like twenty years, I don't know. She doesn't seem to age, somehow. Just sailed in—well, it was almost the exact same time as your company showed up, come to think of it. She turned up one night and set up shop telling fortunes or whatever. I went to see her myself once, actually. I got curious—everybody was talking about her, you know? I gotta say—she said some things—things nobody could have ever known. And I don't mean bullshit psychic stuff—cold readings and that. It's like she knows the inside of your head…" his voiced dropped until I could barely hear him, "and then she tells you what's going to happen." Here he paused for a long time, clearly lost in thought, staring out toward the water. Finally he went on. "I don't know…she was right about me—haunts me even today. I hate to think I'd believe in something like that. But, anyway, I told them both—Mary and Ella—I told them to talk with her when they stopped listening to me. I mean, I just figured that talking to her would give them something else to…lean on a little bit—I don't know what I'm trying to say—just so they'd hear somebody else's voice besides their own…even if it is maybe talking gibberish. You just have to get out of your own head sometimes. But, they wrote her off. Superstition, they said."

With that, he stopped and gave me a piercing look like he didn't want to keep talking for the moment, and drained his mug. I sat there, not wanting to press him on in the conversation if he wasn't interested. After a moment he got up and declared that it was time to have something to eat, and invited me to join him.

"Just fish and breadfruit—about all I survive on," he said. "Sometimes I get the boat guy to bring me some multi-vitamins from Hawaii. I've gotta be deficient in *something*, right?" He led me over to the big kitchen in the hotel. "Most of the appliances are still in working order here, including the fryer. They've never cut off the electricity." He got busy cooking as I poked my head into various empty cabinets. In a little while we each had a plate of something pretty close to fish and chips. Not bad, in fact. We ate it mostly in silence, though I remember him telling me something about the species of fish that we were enjoying and the complicated process of catching them with one's bare hands.

After dinner we just settled back down on the chairs near the window and watched the sun set over the lagoon. We talked at some further length about my family and about his ex-wife. He asked some questions about politics back home, though he also seemed only vaguely interested in the answers. He, in turn, explained the fairly simple Milauan political system to me, not that I remember many of the details. Despite getting increasingly tipsy, the Doc kept telling me that we really needed to finish that whole bottle of Scotch so as not to make a liar out of him. But we were both content to take the task pretty slowly. I think we were on our last glass when I finally asked him something I'd been wondering about.

"So," I said, "what do you actually…*do*…all day up here?"

"Huh?" he said as if confused at first. "Oh…yeah…um…well, I get up and look at the ocean, drink my coffee, read Seneca, drink my whiskey, and contemplate suicide. Same thing everybody does." He laughed hoarsely.

"Really?" I asked. I couldn't tell for sure if he was serious.

"Yeah," he said, this time without a laugh. "Yeah, that's really what I do. Ha! I tried to tell 'em this, you know. I tried. The thing is, you see, the thing is that there are only two hypotheses. And I'm trying to decide between 'em. What I mean is…I mean…what is that blackness out there?" He gestured into the ocean night, "What is that ocean? Is it nothing at all? The abyss? Is it, Hill? I mean…is it just chaos, uncontrolled and fucking insane? And if it is, is it a beautiful chaos, beautiful and deadly like the thrill of a narcotic—the real totality of death? Or an ugly chaos that just drags on like white light made from the spectrum?

"Or is it the other thing—the other hypothesis? I mean, is it there, in there, when we've really turned all the lights off…you know…accepted it, that we actually see anything—that great order, I mean, which maybe does reach into everything? I mean…is that…is it an ocean of salt water, Hill?—the water that kills sailors who go mad with thirst and give in to drink it? Or are we, right here…I mean…without knowing it…are we actually standing back where you and I both come from—back on those…those lakes—sweet water as far as the eye can see where the trappers just dipped their hats right on in whenever they were thirsty? Where are we standing, Hill? Which hypothesis?" He paused for a while, looking out into the night, his head swaying slightly. "Well, maybe it makes no difference. Maybe I should bend down and drink either way. Maybe standing here just thinking about it is just for cowardly shits. But I can't help it anyway. So, yeah…that's what I do. I'm just sitting out here trying to figure what a drink is going to do to me…just so I'll know it in advance. Death or life. Maybe that way I can make it my choice. Even Nero let Seneca kill himself, you know that? That's the only dignified thing…if that is an ocean of salt water, I mean…it's the only rational thing. But how the hell do you decide without rolling the dice? How can you ever know? I just want to know." We sat in silence for a while looking out into the black. I didn't answer him at all, though I admit I was trying to act like I understood him. After a while he let his eyes flutter closed, a last tiny swig of scotch still in his glass resting on the arm of his chair. Pretty soon he was asleep and snoring peacefully.

Believe it or not, I actually walked back to the hotel in town that night. I probably could have just stayed up at the resort, of course, but it felt a little awkward. I had only just met the Doc, and he hadn't properly invited me to stay. And, even though there were plenty of rooms other than his own, it was, in a way, his house. So, I figured the polite thing was to hoof it back. In the darkness as the moon grew huge, setting over the water, I mulled over what he said as much as I could through the misty tumult of whiskey in the brain. Maybe none of it meant a damn thing. Maybe he was just drunk. Probably that was it.

# 14

My eyes snapped open at 8:01 the next morning and for about three seconds my body lay resting in the last shreds of the peaceful night while my mind raced frantically around the room. I had just remembered what was about to happen. And then, those three seconds later, before that body and mind of mine—those two indivisible elements of a complete person—could quite realign for the day, the walls shook hard, the window rattled like it might actually burst, something fell off my chair, and the sickening power of the bomb rushed through my room and out into the endless atmosphere. To tell the truth, I don't even really remember hearing anything. Maybe it was too loud, or the force of the blast—which you could really feel, as close as we were to the place—just overshadowed it. Either way, I jumped out of bed like a syringe full of adrenaline being tossed aside by some quack doctor. Saturday morning, just like they had said. Well—it was a full minute late—but I can forgive them that.

I probably should have stayed well away for a good long while to be safe, but operating on instinct or something, I quickly got dressed and rushed up towards the plant. Most of the doors in town seemed to be open a crack as people peered out to see if everything was okay. From the sight of it, it looked like there was nothing to panic about. I guess the explosion had been fairly well contained, just like Mary Kis had told me it would be. Running fast I made it up and through the trees in sight of the ruined factory.

I remember as a kid going with my father to watch an old assembly plant get imploded to make way for a new one. It was a really tremendous sight—the whole thing falling in a single go. It cascaded in on itself as if shocked at what was happening to it—like it couldn't believe that a bunch of human beings would do this—build it up just to rip its guts out and knock it back over again. What a thing to be—to exist or not to exist at the whim of some guy in an office, deliberating, weighing the options, and deciding on your demise. And then, on your last day on this earth, everybody comes down, brings their kids even, to watch you collapse—but not in order to offer you some solace. They come in order to celebrate the new thing that's going to be built on top of you. That might be alright, even, if they gave you good riddance—but they stand there behind perimeter fences with their minds consumed by thoughts of something not even built, existent as only a sketch, and for that reason they're not even really thinking of you at all. They just cheer as you lose out to something that isn't even there and which, when it finally does exist, will be granted the same pride you remember from your youth for only a short lease before it, too, is packed with C-4 and swallowed by the juggernaut—that great shuffling around of nothingness that is the "new." We watched it, me and my dad, as it tumbled down. I felt like I was the only one sad to see it go, and I probably was. It was filthy and ugly and old and out of date. Only a kid could mourn something like that.

Seeing the pickle plant as it was that morning was nothing like any of that. It lacked all the tragic bumbling elegance of the collapsed behemoth from my childhood memory. For one thing, it was mostly still standing, clutching at a hulking gash in the wall to the cleaning room like a guy trying hopelessly to hold his guts in. The windows, instead of blinking off into oblivion, were there looking shocked and much too alive—busted out, with shards all over the ground. The exterior walls, the ones that were still there, were leaning in over the blast area contemplating suicide. There was a river of piss-yellow brine and vinegar flowing under my feet, broken jars and lids scattered like vomit, and the odd coughed-up pickle in a few of the lower branches of the trees. Everything smelled like sulfur and cucumbers. It was shock and carnage. It didn't mean anything. It was just a damn mess.

I poked around the place for a few minutes, and then, starting to really wake up for the day as my nerves cooled off, I began to wonder what I was even doing there. Given that I had already arrived, I circled the grounds once and gave a few calls to see if there was anybody hurt. No sign of anything. Well, they had advertised, so…good. Content that the damage was material only, I decided to head back to the hotel and…well, just see about breakfast.

When I got back, Doug and Martha were hurrying down the stairs, looking disoriented.

"You alright?" Doug asked, "everything okay? Where were you?"

"I just ran up to check it out. Nobody there—the plant's dead, of course."

"Jeez…good," he said, "I was worried for a minute when you still weren't in your room. So…do we need to go up to there with you again—should we?"

"No, probably not. It's probably not really safe there anyway, and if there's nobody hurt over there, then what can we do? I was just about to get something to eat, actually."

"Alright," said Doug, taking a deep breath and trying to calm down. "Okay…breakfast, then. Sure."

We shuffled into the restaurant past the girl at the desk…yes, reading her book. The waiter seemed a little rattled, but nothing serious. He brought the usual roe and toast. I was starting to hit that stage, as you're calming down from something, when you get to be pretty hungry, so I ate. Doug and Martha still weren't quite up to it, it seemed.

"Where were you last night, anyway?" Doug asked, a little irritated, "we looked all over for you at dinner time."

"Oh!" I said, "yeah, sorry about that. I didn't expect to be gone all evening." I explained what I had been up to at the old resort. Martha, who naturally knew about the Doc, was able to explain to Doug that there was indeed a pleasantly misanthropic ex-professor residing on the property. I related a little bit of the history lesson the Doc had given me. Doug didn't seem particularly interested.

As I was wrapping that up, we were surprised by the sound of someone hurrying through the front door of the hotel, the little entry bell ringing impatiently. In a moment Reg Stryker, of all people, stepped quickly into the dining room, and, spotting us, made his way to our table.

"Did you see it?" he said hurriedly. He was waving a copy of the morning's newspaper. "With a photograph and everything."

"No…what is it?" I asked as he arrived next to us. Stryker dropped the paper on the table.

I straightened up and we all peered at the page, complete with poorly xeroxed photograph, and read through the headline. "Vote Fixing Plot Confirmed—Phony Ballot Box Discovered." The article basically said that a member of the Black Salmon had broken into the embassy the previous night and recovered the ballot box in question, already stuffed. The contents of the box would have the MEP winning a small majority of parliament and retaining the presidency.

"How did this happen?" Stryker was asking in obvious frustration. "Do you tell them something, Hill?" He turned to Martha, and pointed at her sternly, "Did he tell you something? Don't think I'm clueless."

"No," I said, "I didn't tell anyone anything. They were already accusing you of fixing the vote before I ever knew about it. That's why you told me at all, remember?"

He stared at me long and hard, sizing me up. One thing I've always liked about telling the truth is that you know you're giving a hell of a poker face. Well, it's technically not a poker face, I guess, but you know what I mean. After a long moment, he seemed satisfied.

"Okay…good. But, it doesn't matter now anyway. They've got what they've got."

"Where was the thing?" Doug asked quizzically.

"In my office," said Stryker.

"You mean…like in a closet or something?"

"No, just in my office where I could see it."

"And…" Doug went on, "why did you have it stuffed already? Seems…dumb…"

Stryker shook his head in and took a deep breath. "We didn't want it hanging over our heads on the weekend," he said quietly. "Figured we'd just get it out of the way." He stopped and put his hands up in his hair in frustration. "Look, that doesn't matter now. The cat's out of the bag on the plan, and we've got bigger problems. Turn to page two."

We flipped our papers over loudly and examined the next story. We were greeted by the delightful news that the Black Salmon had prepared a response to the vote fixing. They would hereby assume that a victory for president Turner could only be a certain sign of election tampering. So, if the opposition lost, the American embassy was to be summarily destroyed in retaliation. And, they noted flatly, all representatives of the US government would be immediately executed. So, there it was: a right proper terrorist threat…probably the one Mary Kis was vaguely alluding to at the festival.

"They've gone and done it," said Stryker. "Our lives are in danger—every one of us." Martha was visibly agitated, but said nothing.

"Shit…" said Doug quietly. There was silence for a long moment. "What are we going to do?"

"Well," said Stryker, "that's why I wanted to find you. I'm getting a plan together to get us out of here if necessary. I want you both to keep your bags packed, and be ready to go at a moment's notice, okay? I'm heading up to talk to the Captain right now, and my wife is on high alert."

"But…" said Doug, "we're only in danger if the MEP wins, right? Are you still planning to rig the election or something?"

Stryker shook his head. "No," he said, "no, we're not. It's too late for that—it won't work now."

"So we're probably fine then, right?" Doug asked, looking over at Martha. She gave him a subtle nod. "I mean, there's no way for the opposition to lose unless you cheat, right? They're running at close to ninety percent now."

"Maybe," said Stryker, "but just be ready, alright? Anything can happen." He turned around to leave.

"Hey Stryker," I called as he neared the door, "assuming they do win like they're supposed to…what's going to happen?"

"I don't know," he said somberly, "I guess they'll just follow through on their idiotic plan. We tried to stop them. There's only so much you can do." He gave Martha a resigned look, and after making sure she had taken notice of it, he left without saying anything more.

As soon as we heard him go through the main door, Martha dropped her head into her hands. "I'm so sorry," she said, her hair shaking back and forth.

"Why?" Doug asked.

"I told you…" she said, "I'm not sure anymore. How can we drink glasses of poison and think we will live? I did not join for this…" she trailed off.

I gave her a moment before I asked. "What do we do now? I mean between now and tomorrow night?"

"Nothing," said Martha firmly, looking back up at me and appearing to feel more confident at the thought. "Nothing. It will be alright. As long as your ambassador is being honest. We will win, and then we will all be safe."

"So…we just hang tight, then?" I confirmed. "Lay low for the next two days?"

"Yes," said Martha, "yes…that is what we should do. All of us. We will just wait it out. That is all."

"Okay," I said, "and then what? I don't think I want to be on this island too much longer. We've got a week and a half until Tom comes back."

"Well what else can we do but wait for him?" asked Doug.

"I don't know," I said, shaking my head. "Maybe take a boat or something? Alexander mentioned he could get us to Hawaii…"

Doug shook his head. "No…no, let's just see where things stand…and go from there. I don't want to do anything rash."

"Alright," I said, then fell silent for another long while. "I guess I'm going to go take a shower or something then."

"Okay," Doug said, "maybe I'll come by later tonight if you want to go over to the bar."

"Wait, Hill," Martha said, stopping me, "why don't you come too. To dinner today—with my family—in a few hours. It will be a large gathering—it is traditional on Saturday here. Doug is coming already. You can join us."

I thought about it for a minute. It would certainly be something to do, and by this point I really wasn't feeling afraid—just unsure more than anything. "Alright," I said, "that sounds fine. When?"

"We will knock on your door—about three o'clock." She smiled.

"Sounds perfect. I'll be ready." With a little wave I headed back up and settled down in my room. I feel asleep, believe it or not, and got a good bit of shut-eye before the afternoon arrived.

---

The knock came right on time. Martha and Doug were standing there looking happy, and slightly dressed up. Doug had on a pressed collared shirt from who knows where, and Martha was wearing a really lovely blue gown with an array of pink flower patterns. They led me out of the hotel and around the corner toward the church, stopping at a small house across the street. The door was open and you could see a pretty big gathering of people inside. The smell of roasting goat poured out on us.

We entered to lots of noisy greetings and hugs all over the place. A slew of people whose names I never learned were swirling about the two little rooms that made up the house so that you could barely stand. There were kids jumping around in most directions too. It was one of those pleasantly chaotic scenes where it's pretty easy to just fold yourself in as a stranger and go mostly unnoticed. Martha introduced me to her mom, her dad, her brother (his name was James, I think), and something like seven grandmothers. Given that Milauan reproductive physiology appeared by all accounts to be the same as anyone else's, I assumed that some of them must have been great aunts or something. Everybody asked little questions, especially of Doug, in whom they were far more interested than in me. It was pretty clear that he was making his debut as a serious suitor.

Just like practically every other place on Milau, there was a statue of a god in the house—near the door in this case. It was an angry looking female, sticking her tongue out at the world. She had a massive crown on her head, and what looked like a couple of lizards crawling up her legs. "It is the goddess of fish roe," someone told me when they noticed me looking at it. I complimented it, as always, and received a warm smile in return.

They gave me some tea, a large offering of pickles, and at one point somebody handed me a baby, a happy little girl she was. Eventually, more substantial food was circulated around, and people ate standing, or sitting wherever. I ended up squeezed against a fat uncle and an exterior wall so that I only had use of my left arm to eat. That was tricky since I'm right handed, but I managed. Goat, fish, fried breadfruit, some kind of fermented mush with a strong smell, jell-o, and pickles—classic Milauan fare, served piping hot (and that included the pickles…first time I had seen that). It all got passed around and scarfed down loudly and messily by everyone in the place. I tried my best to chew with my mouth open, and a couple of the older ladies smiled sweetly at my pathetic efforts. People always seem to like it when you try to adapt. They'll forgive your failure pretty much every time.

There was a holiday feel to the whole thing—that drowsy sense that nothing else needs to be attended to in the outside world. I needed that—we all needed that, really, given how bananas things had actually become in that outside world. There was one notable little conversation I had, though, while I was sitting with my tea over in a corner watching the world go by. Martha, separated momentarily from Doug for some reason, came over and sat down next to me.

"Hill," she said a little quietly, as if she would prefer not to be overheard. "How are you enjoying everything?"

"It's all lovely, thank you, Martha," I answered.

"Good. It is a pleasure to have you with us. To me, you are nearly a part of the family already—it is the blessing of being a visitor."

"Thank you," I said.

"Hill, I wonder…I have spoken with Doug a great deal about it. But—I wanted to ask you. Can you tell me what is it like in America?"

"Oh," I said, taken a bit off guard. "Well…that depends…where you are, I guess." She sat waiting for me to say something meaningful. "It's a very big place, you know. Thousands of miles across. So…where we're from, is up in the north. It can get quite cold—lots of snow in the winter. But summer is hot there. Let's see….our part…has a lot of water. It's surrounded by big lakes…they're so big that it's like looking into the ocean. It's beautiful, really. And there are forests up there, too, and some hills and stuff in the northern part."

She nodded in smiling approval. "Doug says this, too—but he says it is not good, living where you are. He says we would go somewhere else. Are there many people in your home? Like New York?"

"Well," I said, "not nearly as many as New York…but a lot of people compared to Milau, yes."

"With tall buildings—sky scrapers?"

"Yes," I said, "pretty tall. They would be very tall to you."

"Ah—I think it would be nice, then—not so bad, like Doug says. He says there is no future where you live, but perhaps somewhere else. But can it be true? There is no future *here*—is it really this way where you are from?"

"Uh..." I said, "no. No, not like what's going on here. Doug just means...I guess it's not really a very prestigious place, is all. You can't get very rich or famous. And I think that...for him...he feels like it's time to move on to something else. You can get tired of it—where we're from. It takes a lot of effort to like the place."

"I see," she said with a smile. "He is a man of many dreams, yes? He tells me—many buildings he would like to draw. It is maybe that...he cannot do these things where you live? I suppose I will not mind wherever we go. I do not know the difference yet. I only wished to know, for it seemed to me that it sounded beautiful where you live...because of the water. It is good to have water—you can find your way. You know which way you are going."

"Yeah," I said, "I know exactly what you mean."

She nodded gently and looked over at where Doug was chatting with her brother across the room. "I wonder why that would not be enough. But, as I said, it will all be new to me anyway."

"So...you're thinking of...moving back with him?" I asked, quite surprised. "I had no idea that you two...I mean I understood that you had...made a connection, I guess, but I didn't realize..."

"Yes," she said quietly but with certainty. "It is not love, Hill, if that is what you are thinking—not for me. Maybe for him, I do not know. It does not need to be love. It is good enough to be content. The old island is not my home. It was my grandmother's home, yes, but not mine. This island is the only place I have ever known—even for a moment. And even here, it is only a place to stay. So—where is my home? I think perhaps it is nowhere. Maybe America is where I would find it. If I do not, then what have I lost?"

"Yeah," I said in a murmur.

"I am a daughter of many things," she said, "of this family and the coral sand. But I am a woman, also. He is very alive. He is not everything he could be because he is wild, a little—young, a little. But my people always say that that is how it is with the strongest birds—they are wild when they are young. He will be some things he could be, and not all of them. Do you know him well?"

"Well, no," I said, feeling a bit of compunction in realizing it, "no—not really. We're work friends, basically."

"Yes," she said with a nod. "I know him only a little, though perhaps more. My family have been asking—they are surprised at me, why so quickly to choose him? I am a little afraid, but I think it is sensible in its own way. It is not that I am sure—it is that I am sure enough." She looked back at Doug again with a surprisingly real peace in her eyes. "And…perhaps I should not say as much…but I have been to see her. The little girl. You know of her, yes?"

I nodded.

"It is not in my nature to trust someone like her. But she showed me—it was like I was there—remembering the day I set the bird free—the one I raised when I was a girl. I could not describe it very well. She knew it like she had stood where I stood. She told me that I will go with him. I feel that perhaps I do not have a choice after something like that. Many things she has seen—they come to pass."

"Oh," I said, a little bit skeptical, I guess, "well…but—do you *want* to go with him?"

"Yes," she said firmly, "I do."

"Well," I said, after a long pause, "then…yeah. Why not? Home…America…it's not great, Martha. But it's not that bad. You'd get by fine, I think…as long as you don't forget why you're there. I mean, knowing you even as much as I do…you'd do fine anywhere. And love…well, I don't know what I think about that. What you're doing probably makes as much sense as anything, as long as you think you two could get along."

"Thank you," she said, turning back to me, her half-moon smile on full display, "your blessing means a great deal to me. You do not know—you cannot see, but we both admire you. You were our first friend together! It means a great deal."

"Thanks," I said, "I'm glad." With that, Martha stood back up and walked over to Doug, taking his arm into hers and inserting herself in a conversation he was having with her brother. I sat in silence for a moment before a huge second helping of goat was shoved in front of my face by a friendly laughing aunt, and I felt forced to dig in again. Around ten o'clock, with Doug and Martha growing ever-happier as they mingled about, I thanked everybody in the place, and headed back to get to bed early. I felt pretty calm that night. It was a moment of real respite that I had badly needed.

# 15

The church bells woke me the next morning, feeling refreshed. For a little while I thought about actually going down to the church to check it out. I decided against it, though. Best to lay low, like Martha had said. I made some coffee in the room and sat out on my balcony in boxer shorts and a t-shirt to watch the parade of ladies' hats shuffling into the service. From where I was sitting with my coffee, I could see a bunch of guys setting up a tent on the beach again. It was the same tent as the one they had used for the festival (I actually wondered why they had bothered to take it down) but they didn't seem to be putting many tables inside this time. I could make out a little ballot box placed near the center, and so deduced that that was where the election was to take place. The big wooden statue of the god of the moonlight on the lagoon (as Mary had identified it) had also been set up again and was towering over the scene, looking somehow a bit menacing in the daylight.

Doug knocked on my door and I told him to come in.

"Hey," he said, "I brought some food for breakfast. Restaurant is closed again." I recalled that from the previous Sunday. Doug had a little styrofoam box of leftovers from our dinner with the Toks the day before. I politely declined anything.

"Martha says it's probably okay if we watch from up here," he said, sitting down and taking a big bite of cold fish.

"Watch what?" I asked.

"The president's speech," he managed, his mouth almost completely full.

"Oh?" I said, "I had no idea."

"Yeah," said Doug, "I guess it's traditional for her to give a final address just before the polls open this afternoon. Incumbent gets the last word, I supposed. Anyway, that will be about noon—after the church lets out—and then people have six hours or something to come and vote. Martha says if we just stay up here and watch from a distance, everything should be fine. I mean, I'm curious, aren't you?"

"Sure," I said, "especially since we don't have anything else to do for the day."

"You sure you don't want any breakfast?" Doug asked, his mouth stuffed again. He was really getting into the swing of Milauan eating habits. I told him I was sure, and he left again, saying he'd be back to watch the speech from my balcony.

A couple of hours later, as the parade of hats was leaving the church, Doug reappeared holding his computer. "I figured we could watch a movie or play chess or something in the afternoon since we're stuck here," he said. The clock showed five minutes to noon. Doug stepped out onto the balcony, pulled a chair into a good position near the railing and sat down next to me.

A pretty big crowd had gathered in and around the tent on the beach. I had been enjoying the people-watching as everyone dribbled in from all parts of the island, especially when the parade back out of the church filtered past, hats now slightly disheveled. The president was getting herself ready in the middle of the tent, laying out a bunch of papers or something on a little table and testing the microphone. She kept looking impatiently at her watch, and, when it evidently read exactly noon, she straightened up and looked around, then picked up the mic and got started.

"Dear people of Milau," she began, her voice coming over the speakers so loud that I thought they might blow. Doug and I clapped our ears covered while an an audible gasp went up from the crowd, followed by a squeak from the microphone. A young guy frantically turned some knobs on a mixer we could just see. "Is that better?" the president said after a moment, looking at the sound guy. It was better, though we could still hear her quite well from where we were sitting. We uncovered our ears. "Good," she said, turning back to the crowd. "Dear people of Milau. It is customary for your president to address you just before the opening of the polls, as you all well know. In years past, there has often been very little to say at the president's election day address. Quite often, the president simply wishes you all well, and reminds you of the importance of your work in deciding on a future for our island.

"This year, however, is different for us. Not only is this the most important election in the history of Milau, but this year, perhaps for the first time ever, I have decided to make a critical announcement at this address instead of simply offering my regards. I have decided to reveal to you something which you will need to consider as you make your choice this afternoon." Here she paused for a long time, giving some real dramatic effect. "People of Milau," she finally went on, picking up some kind of document from the table next to her, "I hold in my hands a classified report, from the government of the United States of America, which contains information that has heretofore been a secret, but which I choose to reveal to you today, in spite of the insistence of the American ambassador and all other officials involved." There was a murmur from the crowd, and I looked over at Doug in some concern.

"This report," the president continued, "contains details and assessments concerning the current state of affairs on our former island home of Old Milau. Many of you are under the impression, perpetuated by the National Front, that it would be a simple matter for us to return there. The opposition, as you all know very well, has publicized a number of studies on nuclear decay that suggest that after so long a period, our old island should now be safe, so long as a few simple remedial measures are taken by us in moving there. On the basis of such studies and assumptions, the NFMLA has argued that, in light of the ecological disaster which is certain to occur on this island, New Milau, we are best advised to do what we always would have preferred and return to our home.

"Now, people of Milau, there has been much support for this plan, and there has been much speculation among you as to why the Milauan Essentialist Party and I would oppose it, favoring instead an offer by the American government to build infrastructure to allow us to remain here. To this point, I have only been able to say that I am severely skeptical of the NFMLA plan. But now I feel forced by circumstances to reveal to you the real reason for which I have so staunchly insisted against a return to our island.

"Here, in this detailed report, of which I have made several hundred photocopies for you to examine, you will find not speculative studies on what the likely state of our former island home ought to be, but the results of tests and analysis of its actual state. As you will very clearly see, radiation levels on Old Milau are even higher now than they were when the first nuclear detonations took place there many decades ago. The reason for this is simple. Since our move to this island, our current home, the American government has continued to use Old Milau as a repository for various forms of nuclear waste." There was a kind of collective low shriek with a eerie and haunting timbre that arose from the crowd. A buzz of chattering voices filled the air.

"This information," Turner went on, raising her voice to regain everyone's attention, "has been classified by the American government, and it remains classified. I reveal it to you in violation of American law and numerous treaty agreements. It is quite possible that in light of what I have done, I could be tried for treason or espionage—and I could even be executed for these things. But the future of our people is at stake. If I am arrested and taken away, then so be it, for I will have saved the lives of everyone on this island, and secured the only possible future for our people that there can be.

"People of Milau," she said, her voice reaching crescendo in a triumphant declaration, "we cannot return to our former home. If we do, nearly every one of us will be dead within a year. Spending even just a few days on the island would do enough damage to begin the process of a slow and agonizing demise for all of us. I urge you to reconsider your support for the opposition. I urge you to hear me, and speak with any of your friends and family not here at the present moment, to spread the word about the truth. The plan of the National Front cannot go forward!" There was a rumble from the people below, like a pulse of applause was stuck in the crowd, unsure of how to make itself felt, or whether it wanted to be heard.

"Well, holy shit…" Doug said to me, leaning close and whispering even though nobody could possibly have heard us. "Just went right for it, didn't she?" He got a little proud smile on his face. "Good for her." I nodded in agreement. "This could change everything, though," he continued to whisper.

"We'll just have to wait and see," I answered. "Nothing we can do—just stay here."

"Now," Turner was continuing, "people of Milau, in light of all this, I wish to remind you of the course of action currently proposed by me and the MEP for our future. As we have made clear time and time again, if proper measures are taken against the rising sea levels, we can continue to live here for twenty to thirty more years, with no risk of radiation poisoning, maintaining the way of life to which we have already long been accustomed. Given some extra time, it is possible that sea levels will cease rising, or that…somebody will think of something…I mean that yet newer technologies will present another, better solution to our dilemma." Here she paused, and stood up very straight, getting herself ready to deliver the big whammy of her speech. "People of Milau," she said, her voice growing strong, "today, election day, the MEP and I remind you of our promise to you. We hereby re-establish our opposition to the NFMLA plan which would spell death for all our people, and we hereby forward as our platform in this election the plan of maintaining our lives on this island as they have been, doing so by use of the funds already secured for this purpose. In light of all these things, let me make the simple and humble request that you cast your vote today for me and the MEP." With that, she was finished. There was a long, pregnant silence all around and then, just as a bunch of Striped-Footed Boobies started into a mating call, the whole crowd of people standing in front of the president burst into cheers that rang over Milau city and out into the lagoon, sweeping everything up in exuberance as if every couple on the island had all just had a baby at the same moment. I remember applauding myself, though why I would have been happy about the announcement, I don't know. Maybe everyone else in the crowd would have said the same thing.

The cheering and shouting went on for a little while, and eventually Turner stepped away from the tent and headed off somewhere. Most of the crowd seemed to hang around while two men in bright white suits, with equally bright white gloves, stood up and readied the ballot box in the middle of the tent where she had been standing. Once it was set, the two of them stood next to it with an attitude of regal duty, and signaled (we surmised) that the polls were open. There was a lot of busy movement, and the gathered crowd shuffled around filling out ballots wherever seemed convenient, and putting them into the box. They dipped their fingers in some kind of ink when they were done, I guess so that they wouldn't vote twice. Election day was in full swing.

Doug and I mostly sat on the balcony and played some chess on his computer during the afternoon. At some point, Doug went back to his own room, and shortly thereafter there came a knock on my door. It was Martha, looking for both of us.

"Is Doug here?" she asked as she entered. I told her that he had stepped out. "Okay," she said, "I'll knock on his door next. Did you see it? Did you see what happened?"

"You mean the president's speech?"

"Yes," she said, "no one can stop talking about it. Word is spreading on the island like a pox—it is everywhere. This…this is…we did not expect it," she stuttered through her words in agitation, "I don't know what will happen. Hill…I don't know. I…" she fell silent for a moment. "I voted for her…I cannot tell you. I cannot believe myself. I voted for the MEP!"

"What?" I asked, "really?"

"Yes, I know," she said, shaking her head. "But…we didn't realize—I didn't realize. She left the report for us—I read it myself. It is true—and everyone says it is true—they have looked at all the documentation! We need more time. The president is right."

"Well," I said, "maybe she is. If so, I guess you made the right decision, then. That's alright, Martha. People change their minds."

"I know," she said, "but…what do you think it means? Perhaps they will win. Many other people are saying they will change their vote."

I shrugged my shoulders. "Then, they'll win, I guess."

"And you will have to evacuate, won't you?" she asked, obviously worried by the thought, "You will have to flee…from our…from their threats…with the ambassador."

"Well," I said, "I guess so, yeah—if Stryker says so, I mean."

"I need to go and see Doug," she said, hurrying back out of my room. "Don't leave this room. Just stay…you are safe here." I agreed and looked back out on the activity down near the beach. A steady stream of people, evidently from other parts of the island, had been trickling up to the ballot box since the morning—just a few at a time, a few in cars, and at least one guy riding a goat…awkwardly.

Afternoon dragged on into evening. Martha and Doug eventually came over to my room again. Martha had calmed back down, and I didn't bother to inquire about what they had said to each other in his room. We sat out and watched the sunset together, not really talking about much.

"What time do the polls close?" I asked Martha at some point. She said that voting ended at six o'clock, and the votes would be counted by nine at the latest. Then the winners would be announced. Pretty nice system if you like instant gratification.

Indeed, with the sun almost fully below the horizon, and the clock reading six, one of the guys in white suits took a watch out of his pocket, and looked about to see if anyone else was coming. Seeing no one, he pulled out a little whistle and blew it loudly three times. Then he announced in clear, loud English that voting was over. There were still quite a few people milling about along the beach and on the road up into town. Martha said that people from what she called the "country-side" would just wait around to hear the results. The two guys in white suits picked up the ballot box and headed off, though I'm not totally sure where they went (Martha didn't seem to know either). And that was that. A national election in about six hours.

Once the ballot box was taken away, Martha offered to go down to the restaurant and get them to send up some food. I, however, was starting to feel a bit of cabin fever sitting around all day, and persuaded her that it would be alright to go downstairs for dinner, as long as we didn't actually leave the hotel. She was hesitant at first, but eventually we went,

Martha taking the lead nervously as if to protect us from some unseen head-on attack.

When we got downstairs the dining room was completely full for the first time since we'd been there, and there were three waiters taking orders and the like. In fact, there was a line of about ten people waiting for a table, but we were whisked directly into the restaurant, to an empty table that had evidently been reserved just for us, the actual guests of the hotel. Well, that was nice of them.

The place was completely abuzz, but, when we came in, everybody seemed to start speaking Milauan and so we had no real idea what the conversation was about. People kept glancing over at us with some suspicion, or maybe it was worry, any time there was a lull in their conversation. It made it pretty awkward to sit there and order, drink, eat—and certainly it was impossible to talk to each other. I was starting to think that it might have been better to get room service after all. Maybe Martha was just protecting us from social anxiety rather than physical danger.

Anyway, round about the middle of our meal, we heard the bell for the front door ring loudly, followed by a series of grunting and pushing sounds accompanied with profuse apologies, and through the still lengthening line to get into the restaurant pushed a very flustered and nervous looking Baya Vin. His face was flush and pale, and he glanced quickly around the room before spotting Martha, and hurrying over to our table.

"Martha," he said a little out of breath, "I've been looking all over for you. Thank goodness I found you. Have you heard? Did you hear it?"

"Hear what?" she answered. The whole room had fallen silent and was staring right at us. Thanks for that, Baya.

"The election—the votes…" Baya stopped suddenly, realizing that he was the center of everyone's attention, then seemed to shrug that fact off, continuing with what he had to say, "the MEP are going to win, Martha."

"Impossible!" came a shout from the corner of the room, but it was met with a shockingly loud series of hushing noises and "quiet"s that really shut down whoever had piped up.

"No, it's true," Baya responded to the room in general, though he was still only looking at Martha. "Listen—you need to come with me. We all need to meet—right now—before they make the announcement. We are making plans—quickly. Every member must come."

Martha looked anxiously around, and then looked at us, especially Doug. She took a deep breath. "Baya," she said solemnly. "I am sorry. You will have to go without me. I am sorry."

Baya froze where he stood and stared at Martha. "What?" he said after a moment, with the breathless tone of a man who has just proposed marriage and been declined, "what do you mean? I don't understand."

"Baya…" Martha said, casting her eyes down on the table. "I am sorry. Please go."

"Martha…" he stammered, "you…but…don't you realize? It's…Mary will not…she will not tolerate this!"

"I know," said Martha quietly.

"She will think it is insubordination! She will excommunicate you—or even worse…even worse! She has fire in her eyes now. She could do anything. Come with me—come now, Martha!" He lifted a hand as if to raise Martha from her seat by telekinesis.

But Martha did not stand up. She did no look up. She just looked down at the table, as she had been doing for several moments already. Her eyes were sharp and hard, her mouth quivering slightly at the corners, her hands now rolled into fists on her knees. She said nothing. Her silence crashed and cut louder and deeper than if she had smashed her plate on the ground and thrown the shards at Baya. She was like a woman strangling down a lion, clenching all the tighter in the final moments to make certain its last breath had come. On Baya's face you could see a mix of fear and anger, but mostly it was fear—abject terror at the thought that Martha would thumb her nose at them all. His fear spread to me, and probably everybody else in the room. There was a gravity about it all—a sickening gravity that no moment should ever possess.

All Baya could do was murmur a few words to himself, tossing ideas around maybe. His face turned momentarily red, then went back to pale white, then seemed almost blue for a moment. Then, with a swift, almost crazed shake of his head, but without another word, he turned and pushed back through the line to the restaurant the way he had come.

Everything was dead quiet for a few minutes. Martha sat there, her face burgundy, for as long as she could take it. Then, standing up quickly, she excused herself under her breath and walked out of the room. We could hear her feet on the steps leading back upstairs, which I'm sure Doug took to be a very good sign. He, quite naturally, followed after her, leaving with a brief apologetic look back at me.

So there I was, sitting by myself at a table that really should have gone to someone from the long line, with three plates of unfinished food in front of me, and what felt like the population of an entire nation staring right at me. It was a moment so acutely, so excruciatingly embarrassing that my body just let go and relaxed, as if slipping into a mode of animal consciousness in which panic dissipates as both fight and flight become utterly impossible. I smiled a big, broad, certainly ridiculous smile at everyone around me and, lifting a glass of Aijee, I offered a silent toast to…well, the sheer beauty of heroic will, I suppose…and started eating not just my food, by Martha's and Doug's too. The rest of the people in the place, as if they had only been awaiting my royal decree to lift the tension, lifted their glasses, too, and in a moment's time had fallen into rapid and excited conversation about who knows what. Well, you could make a pretty good guess as to what, come to think of it.

# 16

When I had done some justice to all three plates of food as well as the tray of dessert pickles they brought me afterward, I started making my way back upstairs to my room. Just outside the door of the dining room, however, I was stopped short as the front door once again rattled open wildly and another flustered person charged through it. This time it was Linda Stryker, looking totally disoriented. She actually walked right up to the girl at the desk (still reading) and asked what room I was staying in before the girl simply made a nod over to where I was standing about two feet away.

"Mr. Hill," said Linda, practically gasping for air, "I ran over here…I'm sorry. Reg sent me—he's going up to the base—we need to leave. Get your bags ready. We have to go. Now. Tell Bacon. We need to get out right away."

"Take it easy, Linda," I said, "one thing at a time. What's happened so far?"

"I don't know!" she practically shouted at me, "Reg just said that they lost…somebody lost the election. He said you'd understand. He said to hurry! They're going to come down for you—someone from the base is coming in half an hour. Go and pack!" And, with sweat beads beginning to appear on her brow, she rushed back out of the hotel and away into the darkening air.

Honestly, I felt mostly relieved. It was a little scary, of course, but having a ticket off the island was definitely good news. I headed upstairs to deliver the message. I was still in that state of over-taxed relaxation, so I didn't much hurry. I knocked and Doug came to his door and opened it just a crack so I couldn't see whether Martha was in there (though I assumed she was).

"Shit," said Doug when I told him what had just happened, "well, I guess that's it, then. I guess we're out of here for sure."

"Yeah," I said.

"But, nobody rigged the thing, right?" Doug asked, "I mean, it sounds like the president won fair and square, most likely. They shouldn't attack if it was fair, right?"

"Doug," I said, "I have no idea. I can't tell you what they're thinking. Linda said Pickett—I assume she meant him—is supposed to come down and gather us together to get out of here. I mean, Doug, maybe there's a chance nothing will happen, but it's not safe here right now."

Doug didn't say anything. He looked like he was thinking pretty hard. After a moment he gave a simple nod and closed his door again. I headed back to my room to pack. I hadn't really jumped to get it done when Stryker had first mentioned it, but then again I didn't have all that much stuff with me anyway.

After about twenty minutes there was a knock on my door, presumably from Pickett. "Early," I thought to myself in mild worry. I hadn't quite finished getting everything together. I opened up and there, with a grim but not, in fact, entirely psychotic look on her face, stood not Pickett, or Doug, or even Stryker…but the old hag who had spit in my face a few days before and told me to go see the little girl on the night of the festival. She seemed quite calm, as she had the most recent time I saw her, but still very clearly her crazy self.

"What the…?" I said, looking her up and down. "What the hell are you doing here?"

"Oh yes," she said sternly, "We know where. You think you hiding?"

"What?" I asked, "no…but…well, just answer my question—what the hell are you doing here?"

"No, no, no, no," she said, clucking her tongue at me, "what are you doing—answer!"

"I'm packing," I said, trying to brush the question aside and not really realizing that I had just plain answered it.

"Packing for what?" she asked, bobbing her head around to try and look into my room.

"We're leaving…all of us…we're getting out of here."

"Oh?" she said curiously, "Even you? You think you're going?"

"Yeah," I said, "of course I am."

"No!" she declared, pointing a finger in the air emphatically, "you are going to stay! That's why I come—to take you down there…to see her. You come speak with the little girl now. Time—it's the time!"

"What?" I said, considering whether to actually shove her and slam the door in her face. "Lady, no. No more of this. Just stop it."

"You have to," she said, looking with her crazy eyes straight at me, "everything is in it! You have to."

I was about to give yet another stupid response, but it was precisely then that Captain Paul Pickett, USAF, appeared at the top of the steps in the hallway, walking quickly but calmly toward me. He was decked out in his full dress uniform, complete with hat. Strips of toilet paper, indeed! He was clean shaven, with jacket nicely pressed, and medals proudly displayed. He was relaxed and tempered, holding his arms down at his side like he was getting ready for a ceremonial drill. It would be hard for me to imagine anyone less like the half shell-shocked tweak that I had met twice before. There was a shine in his eye that said that somewhere in the private alley-ways of his mind he, too, was greeting his forgotten self like an old friend come back from the dead. It was nice to see, frankly—for him, I mean.

He walked down the hall toward my door, then stopped in front of us and reached out to give me a hand shake. "Mr. Hill, it's good to see you." We shook, and he seemed like he glanced at the hag sideways, though he didn't say a word about her.

"You too," I said, "you look…you look good, Captain."

"Thank you," he said, speaking slowly and with extreme formality, "no time for that sort of thing, though, Mr. Hill—I'm on a mission, and that's all. We're evacuating the island—all American personnel, along with any visitors. There is an extremely serious risk of terrorist activity here, aimed at the consulate, and potentially any other Americans on the island. The expected results of this evening's election are likely to put you in jeopardy. I assume you got the message from Linda Stryker, is that correct?"

"Yes," I said, "she told us to pack. Can you tell me specifically what happened?"

"Well, it's no great concern of yours, other than the danger. However," he paused and dropped his voice a little lower into a more informal register, "as far as we can tell, the MEP are going to win…fair and square. Stryker tells me that president Turner revealed some things…that she was not supposed to reveal. We'll have to deal with all that later. But now, even though he says they didn't rig anything…it looks like the Black Salmon are going to have their backs against the wall to follow through on their threat anyway."

"Yeah…" I said slowly, "that's what I thought. What a mess…"

"Yes," said Pickett, straightening back up and looking official again, "But let's not dwell on those things. Are you ready to leave?" he glanced once more towards the hag, still not fully acknowledging her.

"Uh…" I said. "Not…just yet…I need just a few more moments."

Pickett nodded to me and turned around, stepping over and knocking on Doug's door. It flew open, banging hard into the wall and you could hear something falling over inside the room. Doug and Martha appeared with a couple of bags each.

"Mr. Bacon," said Pickett with the same rehearsed formality. "Are you aware of why I am here?" Doug nodded, his eyes huge with fear. "Are you ready to depart?"

"Yes," said Doug, breathing rather hard, "yes, we're ready to go."

"I'm sorry Mr. Bacon," said Pickett, pausing for a moment and turning to Martha, "I am only here to escort the United States citizens registered with the consulate on the island. I'm sorry, ma'am, you will have to remain here."

"No!" said Doug with some panic in his voice, "no…she has to come with me. We're…married. She's my wife!"

Pickett stopped cold and looked disoriented for a moment. "Oh…" he said, touching his hat, "I…didn't realize. Then…oh…" He didn't seem to know exactly what to do. "Well…okay, then…" he said slowly, "I suppose we can let you join us and…sort everything out later…since…we do have room on the plane for you, ma'am. Though,

I'm not sure. I suppose my duty requires me…to allow you on board?" He sounded like he was asking himself, but it appeared by the silence that followed that this was going to be his decision. Doug's features relaxed and he smiled happily at Martha, who looked back at him like she had just let out a breath she was holding since birth.

"Good, then," said Doug, "then we're ready to go…right now."

Now, you are doubtless wondering if Doug and Martha had really gotten married at some point, or if this was just some kind of scheme they had cooked up to give her an outside chance of getting off the island. I don't know which it was, and I never had a chance to ask Doug. If you can find him, or them, I'm sure they'll tell you. To my mind it was most probable that they had come up with the plan on the fly, and Doug was fixing to refuse to go with Pickett if it didn't work. But that's really just a guess. It's also entirely possible that they really had run off and gotten married the night before, with some justice of the peace, or ancient priestess, or the minister from the church, or the captain of a fishing boat bobbing up and down on the lagoon, or just a Striped-Footed Booby with a judge-ship. I don't know. Anyway, whatever was really going on, Pickett, like I said, played ball.

"Mr. Hill," the captain turned back to me, "if you please—we don't have much time. Another two minutes at the most please. If that is not enough, you may have to leave a few of your things."

I was still just frozen in my doorway with my bags nearly ready to zip up in the bedroom behind. I looked at Pickett, standing there with his new found air of purpose, bearing on his face the look of someone in whose hands you know you're completely safe. I looked at the old woman, star-ing at me with a dribble of saliva now running down the corner of her mouth. She shook her head "no" and looked into me not with a sense of ultimatum, but of foreknowledge, like she was presenting to me some kind of serious option that she knew I couldn't refuse. And that meant that somehow, staring at the two of them, I had to make an actual choice between the sensible and the absolutely insane.

There are times now and then when you discover yourself selecting between two things after only really thinking about one of them. This happens to me most often if I've had a few drinks. But I wasn't drunk that night. I only bring that up to try and explain what it was like inside my mind when I did what I did. By all accounts—and I mean all accounts—I should have told the old lady to get out of my damn way and gone with Pickett and the rest of them. The plant that I had come there to inspect had been destroyed, every other American besides, I figured, the Doc, was getting out of dodge, along with my only formal contact on the island. I had been aching to go home anyway for days if not a full week already, and the only pressing reason I had for staying there was to follow some raving hag out into nowhere in order talk to some kind of mystical pre-teen prophet. But, somehow, the only choice I could really make clear in my brain was that second one—to follow the old lady. It looped back and shouted at me every time I tried to set it aside. It was all that I could think. And so, in the murmur of a man in a trance, I heard myself saying aloud, "I'm going to remain on the island. Thank you, Captain," with a polite smile.

Pickett somehow didn't seem surprised. He just nodded to me and said, "Very well, Mr. Hill. You understand that all consular and military personnel will be leaving effective immediately? And that as such you will be without any recourse to any services previously rendered on this island by any persons associated with the United States government?" I told him that I understood that. "Very well," he said again, "I have no right or authority to compel you. Please understand that I do not advise you to remain here. It was a pleasure to meet you, Mr. Hill." He made a little respectful bow, and with that, Captain Pickett turned back to Doug and Martha, invited them to follow him, and started making his way down the stairs.

Doug had a look on his face that I'll never forget, mainly because it was the last time I ever saw him. It was a look built of shock mixed with concerned terror and topped off with a touch of frothed outrage and confusion. The guy probably could just as easily have killed me, kidnapped me for my own good, or written me off as crazier than even that old hag and happily left me for dead. I mean, what could it have all looked like to him? What did it seem like I was all the sudden staying to do mere moments after telling him we definitely had to leave? To this day, part of me hopes that the old woman wasn't even real—that she was just a symptom of some kind of psychotic break I was having for reasons I cannot discern. I would have looked a lot less crazy to Doug in that moment if she weren't actually there (and I still would have looked crazy, to be sure). He stared at me long and hard, like he was trying to figure out some way to help me, or at least understand. But, falling short, he turned back to Martha (who for whatever reason didn't seem surprised at all), looked back to me again, shook his head, and simply followed Pickett down the steps and out of the hotel. We didn't even say goodbye. Maybe I should feel some regret for that.

"Good," said the hag when everyone else was gone. "Now you can come. Come!"

It was already quite dark out as the old woman led us past the now dwindling crowd at the restaurant and out of the hotel. For the first time since I'd been there, the sky had grown overcast, and only a little bit of diffuse moonlight was visible through the clouds. We walked down the main road out of town, past the small dock, and up toward the interior part of the island, curving in away from the water just past the ruin of the pickle-factory. As we went, the road became little more than a narrow strip of dirt cutting through a fairly thick wood of trees.

The woman was walking in complete silence, right in front of me, clearly leading me somewhere rather than accompanying me. She moved rapidly and nimbly, almost running at a few moments, so fast, in fact, that I could barely keep up. At one point I actually tripped and hit the deck, and I was basically expecting her to just disappear in front of me. She did stop, however, just long enough for me to regain myself, before she started again to hurry on as before.

After walking like that for maybe fifteen minutes, we finally cut through the trees into some kind of clearing where the woman stopped and stood completely still in front of me. She looked around a bit, and even sniffed the air, like she wasn't sure about something and then, appearing confident that she had gotten it right, called me forward next to her

"Here," she said, "stand right here. You not gonna move from this spot, hm? Don't go up to her…an' don't run. Okay?" She looked at me waiting for some confirmation.

"Okay…" I said, not knowing what I was agreeing to. The woman stepped out into the dark clearing in front of me so that I could just make out her back where she was standing.

I stood still, breathing lightly, my mind not even really processing what was going on. I looked out into the dark, waiting for something to happen. And then, something did, but not, I think, what the old woman was expecting. All of a sudden, I felt myself practically knocked over by sheer sound bursting through the trees; it was a noise so powerful that it actually pushed me, like a wind, and buckled my joints from head to toe. It wrenched and cranked and cackled—a magnificently loud, screaming, mechanical roar that dimmed the whole of the woods into terrifying deafness. It took a moment for me to understand what it was. It was the sound of the engine of an airplane so near that I instinctively started to duck. Then into view, practically right on top of our heads, literally scraping the trees as it went, passed the shrieking hulk of a small silver plane struggling to get altitude. The noise of the engine and the sickening snap of branches ravaged the clearing for a moment as the plane passed the clearing, jumped slightly higher into the sky, banked while I could still see it through the trees, and was gone. The loud agony of the engine began to fade, as the full, round smell of burning oil and mown grass hit my nose. They had damn near crashed the old heap. Damn near. The thought raced around in my head: just a little extra weight—one man and a couple of bags. Well, for all I know about airplanes it wouldn't have mattered. But still…I can't shake the thought. I can't shake it even today. I stood there in the woods, still crouched, pulsing in raw physiological terror.

Soon, though, there was silence again. I tried to take a deep breath and get my heart back under control. The hag seemed basically unfazed. After watching the plane for a moment like she was just looking at a bird, she turned back again towards the clearing, and coughed loudly. She took a deep breath, and then shouted some odd string of syllables that sounded a little bit like Milauan, though it wasn't, I don't think—not modern Milauan anyway. She clapped her hands three times, and then fell silent again.

"Hello?" came a little voice from somewhere I couldn't see. "Who is it?"

"Mr. Hill," the hag shouted back, like she was a secretary talking to her boss.

"Good!" came the voice. There was a shuffle of leaves. "Can you see alright?" the little voice asked me. I shook my head.

"Old woman," she called to her, "please—light the fire."

"Oh!" shrieked the hag gleefully, as though this were the best conceivable news, "let me light it, then, let me!" There was another shuffle of leaves as the old woman walked away from me and into the clearing. This was followed by the quick flash of a match being struck. Then, in front of me, erupted a burst of flame as a pile of kindling took light.

"Better now," the woman stated, "now you can see."

The fire sprang out orange and red, playing flickering little games with all the trees around us. I could see now that the clearing was an almost perfect circle such that it must have been deliberately cut into the trees by someone. On a little stump near the edge of the clearing sat a girl, about twelve years old. She was eating something out of a bowl with a wooden spoon. She had a happy smile on her face, like she was just an average kid finishing up her dinner by the fire-side at home with mom and dad. She wore a simple brown dress, quite clean, and her black hair was neatly cut and smooth. Her eyes danced with a playful joy that you could see even from afar. She looked up at me and, after taking a last bite of whatever it was, set down her bowl and spoon.

She stood up and strode toward the fire. She had the walk of an elegant adult woman. She sat back down cross legged right next to the flames—so close, in fact, that I was worried her clothes might catch. She smiled at me again and with a wave of her hand, she spoke. Her voice was clear and staid, but still childish—still a twelve year old's voice, I mean, but with a maturity in the words somehow.

"Hello again," she said, looking directly at me, "thank you for coming here."

"No problem," I said…probably the most awkward response to a greeting I've ever made in my life.

"Mr. Hill," the little girl said, "I am very glad you listened. You could have left with the others. I am not certain, for I do not see things very clearly which are not to come to pass. I do not know what would have happened, though it is a frightful thought."

"Yes…" I said slowly, my mouth not really wanting to cooperate with the project of speech. "I…it would have…" I gave up on that thought and fell silent for a moment. "Why am I here?" I managed eventually.

"Yes, of course. Please, don't be alarmed. I only wish to tell you—to show you, because you will need to know. You will see—you will be glad that you know. Your people, but for you and the other American, have left the island without you, and now my people are going to leave just the same. Would you have tried to come tomorrow, we would be gone, and you would be lost to wonder. But I do not want you to be afraid. It is easy to see what will become of you. The old woman has told you already," here she signaled the hag, who was now standing silently by her side. "Most people are not so clear to see. You are a very unusual man. I do not know if you are more empty or more full than other people. Do you know, Mr. Hill?"

I had no idea what she was talking about, and I only stammered out nonsense for a second.

"No, do not worry to respond," she said, holding up a hand for me to stop, "do not worry. You may perhaps be one of these things now, and become the other later. Perhaps it is for you to be both, in their own time, and that is why you are very clear—very easy to see. You will find that out of your own, let it be. But this is not why you are here." She fell silent for a long moment, looking around like she was distracted and maybe had forgotten that I was even there.

"Why…then?" I asked finally.

"Oh, yes!" she said, looking back at me, "it is because of what I have already said. Because tomorrow we will be gone—every one of us—all my people, and I did not want you to be alarmed. I thought, too, Mr. Hill, that perhaps someone should know—for it is not a simple thing to vanish—not for those who remain, I mean. When people die, Mr. Hill, it is customary to seek a cause, is it not? Someone will seek a cause when we are gone, even if we are not dead. We are a small people but not so invisible that we will be totally unnoticed. So, it is good that you will be here and you will see."

"What do you mean? What do you mean 'gone'? The old woman said the same thing before…" I motioned to the hag, who smiled as if she were flattered that I had remembered her previous appearance.

"We are leaving, Mr. Hill," the little girl said sweetly, "out into the sea. The boats are already coming for us. What the others wish—to stay here, or to return to our old home—these things cannot be. These are only dead ideas. Our old home would kill us, and here, we are merely waiting for death. Your people may try to help us…but they cannot do so forever. And when those two women are gone, after tonight, there will be no one to build what they call a future even if we wanted. No, we will leave, like our ancestors did long long ago, in the boats that are coming for us—the old boats, wide and long—to test the will of the black ocean."

"I don't understand," I said, "You're all just going to get on boats and…just…sail away?"

"Yes," she said flatly.

I gave her a look of confusion and disapproval. "That's nonsense. Why? Where are they going to take you?"

She paused and looked at me deeply. "Let me ask *you* something," she said after a moment, "how do you know you are not dreaming, Mr. Hill?"

"You mean…right now?" I retorted. "Right now I'm not sure that I'm not dreaming, frankly."

The little girl laughed a trill of bright, childish laughter. It would have been utterly delightful in another context. Now it just seemed incongruous. "Indeed…" she said, "then when you are certain that you are not dreaming, how do you know?"

I thought about it for a while. "I'm not sure," I said, "I guess I just know…"

"You know," she answered, as if correcting me, "because the lines are sharper. The edges are all clear on what you see. When you dream, you are only in your own mind. The images in your mind are not as sharp, for they do not have your eyes to correct them. Many people do not under-stand—but, to see is to have your eyes tell you 'no!' Your mind runs off to things as it would have them be, but your eyes do not let you. In dreams the edges are not clear because all things are made only of the possible, never of the real. For my people, Mr. Hill, this island is a place of dulled edges—a place where our eyes cannot tell us 'no!' And our real home is far gone. We may live there now, but only as one lives in the past. Only in memory is it a place of living beings, people and animals and gods. Ah, it is much the same to us as your home, in fact. It is only a world from stories whose real weight could never be conveyed to us until it was crushing our chests and stamping us down into nothing. The gods of your home, though, are at least alive to give you the comfort of their fantasies. It is no small solace. The gods of our home, Mr. Hill, have nothing more for us—not even that. They will die, too, and are already nearly dead. We were a people of our gods before we came here, like you. We attended to their whims—under every nook and cranny a god to serve. We loved that numb life as much as you love your own. But now, your people have seized us from them, where they cannot follow. We have left them, and their corpses lie unburied on Old Milau. There are those times when one is blessed by the actions of a fool doing what is wrong. Do not think that there is nobility for the fool in such a case, but neither mistake the goodness of the result.

"Yet, Mr. Hill," she straightend up as she went on, "even I would far rather have my people merely fail to see. Even I would have us crawl into the passing safety of a few extra years here, on Mamaoht, the land of ghosts—but better to be translated as 'the land of the blurred edges.' Even I might let us return and simply face the dead gods and our own fate. But it is stolen because these would not be our hopes. We would do these things with a different intention, and so they would be empty. To spend another day here is to wait for a dream to be real. To go home is to hope for dead gods to undie. Tragedy is one thing, and delusion another. That is why it is time to leave—out into all that is left for us. They take pity on such as us, and they will come to take us back."

"So that's it, then?" I managed to ask, my bizarre astonishment bestowing a sudden burst of strength upon my lips, "You're just talking about killing yourselves, right? There's…there's nothing else out there—there are no more islands. You'll die—that's all you'll do. You'll die."

"No, Mr. Hill," the little girl smiled at me tenderly, "That is the one thing that is certain: we will not die. But I do not expect you to understand such a thing, and I do not bring you here to convince you, for you are not one of us. But maybe…" she paused and gave me a long—very long—soul-piercing look. "We speak of dreams now…" she said after a moment, "and…you had a dream not long ago, yes?" Her face perked up like she had stumbled upon something that could really help me to understand. "Or…it is a memory, is it? It is a memory which has become a dream—ah!" She tossed her head back, her eyes rolling up into their sockets, before she looked back down at me, a clear-eyed little girl again. "Yes, that is it. A memory which you have often dreamed. Did you dream it last night, or will it be tonight, Mr. Hill?"

"I have no idea what you're talking about," I said.

"Tonight, then, or you would remember—for I can see that it stays with you—you would know. It has perhaps been a long time. The dream of your mother's grand-mother, yes? Her funeral, do you remember it? It follows another dream of yours—from when you were very small."

What it was like, I can only put roughly. When she said those words, my mind was flooded, almost attacked, by something both terrifying and familiar. It was an experience of absolute and unutterable size. It was upon me—the immensity of…what…of something…I can't tell you. I remembered it—the feeling. It was an old nightmare from my childhood. Standing before pure immensity, I was pierced by my own absolute smallness—a smallness not present by comparison to something, but a smallness existent unto itself. I felt myself so tiny that I was folding in, and pouring back out onto the other side of a line between me and non-existence—not in death, but in utter ceasing to be. I remembered it well, that old terror. I remembered waking up in the middle of the night screaming as I felt it. I remembered trying to tell my parents what I had dreamed. I hadn't felt that way since I was a boy—hadn't really felt it, though I could recall some shred of its weight. But there, standing in front of the little girl, it was upon me in full.

I don't know if I called out in terror in those woods. Maybe I did, but it doesn't matter. The feeling didn't last but a few seconds—a few blind seconds where I could see and yet could not discern the same flickering dance of the light in front of me. It was only a prelude—a little overture. After the brief moment of its presence another feeling came upon me with the same impossible force—actually happening to me, not in memory, but in fact.

Now, I was standing there, eight years old, at her funeral—my great-grandmother's funeral. My parents and I had traveled across town, to the west side, to her little church. It was not a place I was used to. My great-grandmother was a Russian, come to America many years before with her husband, himself long dead before I was born. The tiny chapel of her church was something foreign and elsewhere, a place I had only been perhaps twice before. We were there to watch them pray over her body.

It was night, the night before they buried her, when we shuffled in. No electric light in the place, the smoke of incense, the flickering light of candles making the eyes on the old icons move this way and that. It all shook me as a boy—it was all strange and eternal and frightful. Her coffin stood, closed, and we stood in the tiny box of a room, looking up at an ancient priest, dressed in black but for a thin red stole around his neck, facing the body, scowling through a wild white beard, and chanting something, practically under his breath, chanting over and over, something in a language I could not understand. As a boy I was afraid in a way I had never been before. I began to cry, and my mother picked me up—to comfort me like I was simply mourning the passing of her grandmother just like all those around me. To her it was not brand new, like it was to me. To her it was simply there. She didn't see it, and could not have seen it, like I did, with virgin eyes.

As I stood there back in the woods, I could feel, once again, the black awful feeling I had had in that church, as clear as the very first day—as clear as it was in my mother's arms. It was a terror, the inverse of that smallness from my other nightmare. It was a terror of emptying out into something you cannot ever control—something that is all too completely there. It was a terror not of cessation but of too much being. I had not understood that as a boy, nor ever before in my dreams, but as I stood there before the little girl, I knew it. I knew it as I looked again into the eyes of the ancient priest, as if he were really in front of me. I knew it as, in those eyes, I saw the cold awful fact that his would be the next coffined corpse to be wheeled into a dark chapel while whatever else there was in him gave way to the pull of that total, maddening consciousness that he was invoking now. I embraced my mother, wanting to beg her to take me away, but unable to find the words. I wanted to cry to her that it was not that woman, not her grandmother who was gone, but we…we who were gone—that we had to flee, had to run out into the snow outside and drive home to forget, and ever, endlessly forget what I had seen—what I would see in the depth of certain nights for the rest of my life as a dream unshaken and unfaced.

"Do you remember?" the little girl was asking, her voice ringing through to me as if it were far away at first. "Do you remember your dream?"

I looked up at her. I was on my knees in the woods now, though I could not tell when or how I had fallen down. There was a pool of vomit in front of me, and my stomach was turning over and over. "Yes," I said, trying not to weep.

"Please, Mr. Hill," the little girl said, "stand. You may stand…please." I got to my feet, starting to feel like I was really there again. "Please. I only remind you—so that you can see. For I have seen it myself, I have dreamed your dream with you, and it is with you—it comes back to you because it is a memory of what it is that is waiting for us. That is why I show you. It is your memory of the place that we are going…that was your question…I wish only to answer it. Forgive me, Mr. Hill, it is perhaps too much."

"No," I said, trying to stem another wave of nausea, "no, it's not. I just don't know how…I don't understand how you can know any of that…"

"But I have already said—it is so easy to see with you…" she said innocently, "there are not many people who have such a memory as you. There are many who have not feared this fear. It is easy to see it when a person does. It was an old man who taught it to me, as well, an ancient man—the same black garments, the same black night, and I first, like you, I did not understand. I am sorry Mr. Hill, to call your mind back to this. I only wanted you to know."

My stomach came back under control for a moment. I tried to straighten up, to face her somehow, or show my strength—I don't know. I tried, and I managed to ask it. "Who are you? Who *are* you, little girl?"

"I am so sorry," she said with a look of piercing kindness, "it would not help for me to tell you that. It would be only words to you. It is a thing you see, not a thing you are told."

"What are you *doing* here?" I managed.

She nodded slowly and almost sadly. "I have come from the same place that they all come. Over the water. We cannot leave them without a voice. It is too piercing to see people that way. We cannot live with it. But, Mr. Hill, do not ask further. I cannot make you understand." She smiled weakly at me.

With that, the nausea struck again, and knocked me back to my knees. "I…" I tried to respond, tried to think how to ask—*what* to ask—tried to even think of what I wanted to know in the first place. But there was nothing there. "I'm sick," I finally managed, "I feel very sick. I am sorry…I don't think I can stay here."

"No," she said tenderly, her voice becoming rich and deep, like a mother's, but not my own mother's. My mother's voice was sharp, even grating…never much comfort. This was the voice of a mother that I felt I knew once, in another dream maybe. And yet, still the voice of the little girl. It folded around me heavily. "No, do not stay any longer," she said. "Go. Go back now. But I must tell you…the thing I wanted to tell you to begin with. The reason I wanted you to come. I only wish to comfort you a little, and tell you what to do. You know him, I believe, the professor, yes? Who lives in the north?" I just managed to affirm that if she meant the Doc, then I did indeed know him. "Good," she said, "like you, he is not Milauan. Sleep tonight, even after it all. There will come no harm. And in the morning, find him. Then you will be able to return home, and have your son—ah such a beautiful baby boy! It is good that you listened." The little girl smiled a warm and intoxicating smile. A wave of peace struck me powerfully—the nausea dulled with its presence. She said nothing more, only stared at me for a long time, while I looked back at her, the firelight dancing, the overcast night swaying around us.

Then, after a long moment, the old hag approached me slowly, and grabbed my arm with a gentle compassion that I did not expect. She helped me stand up fully from where I was hunched. Her gesture was comforting because—I don't know how else to express it—standing there the old woman smelled to me like a rose lit aflame, sweet and smoky, something you almost taste. She looked back to the little girl with a nod, and turned me around. The darkness of the forest took over my field of vision, and the little girl was gone from my sight. The old woman led me, slowly this time, back through the woods and out onto the main road. It took a long time. My nausea still hit me once or twice as we went, and we were forced to stop. But she waited patiently for me then, helping me back to my feet when I fell. As we got further from the clearing, I felt stronger and more myself. When we came in sight of town, she turned and looked me in the eye as if to inspect me before my release.

"I'm feeling a lot better," I said, which was true. "Thank you."

The old hag only nodded at me and pointed down the road toward the hotel. Her eyes flickered one last time, like she was still looking into the fire in the clearing somehow. The madness was gone from them, like it had all just been a show. Now she looked wise and peaceful. She pursed her lips and smiled slowly and gently. Then, without a word, she turned where she stood, and disappeared again back into the trees. The few lights of town struck me, in that moment, as perhaps the most inviting solace that I have ever known.

# 17

I didn't stand long on the road. I made my way straight toward the hotel, figuring I would just lie down and rest for a while. But, as I was getting close to the door, a flurry of people suddenly burst through it on their way back outside. Doors were flying open all around town, in fact, and there were shouts and calls to get down to the beach. The crowd of people rushing out from the hotel basically absorbed me—I think someone might have even grabbed my shoulder—and I found myself making my way to a spot on the road near where everyone was going.

It quickly became obvious that the frenzy was because the winners of the election were about to be announced. In the voting tent, the two guys in white suits had returned, carrying the ballot box again, one of them holding a large envelope as well. In the tent stood Ella Turner, Gavra Kis, most of the members of parliament I had noticed at the festival, and various and sundry other people. There was a real nervous energy radiating out from them all. We waited for a few minutes while some others arrived, and the two guys got themselves situated. Finally, the taller of the two stood in a very formal pose, and opened up the envelope.

"People of Milau," he announced loudly, "it is my happy duty to announce to you, on behalf of the parliament of Milau and the office of the president, the result of today's election for all national offices and parliamentary seats. We apologize for a delay in counting the votes.

Voter turn-out today was much higher than ever in Milauan history, and the results were very close. I will announce first the general results for parliament. Of the twenty seats, the election at-large has delegated one seat to independent candidate Anyu Kasta…congratulations. Five seats go to the National Front for Milauan Liberation and Ascendancy. Fourteen seats to the Milauan Essentialist Party."

There were some gasps from the crowd, some scattered applause, groans, laughs, and all manner of other reactions. Everyone quickly calmed themselves, however, and turned back to listen to the guy in the white suit.

"In the election for the national judgeship, his honor, judge John Tok, retains his bench." There was scattered applause. "And, for the office of president…President Dr. Ella Turner retains the office by a margin of three hundred and seventy nine votes." He put down the envelope and smiled broadly at Turner like he was speaking at some kind of awards show. The crowd, however, gasped again, with a few more claps rising up after a moment, and a general buzz of confusion spinning around the place. The sound started rumbling louder and louder as Turner stood up to address the crowd. The tall election official moved over, motioning to her where to stand, and making a little bow.

"People of Milau," she said when she was in place. She had to basically shout to be heard. "Thank you for delivering this victory to me and to the MEP. We have made the right choice about our future!"

"Fraud!" came a shout from the audience somewhere near.

"Lies!" came another shout.

"No…no…it's the truth!" a third shout.

"Yes, free and fair!" rang another voice, "we have changed our votes freely!"

"I can assure you all," said Turner over the rising din, "that this election was not tampered with. The opposition themselves had their own representatives certify this result—that is unprecedented, but we wanted to assure you all of its legitimacy. The Americans have already left the island. There has been nothing untoward. The people have spoken!" The crowd began slipping into chaos, with people talking over one another, more shouts of various sorts rising up, and generalized movement in most directions as the confused mass tried to find its center.

As this was going on, however, there came from behind us, somewhere in town, the piercing shriek of a woman's scream. She called out several times hysterically, and then, above her rose a man's voice, clear and strong, bellowing with all its strength a single word. "Run!"

"No!" came a shout from down on the beach, "no! They cannot! No! Stop them! Stop them!" But in spite of whatever protest could have risen above the crowd in that moment, people began to move—several pouring out from the center of town, and others heading quickly down the beach. I caught a glimpse of Gavra Kis, still in the tent, talking rapidly and in great agitation with someone I didn't recognize. He pointed up toward town, trying to communicate something quickly, and waving wildly about in clear anger. His interlocutor was not listening, shaking his head with a look on his face that said it was out of their hands now.

Indeed, if Gavra had intended to call off the plan, it was too late. At that moment he was only one of the crowd, watching it. It was now a thing of its own, a freed animal that would carry out its instincts—a mind unstoppable, given life and destiny, and intent upon exercising its will in the only way granted it by its creators. There were no considerations now. The bomb would go off.

I stood there, looking back towards the embassy and waiting. Some people were still trying to get further away, but I just let it go and watched. A flash of light burst up and drew its fingers across the satin sheet of the overcast sky. In the same moment there rose a fantastic crash that could well have broken a few ear-drums, and certainly left my head ringing. It was all one together: bursting glass, some rending steel, and the clatter of bricks or concrete or who-knows-what tumbling to the ground. Everyone turned who was not already looking—turned towards the noise, in time only to catch a wisp of smoke and a few tongues of flame rising up from the embassy. They had done it. They had to have packed the place with explosives hours before—maybe even days. They had to have been standing there holding the button while the results were read out. But, they had forced their hand by giving their word, and sold now into slavery to their own intentions, there had been no reason to delay; they were right on that account, at least. I took a deep breath and gave a grateful thought to the image of the plane carrying Doug, Martha and the rest of them off the island without me.

The crowd now went into an immediate frenzy. People were rushing back up toward the embassy, or over to their houses, or just high-tailing it even further away. Shouts began to rise up aimed at Turner in the tent, or the guys with the white suits, or the ocean itself—who could tell? Several people seemed to be rapidly organizing some kind of bucket brigade to put out the fire beginning to take shape in town. I turned back to the tent, a sense of collapsed acceptance in my mind, and gazed at the god of the moonlight on the lagoon next to which Turner still stood in silence. Everyone raced around us, three shocked watchers. It was then that she strolled up calmly, unnoticed (as far as I could tell) by anyone but me, walking out of a large group of people on the north end of the beach, and right up behind the president. It was Mary Kis, in her usual black sari, openly wielding the same massive hunting knife she had pointed in my face the first time we had met.

While everyone continued to look in some other direction, I witnessed it—wishing I could take my eyes away, or get someone's attention…or just do anything but stand there. But I was nothing more, in that moment, than a statue cursed with consciousness. I simply stared ahead of me as Mary lifted the knife in her hand and plunged it into Ella Turner's back—once, then again—and Turner fell to the ground with a piercing scream that silenced everything around her, and turned the attention of everyone on the island of Milau to her body as it crumpled.

Mary Kis now stood alone, almost exactly where Turner had been standing, bearing a somber and broken hearted look on her face—a look both sincerely apologetic and severe in its resolve. She held the knife up in the air, enrobed in blood and still poised for a third strike. Turner's body lay on the ground, already dead, her eyes empty and shocked. There was silence—utter silence as I was hit again with a wave of nausea, worse, in fact, than what I had felt in the woods less than an hour before. We stood, we all stood, one people for a shining moment—one people betrayed, liberated, destroyed—who knows what—we didn't know what, not right then. Mary's eyes said everything—she didn't need to speak a word. She said to us in the silence that this was what she had to do—that the freedom of her people rested on this act—that that dream that her grandson had spoken of, to dance with the gods waiting back on the old island, was more important than anyone's life, no matter who. She said it all to us, and we, thinking as a single being, a crowd of people ringing as if played by one tuning fork in a harmonic so strong, so palpable, that we could hear one another's very thoughts—we looked back at her and we called her a liar. We considered it, standing there—the possibility that the election had been fixed, or that she was justified even if it was not. But we considered, too, the possibility that it had not been, and that she was not, no matter what. And as we mulled this over, whatever direction our predilections led us, we knew that regardless of anything, regardless of who had really won, regardless of anyone's plan, of any future, of any image of the destiny of this people—regardless of it all, Mary Kis stood in front of us nothing more than a common murderer. A moment later, after all this pulsed through that one mind that for a brief moment inhabited us, there was a scream from a woman somewhere on the beach—then another—then a third. The silence broke like an axle bearing far too much weight, and chaos returned.

Then Gavra Kis stood up and shouted. "Grandmother—what have you done?! Not like this—no! Not this way!"

Someone rushed up to the body of Turner, and felt her pulse. "Dead!" he shouted, then paused a moment. "Dead!" he said again.

Then everyone—everyone but me, that is—tumbled into motion. The shouts rose up, "murder!" the first, "murderer!" the second, "liar!" a third, "witch!" from somewhere else. And then, the grave and solemn call giving way and license to the grand and terrible end of Mary Kis. *"To the vats!"*

"Yes, yes!" came more shouts from the crowd, "murderer! We've all seen it! Murderer!"

"But then…then what?!" a woman kneeling by Turner's body shrieked, "she's dead we are lost! We are lost!"

"To the vats—into the brining vats! Let her die like a common murderer!" came the shout of another man, rushing towards Kis.

"And then to the little girl!" an old man cried. "She knows a way! She has spoken of another way!" I turned to look at him, and a flash of recognition came over me. It was one of the men from the conversation I had overheard the morning I met Reg Stryker. His voice bore an authority, and his eyes were brimful with certainty and hope.

The crowd shouted out in confirmation. "Yes—I have heard her say this!" came a woman's voice.

"And I!" shouted a man, "the day Anikka died!" A number of murmurs bubbled to the surface confirming the same.

"Then we go to see her!" shouted the old man whom I'd recognized. "As soon as we are done with the murderer!"

Then, as if they had just been waiting to somehow hammer out these specifics of their plan, the lynch mob descended upon Mary Kis, still standing stock still where she had been. I saw them seize her, a group of mostly men, with a few older women joining in. I saw them strip the knife from her fist. I saw them tear off her clothes, rip them to strips, and bind her with them, practically naked now, rolls of wrinkled fat on display to the lagoon. I saw her look at me—right at me for a moment with a horrified gaze. She had not expected this…she had not planned for it. She did not realize that anyone could turn as fast as she—that she was not the queen and sovereign of betrayal, herself somehow exempt from its whims. I saw them lift her onto their shoulders; she did not struggle. I saw them take her, at a run, down the road towards the plant. And I saw them disappear. That is all that I saw. I was still standing on the beach as the noise of their shouts and feet faded. I was still standing as the rest of the crowd began to follow, as quickly as they were able. I was still standing when there was no one left on the beach or on the road but me—me and the lagoon, the palms, the birds, the looming statue of the god, and the pregnant quiet of air separated only by degrees from a seething crowd now drowning a fat, deluded woman in a brining vat full of pickles.

I was more sick than afraid. I was cursing myself for staying there on the island, cursing them all, every person there. A small, dying fire smoldered at the embassy as I eventually walked down the road past it. The face of a child peered out at me through a window, and I could do nothing but look away. I walked inside the hotel. There was no one there, not a soul. The girl at the desk was gone. I marched into the dining room of the restaurant, through the swinging double doors, into the kitchen. I glanced around for a moment, then seized a bottle of the clear sharp island liquor, a jar of pickles, and a bowl full of ice. I returned to my room, locked both doors tight, pushed a chair up to the hallway door, and the entire bed against the one to the balcony. I sat, staring at the wall, and poured a drink.

# 18

It was maybe two hours later that it happened—the thing that you really want explained. There came a knock at my door. I stood up, barely even thinking about the fact that I had intended to hide, and moved the chair to look through the peep hole. At the door stood Alexander, looking impatient and sad. I opened up.

"Mr. Hill," he said with a weak smile. "Thank you for answering. I wished to see you a last time—I hope it is alright."

"Yes, of course," I said, "come in."

"No," he said with a wave of his hand, "no, I cannot stay. Please—I merely thought it was good to say farewell. We should not depart without any ceremony."

"I'm not sure how soon I'm leaving," I said. "The others are already gone."

"Oh yes, I know," he said, "but I mean us. It is I who will be leaving now."

"Oh," I said, "yes…"

"We have all been to see her—all together," Alexander said, "Mary Kis is dead— it is the worst kind of death—reserved only for the worst of criminals. Dr. Turner—she is murdered…I think I saw you there, on the beach—you saw it?"

"Yes," I said, a knot forming again in my stomach.

"I am so sorry…to witness it…it is not right for a visitor. But it is done now. They are both gone, and so…we are lost—we are a lost people. What else are we to do? We are frightened, even to live through the present night. So, we went to ask her—the little girl. She has always known before. She has told us that we must go to face the sea and find what it wills for us. She showed us our lives—showed us everything. It is time for us. Her people are coming, she says—from where she came—into the lagoon, and they will take us. We are are going down to the water right this moment—everyone else, I mean. I ran ahead to see you first. They are coming down the road."

"Alexander…" I said slowly, "She told me the same thing. But you can't survive, can you? Aren't you afraid?"

"Sir?" he asked, puzzled. "No, sir. We are afraid of this place, not of the water. We must go. Perhaps another island is waiting for us. Or perhaps it is something else." I shook my head slowly and sadly. "I cannot tell you," Alexander said, a tear now in his eye, "but this is our way now. Please…just accept my goodbye with my friendship."

"Okay," I said with a slow, slow nod. "Goodbye, then. May your son…well…may he live, Alexander."

A melancholy smile lit across his face like it would jump past his eyes and inhabit the entire room. "Thank you," he said after a long, brilliant pause, covering his eyes so that I wouldn't see him cry. "It is your blessing again. Sir…thank you. It will pilot him—I know it." He took a long moment before he looked back up at me. We looked at each other for a long moment. I didn't know what to say. I guess he didn't either. Then, he made a deep bow, and with that he turned down the hall to walk away. Just before the stairs he stopped a moment, and looked back. "You may watch us, if you like," he said, "you can see it from here, I am sure." I nodded, not even really knowing what I was agreeing to. Alexander smiled a last time, and descended the stairs—gone.

I shook my head to myself as I re-entered my room. What could I have said? There was nothing. I went slowly to the window. The moon had set, a big bright diffuse light over the water. I looked up at the stars, now cutting through clearing patches in the previously overcast sky. As I gazed out, a crowd of people came down the main road from the city. It looked, at first, like the same small group that had seized Mary Kis. But, as I watched, the line of them began to grow, and it became clear that it must have been hundreds of people at least. They were heading from the south toward the beach, the whole lot of them, a handful of men near the front of the group holding torches to create a little light. And in front of them walked the little girl from the woods—marching with the same elegant walk of a woman far beyond her age—flickering and moving in the light so that I wasn't sure if she was more than an illusion produced by the excitement of the flames.

I decided to go all the way out onto my balcony. I had to move the bed back so I could open the door. I stepped out. What from my window could have been a few hundred people was far more than that. It ran all the way through town and back out again and on and on beyond that. It must have been the whole island—it would have to be. Old men and old women, young children, families with babies—everyone of every shape and size, faces lit by the light of the occasional torches dispersed through the crowd. Many of them I recognized, most from simply seeing them around here and there. Alexander walked with his family, and Baya with his wife. Martha's clan made their way down next to Sam, the bartender. I even spotted Gavra Kis, which surprised me a little for some reason. He was holding hands with the girl from the front desk. As the crowd of people began to grow, I realized that they were singing—voices strong and weak—a verse or two in a language I could not understand.

They were all making their way to the beach, and gathering there. They dug their torches into the sand, illuminating the scene in orange and red. I could see the little girl turn around as if to make sure everyone was still with her. She made a few signals with her hands, and they began. They arrived in silence, out of the dark of the water—first a handful, and then more—dozens and then a few hundred, I'd guess: boats—wide long canoes, each piloted by a single person. They were typical in appearance, by all means—the pilots, that is—men and women, a handful of children, in no particular order, come from nowhere but the dark of the water as far as I could tell.

They pulled their boats in on the shore, and everyone gathered on the beach made their way to them. Then people started to get on, the old and the young, the families, the babies, the children, the people I knew, and those I did not. As the boats filled up, packed to their absolute capacity, they pushed out into the water. The stronger men took up paddles and oars themselves, and the pilots turned each vessel out into the lagoon where they held to wait for the others.

It took perhaps the better part of an hour, but eventually every person on the beach had found their way onto a boat. The little girl was the last to board. She stepped onto an empty fishing vessel sitting on the beach. All on her own, and with a strength impossible for someone her size, she picked up an oar and pulled out onto the lagoon where I could just see her face in the light of the torches. Looking at the water then was like looking out onto an audience in a dark theater. Heads and faces saturated it, blanketed it. Most of them were not fully visible in the diffuse light; only the ones closest to shore could be seen.

The lagoon was calm—fantastically calm—the waters not moving at all, in fact. The little girl lifted a hand in signal, making a simple loop in the air. Oars dipped into the water. Then they all…started to make their way. A few sparse voices could be heard guiding the boats, but otherwise in silence they went out into the dark. Beyond the torch light they began to vanish from my sight. Their form and shape seemed to fold into the water, mix, and invert until their faces looked not like objects above the surface, but like reflections of faces painted upon it. Those reflections seemed to stare up into the sky, but they did so formlessly. The faces lost their sense, I mean—they were less and less clear every moment—like ripples on a pond distorting an image, though the water was glassy smooth. Their eyes shone bright, and brighter. They were looking into something—looking into a light not of the sky, not on the island, not even out there in the water—not to be seen at all. The forms of the people and the boats, the glow of their eyes, the fire of the torches were soon indistinguishable from the arcing pattern of the celestial sheet above them until I couldn't see anything but the stars anymore. They were gone. That's all I can tell you. That's all that I know.

# 19

I woke up quite late the next morning. It took me a long time to get to sleep after they all departed. I kept finding that the image of those eyes, looking out at some light, was haunting my mind. And, like the girl had said, I dreamed that dream about my great-grandmother, and it woke me up. I don't want to dwell on that now. The morning was silent but for the calls of the birds. I opened up the window and looked out. There was no one to be seen anywhere. The pile of rubble that had been the embassy was still smoldering slightly. Everything felt peaceful.

I was happy to see that the water in the bathroom was still running, and the electricity seemed to be working fine. I took a shower, and finished packing up my bags. Thinking back, I'm rather surprised at myself. I didn't even give it a thought. I just started operating on what the little girl had told me the night before; I was already making my way up to the north end of the island to look for the Doc.

Before leaving, I broke back into the kitchen and made myself some coffee and breakfast. Everything was in there—it had just been abandoned as it was. I'm sure every house in town would have been the same story if I'd bothered to check. That's one thing you can confirm for yourselves, if you go out there…or maybe you already have. They'd all just walked away leaving everything but the clothes they were wearing. In the kitchen I found some of the roe they had been serving me every morning in a fridge, made a bit of toast, and sat down near the window like it was any other day, albeit without a waiter. The tall statue of the god of the shore of the lagoon looked down on me, as he had every morning. I even picked up the paper from the day before and pawed through it, just to make things feel as normal as possible. There was another Blondie strip near the back which ended with Dagwood irritating his boss. Always original.

When I was done eating, I headed outside. The air felt a little cooler than normal, and there were some lingering wisps of cloud in the sky. I headed northward down the road out of town. I walked down onto the beach and started making my way to the old resort. The boats left on the beach looked strangely lonely, communicating that essence that clings to abandoned things for reasons I've never understood.

I probably shouldn't have been as shocked as I was. I really was just assuming that there would be no one left on the island but me and the Doc. But, I was wrong. He was there right on the beach, rigging up a boat (it was one with a motor) and tossing a few boxes into the back. It was an old fisherman, and I recognized him as the one who had let us cook bread-fruit on his fire a few days before. My heart stood still for a moment like it couldn't decide whether to leap joyfully at the thought that I had only been hallucinating this whole time, and everyone was still here like normal, or disappointed that it wasn't all really over. I walked up to him.

"Hello," he said casually. He was smoking a cigarette and wearing blue jeans and a worn looking t-shirt. "Heading up there, are you?" He signaled up to the resort.

"Yes," I said, "how did you know?"

"You two and me are the only ones left," he said with a smile, stopping what he was doing and pulling the cigarette out of his mouth. "I figured you probably wouldn't know that some old fisherman would still be here.

But, I wasn't born here. I was born in Guadalajara. You ever been to Mexico?" I shook my head. "Well, that's where I was born. My father was a preacher. Ended up out here. Buried both my parents in this coral sand. But I guess that's not quite enough to make me one of them." He smiled broadly.

"And…what are you doing…now?" I asked, looking at the various crates he was packing.

"Just heading off again," he laughed. "It's been a long time, but I still remember how. Probably I'll just head to Midway and see if I can't get someone to drop me somewhere. No reason to stick around here, is there?" He lifted the last puff of his cigarette to his lips with a smile.

I stared at him long and hard. It all seemed completely normal to him.

"Sir," I said finally, "what happened last night? Do you know?"

"I thought you understood…" he said, getting started again on his packing. "They're all gone. They all went away. You didn't see it? I was watching from up in a tree right over there. Never seen anything like it."

"No," I said, "I mean, yes, I did see it. I watched it from my balcony. But where? Where did they go?"

He was lighting another cigarette and offered me one. "Out into the lagoon," he told me after I declined. "I don't know anything more than you about it."

"Yes, but…from the lagoon…where?"

The fisherman shrugged. "One thing I've learned…from the water…is that if you wanna know *that* kind of thing, you gotta go look."

"You sound just like her…" I said quietly.

"Who?" the fisherman asked.

"The little girl—the one from the woods."

"You saw her?" he asked in some excitement. I nodded. "Well, then what are you asking *me* questions for?" He gave a broad smile with his nicotine-stained teeth. "You know," he went on after a pause, "we think we're living men asking where the dead are now—that's something that makes sense. But think to yourself for a minute. What is it like for a dead man to wonder where the *living* are? I think about that sometimes. I'll probably think about that one tonight on the Pacific. Just a riddle. But, if you want an old fisherman's advice, you ought to quit talking to yourself—look around a little while. It's like fish. You catch whatever's there. Can't be picky. The islanders are not here anymore to be seen. But there are things that are." He shrugged and took another drag.

"Well, thanks," I said. "Good luck on the trip."

"Yeah," he said, "if you want to hop on this boat with me, I'd be happy to have you along."

"No," I said, "I think I'll just head up to the resort."

"Sure," said the fisherman with another shrug. He stood up and started loading the last few things into the boat. "All the best now, friend," he said as I started walking away. Then I heard him shout again. "Friend!" I turned around. "Come back a minute. Here. I ought to give you something. It's a Milauan tradition—they wouldn't have wanted you to leave the island without a gift. Here." He handed me a little wooden statue, small enough to fit in my palm, the smallest I had seen, but just like all the others in every corner of the island. It was a deep red figure of man, hands outstretched but looking toward the ground—the same god I had seen in Baya's living room.

"The god of the cucumber vine," I said to the fisherman.

"You know your idols," he answered with a smile. "Do what you want with it. It's just a trinket. But I don't want it anymore."

"Thanks," I said, not sure if I was really grateful.

"All the best," he said again, and I walked away up the beach.

It didn't take a lot longer to get to the resort. I went through the broken fence and knocked on the big glass door by the pool. After a few minutes, I saw the Doc appear through the windows and open up.

"Good morning," he said, "Let me tell you, I'm glad to see you."

"The feeling is mutual," I said.

"Do you have any clue what's going on?" he asked. "Where is everybody? The fishermen aren't out—nobody's out. Nobody's even on the beach that I can see. And there were bombs going off or something last night. What the hell happened?"

"Well, there's only so much that I know," I said.

"Come in and sit down," he ordered sharply, "coffee black, right?" I accepted the offer, and set down my bags near the chair. "And here you've got all your bags. Go—tell me what you know."

So, I did. He got the coffee ready, and brought a cup over to me as he listened attentively.

"So that's it?" he said when I was through, "nobody left here? Not a soul?"

"Assuming that old fisherman has taken off already, then, yeah, nobody but me and you."

"Huh…" he said, mulling it over. "Well, fancy that. I was half expecting them to leave me here, but I figured they'd be heading back to the old island or something. Crazy."

"Yeah," I said, "no kidding. What do you make of it? I mean…where could they possibly have gone like that?"

"Ha!" he laughed hard, "you think *I'm* the kind of person who would know that? I didn't even see it myself—you should probably be telling me. Who knows. Maybe they're dead."

"Dead…" I said, "I hope not."

"Don't we all? I mean, all the time? Hill, one thing I *can* tell you is don't feel too blue even if they are. How big of a deal would a few extra years have been anyway?" I nodded sadly.

"Listen," I said after a few moments, "I don't know what she meant…by anything…but the little girl said I should come find you. That's why I've got all my bags here. She said you'd help me get back home somehow."

"Hmm," he said, "not sure. I mean…I don't have a boat or anything like that—well, there's that old sail boat out there, but I don't think that'll do us any good. Maybe she just figured you'd be better off up here with me. I mean…somebody must be coming to pick you up, right?"

"Yeah," I said, "in ten days. I mean…I hope he's still coming."

"Oh well," said the Doc, remaining remarkably cheerful. "Only one way to find out. And if he doesn't show then…I guess we'll just have to make some smoke signals or something." I didn't find the idea very funny, though he seemed to think it was a delight. "Well, you can just stay up here until then, and hope for the best. I've got plenty of books."

I nodded, sipped my coffee and settled in.

---

The Doc set me up with one of the rooms in the old resort, and I just hung around there for those ten days, trying to make myself believe I was on a vacation like anybody else, enjoying the sun. I even went swimming in the lagoon a few times just to really play the part. I sat out and looked at the stars each night. I hadn't really taken the time to do that except for the very first night with Doug. They're just incredible out there—completely away from any light. Like nothing you've ever seen. The Doc and I talked a little here and there, but not that much. He seemed like he wanted to just keep to his normal lifestyle which meant being alone most of the time. He spent a lot of the day just reading by the empty pool. By the way, those ten days waiting for Tom were when the Doc taught me that passage from Seneca—the one that I started off with. He told me why I was supposed to remember it.

"He understood something, Hill," he said, "and maybe everyone who was on this island does now too. There's nothing but life and…not-life, that's the thing. You can do what you do, or you can just end it all. You don't build anything—you don't make anything that lasts—that's not the point, even though every jackass in the world seems to think that now, just like Ella did and Mary did. No, you don't build, you don't do, you just be or not—sit through the hours or walk out of the exam. But it's not all gloom—you've got to be able to appreciate that. It's not all just foggy afternoons or something. The thing is, you're here anyway, and what the hell else are you going to do to occupy yourself, huh? I mean, the time is going to go by whether you like it or not—you might as well build the damn pyramids, right? Just don't fool yourself into thinking they're really doing anything to be there. They'll just dissolve into sand. And Seneca is saying if that fact is all just too much, death is a haven from it."

"Do you believe that?" I asked him.

"I'm trying," he said, "but I just keep worrying that maybe it's backwards. Maybe life is the haven. Maybe *this* is our escape from even more life—we wouldn't really know would we? I've got to decide on that, first. Too bad I can't ask all of them, huh?" he motioned out to the lagoon, "They would know."

"Probably," I said. "You sure you want to stay out here, by the way?" I asked after a moment. "There's nobody left here—you'll be completely on your own."

"Sure," he said, "I could get sick, and that could be the end of it. Or I could drown in the waves in a few year's time as they rise up to my chin. But, I already told you—there's nothing for me anywhere else. What would I do back home? I'll just have to start growing my own coffee, I guess," he smiled, but it was clear that he was serious, "and I used to love to go fishing as a kid. I guess I'll just brush off my old skills." Well, I wasn't going to kidnap the guy and bring him back, so that was that. "Really, it's you who should be asking yourself if you actually want to go back. It won't change anything. You'll be looking out on the same damn ocean. Just with a lousy view. Why don't you just stick around."

I shook my head, but I didn't answer him. I didn't have an answer—and I still don't. But, then again, what difference did it make?

I think that was about the last conversation we had while I was there. My heart just about burst open when the *Jet Red Sadie* appeared in the sky right on time. You can be out there, isolated, for a long long time—but you can't do it if you think it's going to be forever. Well, I couldn't have, anyway. I breathed the deepest sigh of my life as I watched that piece of shit plane come down on the lagoon. I had left the resort before the Doc was even up that morning to walk down to the dock and wait. When Tom landed, I just walked out the little pier and greeted him. Tom ran about with his jerry cans, filling the gas tank for close to half an hour, then jumped back in the cockpit and started her up.

"Good to see you," I said.

"You too," he replied. "Where's your friend? Not comin'? Wait…don't tell me. Fell in love with that girl and he's gonna stay forever, didn't he?"

"Well…" I said slowly, "in a manner of speaking, yeah. Anyway, no, he's not coming with us now."

Tom nodded like he had been figuring at least one of us would pull something like that. "You get everything done then? Everything go okay?"

"Yeah…" I said slowly, "I guess I'd say everything is taken care of."

"Good," he said, "quiet day here, huh? I don't see anybody out at all."

I just nodded. The engines roared loud as we floated out into the lagoon. I took another last long look—like maybe I'd see them in there still—in the water, I mean. With a roar and a burst of smoke, the pontoons lifted off gently into the quiet, with Tom already talking my ear off about some baseball trades I had missed. Milau sat silent below us. I could practically hear the bustle of Honolulu in my ears.

# EPILOGUE

There you go—everything you asked for, if I'm not mistaken. As for the other Americans and Martha, about a year back I actually saw Linda Stryker shopping in Chicago, not that I said hello or anything. It was definitely her, though. So, I assume they all made it back. Where they've gone since then, I certainly don't know. Doug never reported to work again, and there's been no sign of Martha.

When I got home I tallied up a report for Saf-T-Set that I think you have. I eventually did discover that there had never been any supply issues with North Pacific pickles to begin with, just a problem in a computer algorithm that some intern probably set up. The jars were all making it from the real plant in Zeeland to store shelves like they had been for ten years. There was never any reason for me and Doug to go to Milau. Anyway, I stapled my two-weeks' notice to the front of my report, and dumped it on Josh Plank's desk. I put the little statue I got from the fisherman right next to it for the company to display somewhere. I figured it belonged with them. I've got another job now and, like I think I mentioned somewhere, we just had a baby. We call him Alex.

Oh, and one last thing. I'm not sure if it's within your bureaucratic protocol or whatever…but if you do send somebody out there again, I wouldn't mind getting ahold of a little more of that coffee, and maybe a bottle of Aijee. I'm sure there's plenty laying around. Just a request. I understand if you can't do that kind of thing. And send my regards to the Doc, if you see him…if he's there to be seen. He'll know who I am.

# About the Author

Caenys Kerr lives with her husband, David, at the southern end of Australia's iconic Gold Coast. Her favourite writing spot overlooks a tidal canal alive with fish, rays and the occasional bull shark.

Other books by this author:

Merry Christmas Liebchen
Her Holiday Fling
Happy with the Millionaire (due for release 2026)
The Salignac Legacy
The Beaulieu Birthright
On Board with the Secret Billionaire

Keep up to date with new releases through Caenys' website:
www.caenyskerr-author.com